# AGAINST THEIR WILL

A THRILLER CONCEIVED FROM TRUE EVENTS

CAROLYN COURTNEY LAUMAN

**AGAINST THEIR WILL**

ISBN: 978-1-7332864-0-4 (Ebook Edition)
ISBN: 978-1-7332864-1-1 (Paperback Edition)

The characters and events in this book are fictitious. Any similarity to real persons, living or dead, is purely coincidental and not intended by the author.

Cover Design by Hampton Lamoureux

❀ Created with Vellum

# AUTHOR'S NOTE

---

# DEDICATION

This novel is dedicated to my sister, Debbie, who set out with me on that fateful trip south so many years ago. It was scary then, for certain, but looking back now, with daughters of our own, I am much more frightened by what could have been. Could have been but wasn't, when our own guardian angel, in the form of a kind and concerned truck driver, stepped in to help us. Be safe, Nicole and Emma. We love you.

# ACKNOWLEDGMENTS

This novel has been forty years in the making, and I'd like to thank the people who helped bring *Against Their Will* to its inevitable conclusion:

Debbie Molino, my sister and friend, for being there from the beginning, for reading the early drafts, and for your unending support and encouragement.

Barbara Courtney, my mother, for fostering my love of the written word from a very early age. I love you!

Maria Pease, writer and instructor, for your invaluable guidance, instruction and friendship.

Kate Schomaker, my editor, for polishing my words and inspiring me to become a stronger writer. I am lucky to have found you!

Hampton Lamoureux for your creative cover design that allows Against Their Will to stand out in the crowd.

And finally, to my husband, Wayne, for your quiet support and unceasing love during the many months I disappeared into this story.

# PROLOGUE

U S Interstate 95 runs from Maine's border with Canada to Miami, Florida, passing through more US states than any other interstate.

Completion of its bypass east of Fayetteville, North Carolina, took place in 1983. Prior to that, as was the case in late 1979, Business 95 ran through a densely populated area of Fayetteville. Lined with service stations, fast food franchises, pawn shops, and roadside bars, this urban thoroughfare both welcomed and repelled travelers heading north and south.

# PART I

*If you want to change the world, start with the next person
who comes to you in need.*

—B. D. Schiers

# LATE SATURDAY, DECEMBER 29, 1979

## FAYETTEVILLE, NORTH CAROLINA

The engine of the aging yellow Subaru sputtered a bit, shimmying the steering wheel in Isabella's hands. "What the hell!" she exclaimed, pressing hard on the brake pedal.

Looking up from her fashion magazine, Maria sighed and said, "Don't tell me we're out of gas."

"Not according to the gauge, but we'd better fill up, just in case."

Signaling her move into the turning lane, Isabella cut in front of a jacked-up pickup. The bearded driver honked angrily, flashing his middle finger.

"Screw him," Maria said as Isabella pulled into a brightly lit Hess station. Looking around, she asked, "Where are we, anyway?"

"Some town in North Carolina. Fayetteville, I think," Isabella replied.

Squirming in her seat, Maria drawled, "Otherwise known as Hicksville. Do y'all think the john's clean here?"

Looking askance at her sister, Izzy said, "Only one way to find out. Go ahead while I pump."

Maria made her way into a grimy, glass-fronted office where a mess of a man sat behind a battered metal desk overflowing with NASCAR and girlie magazines. His scraggly, yellowed mustache accented a mouth with few remaining teeth, and his eyes were red-rimmed and rheumy. More hair sprouted from his nose and ears than his scalp, and what little there was of that was an oily shade of gray.

"Well, hello there, missy," he said, leering at Maria. "What can I he'p you with?"

"Is the restroom unlocked?" she asked, trying her darnedest to avoid looking at the man's teeth or the centerfold of a naked woman on the desk in front of him.

"Naw, but here's the key," he answered, reaching back to grab a ring from a hook on the wall. "Ladies' is the second door 'round to the side. Be sure to bring that back when yer done."

"Yes, sir, thanks," Maria assured him. Turning, she collided with Izzy, who was making her way into the office.

"Done already?" Maria asked.

"Yeah, only took a few gallons. Don't know why it was acting up, but we should be good to go."

The girls took turns using the single-stall bathroom, which wasn't terribly dirty after all, although a disgusting cockroach had been desperately trying to extricate itself from the toilet bowl until Maria flushed it away. After they returned the key to the office, the old man called out to them, "Stop on back, ya hear?"

On the second try, the ignition caught, and with sighs of relief, the sisters pulled back onto the crowded four-lane road. Daylight was quickly fading, and colorful Christmas lights could be seen adorning buildings and streetlights on both sides of the road. Everyone in Fayetteville seemed in a hurry to get somewhere on this late winter afternoon, and

Izzy swore under her breath when a low-riding El Camino braked abruptly in front of them.

With red lights stopping traffic at just about every intersection, it was slowgoing as the girls made their way south. Braking at what appeared to be the last crossroad heading out of town, the Subaru once again coughed and jerked disconcertingly.

"Shit!" cried Izzy, banging her fist on the steering wheel. "This is ridiculous!"

"What's wrong with it?"

"How do I know?" Izzy answered angrily. "We're gonna have to pull over again."

"Where?" Maria asked, peering nervously out the window. "The gas stations are all behind us."

"There," Izzy said, pointing to the dirt parking lot in front of a low, red-brick building that had seen better days. The glass front door, framed by a portico of rotting wooden columns that bowed haphazardly, beckoned passers-by with a flickering neon Budweiser sign.

Maria sighed heavily as Izzy steered the dying car to a stop beside a stand of unsold Christmas trees. A hand-lettered sign, originally reading *All Christmas Trees $59*, had been corrected with red paint to read *All Christmas Trees $19*. The next stop for the remaining few would be the mulch pile.

"What are we gonna do now?" Maria asked, sounding a bit panicked.

"I don't know." Izzy shrugged, watching the neon beer sign flash on and off. "Let's go in and see if there's a phone we can use."

"This sucks! We'll never make it to Florida tonight," Maria complained. "First we drove twice around DC, and now this."

"Shut up!" Izzy snapped, though she'd been feeling crappy about missing that earlier exit in northern Virginia, a diversion that had added over an hour to the already interminable trip. "Let's just see what we find inside."

The girls exited the car, pulling their purse straps over their heads and hugging them tightly to their bodies. With temperatures in the thirties when they'd left Pennsylvania that morning, they were wearing jeans and flannel shirts. Having left their heavy winter parkas at home, they'd tossed their lightweight jackets into the back seat when they'd stopped for lunch earlier in the day.

The parking lot was nearly deserted, with a single tractor trailer off to the left and a rusty old pickup truck parked directly in front of the door. As the girls approached the entrance, Maria read aloud the faded sign above the door: "Jimmy's Joint."

A haze of cigarette smoke, backlit with tacky Christmas lights and buzzing neon signs, greeted them as they entered the building. Johnny Cash could be heard singing "A Boy Named Sue" on the jukebox in the back corner behind a pool table. Three men sat at the bar, their backs to the door.

Resisting the urge to turn around, the girls approached the aproned man wiping down the bar top. He was big and tall, appearing to be in his late forties. A ruddy face and hair graying at the temples highlighted his need for a shave and a haircut, but he reminded Maria a little of Buford Pusser, or at least Joe Don Baker *as* Buford Pusser. Looking up, he tossed the rag over his shoulder and asked, "What can I get you, ladies?"

"Uh...," Izzy started, hesitant at first to continue. "We were wondering if you have a phone we can use."

Hearing the short exchange, the two nearest men stopped their conversation and turned to check out the girls.

"Hello, pretty things," drawled the slighter of the two. Small but mean-looking, he sported a jagged scar across his pock-marked right cheek and beady eyes that darted from under the bill of a green-and-yellow John Deere cap. His unruly black hair, which he'd shoved behind his ears, hung to his shoulders. Dirty denim overalls and a jacket with "Stud" crudely stenciled on the back completed the package. Noting that last detail, Maria shuddered as she grabbed Izzy's upper arm so tightly she winced.

"Mind yer business, Billy," the bartender warned.

"Oh, you're no fun, Jimmy. I'm just being nice. Right, Frank?" he asked the man sitting to his left, who, like Billy, was wearing grimy overalls. Unlike Billy, Frank was soft and pudgy with eyes that didn't seem to focus all that well. His hair was buzz-cut short on top and longer at the collar, a style the girls knew to be a mullet. *Maria was right*, thought Izzy, *we are in Hicksville*.

Stubbing out his cigarette in the overflowing ashtray, Frank slurred, "Yeah, that's right. We don't get many pretty ladies in here. Nice change of scenery. No offense, Jimmy."

"Sure is," agreed Billy, but before he could finish, Jimmy waved the girls around to the side of the bar, telling them, "Ignore those boys, ladies, and tell me what's going on."

With fear threatening to get the better of her, Izzy struggled to calm her voice as she explained about their car. "Maybe we could call a tow truck or mechanic to see if they can fix it."

"Well, honey," Jimmy replied, "that would be nice, but seeing how it's Saturday night, there ain't nobody open to come help you. It's probably gonna be Monday before we can get somebody to take a look."

Eavesdropping on the conversation, Billy chimed in, "Or even Tuesday or Wednesday. Case you didn't know it,

Monday's New Year's Eve. Won't be nobody working over the long weekend."

As Billy's words sank in, the color drained from Izzy's face, and she pulled Maria toward the door. "Let's go," she whispered, her voice a mix of fear and anger. "We'll find someone else to help us."

"Damn you, Billy," snarled Jimmy, snapping his dishrag at the man. "I told you to mind yer business!"

"Stop 'em," hiccupped Frank, leaning unsteadily toward Billy. "We can fix their car."

"Yeah!" Billy agreed, jumping off his stool and stumbling after the girls. "Wait, little ladies!" he shouted. When he grabbed Izzy's arm, she turned and slapped him hard across his scarred cheek.

"Keep your grimy hands off me!" she growled.

"Whoa, now, pretty girl. We was just gonna offer to help you," he said, rubbing his smarting face. "No need to get yer knickers in a knot. My friend Frank here and me know a lot about cars. Why don'tcha let us take a look?"

Izzy and Maria exchanged doubtful looks, but with no other assistance coming their way for who knew how long, Izzy asked, "Do you really know about cars?"

"Absolutely!" Billy replied, drawing out the word as he attempted to corral the girls out the door without touching them again. "Come on, Frank, let's give these two pretty ladies a hand."

At the door, Maria glanced back in Jimmy's direction with a look that seemed to say, *Thanks for nothing.* Jimmy gave an almost imperceptible nod, then shifted his eyes down the bar where the other lone patron had just called his name.

# LATE SUNDAY MORNING, DECEMBER 30, 1979

## DOYLESTOWN, PENNSYLVANIA

Anna and Tony Thomas opened the door into their mud room and heard the phone ringing. Having just returned from morning mass at Our Lady of Mount Carmel, Tony was looking forward to a hearty breakfast, the Sunday papers, and an afternoon watching NFL playoff games.

Tony grabbed the phone off the wall. "Good morning, Thomas residence."

"Hi, Tony," said a quiet voice on the other end of the line. "This is Helene D'Amato, Lisa's mom."

"Hi, Helene. Did our girls get there safely?" he inquired.

"Well, no, Tony. That's why I'm calling. The girls aren't here yet, and we haven't heard from them. I was hoping maybe you'd know when they're scheduled to arrive. Did they get a late start yesterday?"

"No, they were up and out of here by six. They should have gotten to you by now, even if they stopped for the night somewhere," Tony replied, glancing at the wall clock. "It's just before noon now, so why don't we give them a little longer. Maybe they stopped for a bite to eat."

"Okay," Helene agreed. "Lisa's just anxious to get back to

campus this afternoon. Guess she's had too much family time this Christmas break."

"I hear that," Tony said, laughing. "Let's not worry yet, but have the girls call us when they show up."

"Will do, Tony," Helene assured him, and they both hung up.

Taking off her hat and gloves, Anna looked concerned. "Tony, what's going on? Are the girls okay?"

"Of course they are," he replied, drawing Anna into his arms. "Why wouldn't they be?"

# LATE SATURDAY AFTERNOON, DECEMBER 29, 1979

## FAYETTEVILLE, NORTH CAROLINA

Henry Long pulled his rig into the parking lot of Jimmy's Joint, his favorite watering hole whenever he passed through Fayetteville. He was dog-tired and contemplated reclining his seat for some quick shut-eye before going inside for a beer and burger. Thinking of his tight deadline for the load he was hauling, he sighed and jumped down from the cab. *There'll be plenty of time to sleep tomorrow*, he thought.

"Hey, Hank!" called Jimmy as Henry opened the door of the dingy bar. "What's it been, two months or more?"

As Henry's eyes adjusted to the gloom, he conceded there wasn't much to see in here, but the beer was cold and the burgers thick and juicy. Two men sat side-by-side at the right end of the bar, so Henry deliberately chose a stool at the far left. He had learned long ago to avoid eye contact and conversation with the locals in this place—and other places like it. Too often, the drunker the locals got, the more they wanted to prove how tough they were, especially to out-of-towners. Henry was too old to take them up on those invitations to fight, even though he could, he knew, take down a drunken punk anytime, anywhere. A retired drill sergeant out of Camp Lejeune, he'd once been a badass himself. While he tried to maintain his strength and endurance with regular visits to the gym and runs along the beach, at sixty-two, the days of proving his toughness might well be over.

"Yeah, Jimmy, was Halloween—remember?" Henry responded. "Ugly ghouls crowded the bar that night."

"That's right, with some even sportin' costumes!" joked Jimmy. "What'll you have? Same as usual?"

"Sure, thanks," Henry replied, pulling out a stool.

Thirty minutes later, as Henry finished the last bite of burger, he watched in the mirror as two young women walked in. *They can't be older than twenty or twenty-one*, he thought. One had straight brown hair and was tall and willowy. The other had shorter blond hair and was, herself, shorter than the first. Had to be sisters, though, since their faces and figures—not that he purposely took note of their figures—were so similar. *Heck, they could be my granddaughters*, he thought. What were they doing in a place like Jimmy's?

Not wanting to get involved but still a bit troubled, Henry kept an eye on what was taking place at the other end of the bar. *Shit*, he thought, *the girls are walking out with those assholes. Not a good move, but none of my business.* He called Jimmy's name and signaled for his check.

"What was that all about?" he asked as Jimmy approached.

"Girls are having car trouble, and Billy and Frank went out to see if they can get it started."

"Like those two yokels could fix a car," Henry retorted. "They wouldn't know a carburetor from a gumball machine."

"Yeah, and mix in a couple hours drinking, and you've got a real shit show," Jimmy added.

"Shit is right," Henry groaned. "I'd better see if they can use my help." Finishing off his pint, he grabbed his jacket, threw a twenty on the bar, and walked outside.

**4**

## LATE SATURDAY AFTERNOON, DECEMBER 29, 1979

FAYETTEVILLE, NORTH CAROLINA

After opening the hood of the Subaru, Izzy and Maria stood back while Frank and Billy, or "Stud" as Maria now thought of him, stuck their heads under. A lit cigarette dangled from Billy's mouth, and Maria admonished, "You better put that out before you start a fire."

Checking his anger, Billy grinned up at her. "Don't worry yerself, pretty lady, I know what I'm doing."

"I hope so," Izzy added, "but put out the damn cigarette anyway!"

Billy spat the butt to the gravel and ground it under the heel of his boot. "There ya go," he snarled. "Ain't nothin' I won't do for a pretty lady."

"Stop saying that," Maria said, a shiver of revulsion running down her spine. "Just pay attention to the engine."

Shaking his head, Billy pulled out the oil dipstick, looked it over, and elbowed Frank. "Not seein' nothin' here. How 'bout you, Frankie?"

"Nah, me neither," Frank agreed. "Might need to wait til Bobby Stott can have a look-see next week."

"No way we're sticking around til next week," Izzy insisted.

"Don't know that you have a choice," Billy replied, a tad too excitedly. "No need to fret, though. We know a nice place you can stay at while your car's being fixed, don't we, Frank?"

"Yep, we sure do!" Frank answered enthusiastically.

Approaching the Subaru, Henry Long overheard the exchange. "Girls, I'd be happy to take a look myself, if you want."

"No need, old man," Billy warned, puffing out his chest and clenching his fists. "Frank and me got everything under control."

"Yeah, be on yer way, mister," Frank said and laughed, yanking the jacket from Henry's hand and tossing it in the air.

Henry grabbed the jacket before it hit the ground, and when Frank started shoving him toward the bar, Henry pushed back. Stumbling, Frank fell on his ass, yelping, "Hey, man, no need to be an ignoramus!"

Walking around Frank, who looked as if he might cry, Henry whispered, "Ladies, you do *not* want to stay anywhere near this place tonight. How about if I see if I can get your car started?"

"That'd be great," Maria agreed, relief spreading through her as she inched closer to Izzy.

Henry pulled a small key light from his jeans pocket and directed it under the hood. The girls stood close by his side, watching as he muttered and jiggled a few connections. With their attention elsewhere, Billy backed toward the stand of dried-out evergreens. Bending as if to tie his shoe, he came up holding a wooden stake. Brandishing it like a Milwaukee slugger, he crept up behind Henry. Sensing his approach, Izzy glanced over her shoulder, but before she could call out a warning, Billy bashed the stake into the back of Henry's head, knocking him to the ground.

"I said we don't need you, old man! That'll teach you to mind yer own damn business!"

Recoiling, Izzy dragged Maria away from the car. "What's the matter with you?" she screamed. "You could've killed him!"

Ignoring her, Billy snickered as he kicked Henry twice in the ribs. Helping Frank to his feet, he asked, "You okay, man?"

"Yeah, I'm good. Fucker caught me by surprise, is all," Frank answered, landing a kick of his own in Henry's side.

Looking around to see if anyone else had seen the attack, Billy grinned menacingly as he approached the girls.

"Stay away from us," Izzy warned, stepping in front of Maria.

Moving quickly, Billy grabbed her by the neck. "Grab the blonde, Frank, this one's mine."

Clawing at his arms, Izzy screamed, "Let me go! Run, Maria!"

Hesitating at first, Maria debated whether to go to Izzy's aid or to flee. "Run, Maria, run!" Izzy yelled again, so she turned and took off toward the road. Catching up to her, Frank slammed his considerable weight into her back, forcing her to pinwheel forward. Hitting the ground hard, she rolled onto her back, punching her legs upward and connecting with Frank's fleshy belly.

"You bitch!" he grunted as regurgitated beer spewed from his mouth. Grabbing her ankle, he twisted it angrily, forcing her to turn over. Straddling her, he ground her face into the dirt and gravel, threatening, "Don't fuckin' try that again."

Struggling to breathe, Maria called out for help, but Izzy was still straining in the grip of a very pissed Billy. He held her in a choke hold with one arm while pulling her head back by her hair with the other. Izzy scratched at his arms and face, bucking to free herself, but the harder she thrashed, the tighter he gripped.

"Calm the fuck down," Billed growled in her ear, "or I'll break your fucking neck and get Frank to do the same to your friend." Muscling her to the truck, he opened the gate and heaved her in. When she landed with a thud on her back, he jumped in on top of her, punching her hard in the face. Izzy's eyes rolled up, and she stilled.

"Come on, Frank, get her the fuck over here. We'll hog-tie 'em and head to the cabin."

Holding Maria by her collar and waistband, Frank tossed her in beside Izzy. "Get outta here, Billy," he ordered. "I'll tie 'em down while you drive."

"Throw their shoes and purses in the cargo box," Billy shouted through the cab's open rear window. He reversed the truck from the lot, fishtailing northbound when he hit the road's pavement. Frank worked to secure the sisters' hands and feet, and once done, he squeezed himself through the window and high-fived Billy.

# SUNDAY AFTERNOON, DECEMBER 30, 1979

DOYLESTOWN, PENNSYLVANIA

Tony Thomas sat in his burgundy leather recliner, clicking on the TV with the new remote Anna had given him for Christmas. He was still trying to figure out all the buttons, but so long as he could watch both playoff games today, he'd be happy. He thought of himself as a simple man with a beautiful wife and two beautiful daughters. Although he wished he were retired already, his job as an accountant for a local paint factory wasn't so bad. Life was good, and on Sundays, it was great.

Untying her apron, Anna walked into the room, a stern expression on her porcelain face. "Do you think we should call the D'Amatos to make sure the girls have arrived?"

"It's only been an hour since I talked to Helene," Tony responded. "Let's give it til halftime, and if we haven't heard from them by then—"

Anna exploded. "Tony, aren't our daughters more important than a damn football game?"

"Calm down, Anna," he snapped, but as he took in those fiery eyes, his voice softened. "Okay, okay, we'll call now. Get me the phone number." Beautiful but prickly, he thought of his wife. They'd been married nearly a quarter century, but he still melted when she got her ire up.

Picking up the phone on the chairside table, Tony punched in the numbers. Helene D'Amato answered on the first ring.

"Hi, Helene, it's Tony again. Just checking in before the game starts to see if the girls've arrived." He winked at Anna, who sat biting her thumbnail in the chair across the room.

"Hate to tell you this, Tony, but no, they're still not here. If you think it's the right thing to do, I'd like to call the police."

"They'll probably be mad that you're even bothering them, but maybe we should both call. You contact Jacksonville, and we'll call Doylestown," Tony suggested. "Just to let them know what's up. Maybe they can check with highway patrols along I-95, just in case they've broken down somewhere."

At hearing Tony's words, Anna stood and walked to the window. Staring out over their carefully manicured landscape, she wiped a tear from her eye as two squirrels chased each other down the trunk of a towering pine tree.

"Helene, I'm hanging up now. We'll talk again in thirty minutes."

"Okay, Tony. Tell Anna to stay calm," Helene said quietly, then disconnected the call.

Pushing down the footrest, Tony stood and walked purposefully into his study, leaving Anna weeping softly in the den.

# SATURDAY EVENING, DECEMBER 29, 1979

### FAYETTEVILLE, NORTH CAROLINA

Henry Long moaned and rolled onto his back. His head throbbed, and when his hand probed instinctively at his scalp, he felt the hot, sticky liquid.

"What the hell?" he mumbled. Propping himself on his elbows, his vision blurred, and he turned his head to vomit. Burger and beer splattered down his arm, and he fell back to the ground.

"Hey, mister, you okay?" a voice called out. Opening his eyes, Henry could make out the shape of a man leaning over him, but his features were lost in a glare of headlights.

"I'm not sure," Henry admitted uncertainly. "I must've passed out." Holding up his hand, he added, "My head's bleeding, cut wide open."

"Man, you look like shit. Let me get Jimmy to call an ambulance," the man suggested.

*Jimmy. Oh, that's right,* Henry remembered. *I just had my supper. Burger and beer. What happened after that?* He couldn't remember.

Jimmy ran from the bar, kneeling over Henry. "Did you fall, Hank?"

"Maybe. I don't know. My head and chest feel like I was blindsided by a grizzly."

"Might've been a black bear. No grizzlies around here that I know of," Jimmy joked. "Smarter bet is that those two drunken idiots had something to do with this."

It hurt too much to think, but after a few seconds, Henry said, "Last I remember is paying my tab and going after those yahoos and the girls. Can't remember anything else."

"Well, those two yahoos never came back in to settle their tab, so if they had anything to do with what's happened to you, they're in even bigger trouble. Just lay still, Hank, an ambulance is on the way."

# SATURDAY EVENING, DECEMBER 29, 1979

### ALONG THE CAPE FEAR RIVER

S werving around yet another curve, the girls rolled roughly to one side of the truck bed, then the other. The temperature was comfortably cool, but fear-induced sweat plastered hair to their faces and necks. The ropes trussing their ankles and wrists gouged into their flesh, cutting off circulation.

Coming to, Izzy struggled to stretch out before recognizing the trouble they were in. "Maria, where are they taking us?" she asked, her voice panicked.

"I don't know, Izzy, but I'm scared to death." Maria's breathing was ragged. "I can't feel my hands anymore."

"Me either," Izzy admitted, "but we've got to stay strong. When they untie us, run if you can, and don't worry about me."

"I will if you will," Maria promised before silently praying the *Hail Mary*.

As the girls toppled like rag dolls with each bend in the road, Billy and Frank passed a joint back and forth in the cab. With its rear window open, Izzy smelled the pungent smoke and heard the men's raucous laughter. Her thoughts turned to the last time she'd smoked weed. Lisa and she'd been hanging out, talking about how much fun they'd have sharing an apartment during spring semester. *God*, she thought, *I'd give anything to be high now and only imagining this shit.*

The truck hit a deep rut, bouncing the girls roughly. Their heads cracked together, and lightning flashed in Maria's eyes with what she feared was the opening salvo of a migraine headache.

"I think I'm gonna throw up, Izzy."

"Close your eyes, and take a deep breath. Whatever you do, don't let them know you're afraid," Izzy said.

"I'll try," Maria gulped.

"Do more than try, Maria. We can't act like weaklings, or we'll be in worse trouble."

"Worse than what?" Maria's asked, her voice hushed. "Nothing could be worse than this."

The truck veered sharply to the right, slowing to take the turn. Gravel crunched under the tires, and Izzy suspected they'd turned off the main road. The truck engine quieted, and she thought she could hear water flowing not too far away. A dense canopy of trees closed overhead, and a screech owl shrieked somewhere nearby.

Fifteen jolting minutes later, the truck rolled to a stop. One of the men jumped from the cab, followed by the sound of creaking metal hinges. Startling the girls, Frank hoisted himself into the bed. "We're here, pretty ladies. We'll get you comfy real soon."

Billy laughed from the cab, and after the truck moved forward about ten yards, Frank jumped back out to close the rusty gate behind them.

# SUNDAY AFTERNOON, DECEMBER 30, 1979

## DOYLESTOWN, PENNSYLVANIA

After speaking with the duty officer, Tony and Anna sat quietly in the den awaiting his arrival. The officer had told Tony that it was unlikely there was anything to worry about, what with the girls not missing, really, for more than a few hours, but he'd asked to come by the house to pick up photos that he could wire to his counterparts down south.

Hearing the police car pull up the driveway, Anna walked to the piano to retrieve framed photos of the girls taken for their high school graduations. With shaking hands, she slid the photos from their frames.

Tony opened the front door before the officer had the opportunity to ring the bell. Reaching out his hand, he greeted the man. "Tony Thomas, and this"—he gestured in Anna's direction—"is my wife, Anna. We appreciate your coming by."

"Officer Tim Johnson, sir," replied the clean-cut young man in his late twenties. Accepting Tony's firm handshake, he smiled pleasantly. "Nice to meet you both. Why don't we take a few minutes to talk?" Looking around, he added,

"How 'bout the kitchen?"

"Absolutely," Tony replied. "Right this way." Taking the photos from Anna, he motioned her ahead of them.

"Can I get you something to drink, Officer?" Anna inquired. He noticed how slight and pale she was, obviously quite distraught. In her early forties, she was a petite woman who wore her long blond hair twisted atop her head. Anna Thomas was a mother whose apprehension now overshadowed an otherwise graceful demeanor.

"No, thank you, ma'am," he answered politely, although frankly, he could have used something strong to drink about now. This was his first missing persons case—*possible missing persons*, he corrected himself—and he was a little unsure of protocol. His typical Sunday involved ticketing tourists speeding through this small, scenic community. But with the holidays, the desk sergeant had taken the weekend off, and Tim had offered to pull double duty.

"I have a few questions about the girls. Their heights, weights, etcetera, to go with the photos," Officer Johnson explained, holding out his hand to accept the photographs from Tony. "Then I'll let you get back to football."

Anna kicked Tony under the table while smiling sweetly at Officer Johnson.

"Pretty girls," Johnson noted, placing the photos on the table in front of him. "You must be proud."

"We are. I didn't want them to go by themselves, but they begged us," Anna explained unnecessarily, glancing at her husband. Her manicured nails tapped worriedly atop the table. "I was married at Isabella's age, after all, so how could I, we, not let them?"

"I understand completely," Johnson assured her. "I remember how determined I was at that age."

"Always knew more than our parents," Tony added. "We

raised our girls to be independent, but perhaps we should have been a little less permissive?"

"I'm sure you've done just fine, Mr. Thomas. We can't plan for every eventuality that might come down the pike, now, can we?"

"No, I suppose you're right, isn't he, Anna?" Tony asked, taking his wife's hand to quiet her tapping.

Twenty minutes later, with his questions answered and promises made to stay in contact, Officer Johnson placed his card on the table and left.

"I'm going up to lie down," Anna said, sighing deeply. "Come get me if anything happens."

"All right, dear. I'll sit by the phone," Tony assured her, before muttering under his breath, "while I watch a little football."

# SATURDAY EVENING, DECEMBER 29, 1979

### FAYETTEVILLE, NORTH CAROLINA

Henry Long lay on an emergency room gurney, his head wrapped in gauze and an IV tube snaking from his arm. Police Chief Wayne Roberts stood at the foot of the cot, Moleskine notebook open, pencil poised. He was a tall, fit man with well-defined biceps visible under his tan short-sleeved shirt. Close-cropped sandy hair and long sideburns framed a face that featured a strong jaw and hawklike nose. Hazel eyes, vigilant behind a pair of rimless glasses, were creased with intensity as they studied Henry.

"Mr. Long, let's go over this again," Chief Roberts intoned. "Tell me what you planned to do when you walked out of Jimmy's Joint."

"Like I said before, Chief, I'm not exactly sure what I was going to do. Jimmy told me two girls were having car trouble, and I thought I might help."

"And you don't remember anything after leaving the bar?"

"Not really. My mind is so fuzzy, and it pains me to even try to remember."

"How did you hurt your head?" the chief inquired for the second time.

"I don't remember!" insisted Henry. "All's I know is that I fell. It was the doc who stitched me up who said my head looks like it was hit by a bat."

"Well, Henry—may I call you Henry?" Roberts asked. Henry nodded, and the chief continued, "My patrol officer did locate a bloody stake in the weeds near where you were found, so that doctor is probably correct. But more important here is why anyone would want to hurt you. Why do you think that is?"

"Again, Chief Roberts, like I just said, I wanted to help out the girls. Whether I did or said something to royally piss off one of those local yahoos, I just don't remember."

"Yeah, Jimmy told us how Billy Ramone and Frank Carter had offered to fix the girls' car," Chief Roberts said. "Problem is, we got ourselves a mystery. See, we found their car still in Jimmy's parking lot, hood up, but the girls were nowhere to be found. And Ramone's truck is gone, which means Billy and Frank are gone, too. Do you think the two young ladies went off with those boys, and if so, why would they do that with you lying there bleeding?"

"Chief, if I start remembering anything, you'll be the first I call. Until then, I suggest you put out a BOLO for this Ramone's truck. Maybe you'll find your answers faster that way than waiting for my brain to unscramble."

"Well, Henry, thanks for telling me how to do my job, but we're already out looking for them. They've been in plenty trouble before, FYI."

"What a surprise."

"As for the girls," the chief continued, "Jimmy gave us as best a description he could, and we're tracing their vehicle —it has Pennsylvania plates, by the way, a long way from home—and we hope to find all four of them having a nice supper somewhere."

"The doc says I'm not going anywhere tonight, but if I remember anything, I'll be in touch. Oh, and make sure my rig stays safe at Jimmy's. I'm already gonna be late delivering my load; I don't need it stolen, too."

"Will do, Henry, will do," Chief Roberts assured him, closing his notebook. He then stormed from the cubicle, leaving the privacy curtain fluttering in his wake.

# SATURDAY EVENING, DECEMBER 29, 1979

CAPE FEAR RIVER, HARNETT COUNTY, NORTH CAROLINA

Maria and Isabella, wearing only bras and panties, lay side-by-side on a sagging, mildewed mattress. Their arms and legs were tied to a rusty metal bed. The flickering overhead bulb, which had surprisingly switched on after Billy fired up the cabin's gas-powered generator, cast eerie shadows across the room.

Billy and Frank stood at the foot of the bed, sweating and breathing hard, competing looks of triumph and anticipation on their faces. "Well, well, Frankie boy," Billy snickered, rubbing his palms together. "Look at our guests now. Not so snooty, are they?"

Getting the girls from the truck to the cabin hadn't been easy. After untying them, the brunette had tried to escape when Billy, stoned silly, had slipped and fallen on a moss-covered step. When his shin slammed into the tread, his grip on Izzy had loosened. Twisting out of his grasp, she'd run back toward the gate as fast as her bare feet could carry her. Daring to take a quick look back at Maria, she, too, slipped on wet leaves. Billy had grabbed her from behind and smacked her good and hard over the right ear, yanking her arm behind her until the shoulder wrenched from its socket with a pop. Izzy had shrieked in pain.

"I like my women feisty," he'd hissed in her ear. "But only once, and you've already had your chance." After that, he'd dragged her to the cabin steps, forcing her to crawl up while holding her long hair like a leash.

Maria, hearing her sister's cries of pain, had simply slumped to the ground. Frank had thrown her over his shoulder and schlepped her limp body into the cabin.

Blood now trickled from Izzy's nose and right ear. Maria's left eye was swollen shut, and her nose crooked to the right, broken when Frank had ground her face into the gravel parking lot. Both girls were drained from the struggle to free themselves. Eyes closed, Maria whimpered quietly while Izzy, terrified but stoic, lay silent beside her.

"Can I have mine now, Billy?" Frank asked, pulling down the shoulder straps of his overalls.

"No! We're gonna do 'em at the same time," Billy pronounced, his breath quickening at the thought. "Where's that guttin' knife we used when we was up here fishin' with Bobby last summer? We'll use it to cut off their britches."

"Out the shed, I think," Frank answered. "I'll git it, but don't you start without me."

Returning minutes later to find Billy gripping his erection, Frank stopped and stared, his mouth twisted with irritation.

"Whatcha lookin' at, doofus?" Billy asked, stroking the length of his dick. "Never seen such a fine cock before? These pretty ladies sure like it."

"But, but—I told you to—to—to wait for me," Frank stammered.

"I am waitin', jackass, but hurry up with their britches. I don't know how much longer this big guy can wait."

Opening her eyes, Maria spotted the knife and prayed silently that she'd shrivel up and die right then and there. Tears streamed down her cheeks and puddled in her ears, and she began to shake uncontrollably.

"Don't worry yer pretty self," Frank assured her from where he stood over Izzy. "I'm a real pro with a knife. Long as you and your friend here lay real still, I promise not to cut nobody." Slicing through the front clasp of Izzy's bra, he pinched her nipples between his dirty fingers until she bucked.

"Ooh, she's alive after all," Billy moaned from the foot of the bed, his hand moving up and down his cock.

Ripping off Izzy's panties, Frank took a deep sniff of the crotch and quivered. "Sweet," he sighed, tossing the panties to Billy, who rubbed the silky fabric over his erection.

Frank walked around the bed to Maria, at which point, Billy, on the verge of exploding, dropped the panties to the floor and hurried from the room. A few moments later, he returned, swigging from a bottle of moonshine he'd unearthed in a kitchen cupboard.

"Save some of that hooch for me," Frank demanded, pulling Maria's panties taut and slicing them from her body.

"Ooh-wee!" Billy whistled. "Look at that bush! Can't wait to see what's hidin' underneath."

"Hey, I thought she was mine," Frank protested.

"No worries, Frankie," Billy consoled, handing him the bottle. "We'll take turns. Somethin' tells me it's gonna be a long night."

# SUNDAY MORNING, DECEMBER 30, 1979

CAPE FEAR RIVER, HARNETT COUNTY, NORTH CAROLINA

M aria awoke with a start, breathing in the malodorous scent of mildew and sex. The faint light of dawn tinged the cold room in murky shades of gray. She could just make out a swaying tree outside the dirty, rain-streaked window. An angry draft whistled through the uninsulated walls, and a steady drip from the ceiling puddled onto the room's threadbare rug before seeping through the floorboards.

Her body shivered uncontrollably, each shudder racking her naked body with pain. She was parched, and when she tried to swallow, her throat felt like it was lined with glass shards. Fear followed confusion as the horror of last night came back to her. Twisting her head, her eyes settled on Isabella, still out of it. Dried blood zigzagged down Izzy's cheek and chin, disappearing into the mattress. Nasty bite marks, and maybe cigarette burns, crisscrossed her left breast.

"Izzy," Maria whispered urgently. "Wake up. We've got to get out of here."

Izzy didn't stir. As Maria worked to slide her body closer

to her sister, she noticed the sticky streaks of blood smeared across her own belly and thighs. With her arms tied to the headboard, she could lift her head only a few inches, but it was enough to see the dark red pool spreading out from her legs.

"Izzy, wake up, please," Maria pleaded, bouncing a bit to generate movement that might awaken her sister.

Isabella moaned slightly. A gurgle rose from her throat, followed by a rasping cough that rattled the rickety bed.

"Izzy, wake up! We've got to get out of here," Maria repeated in a full-blown panic.

Izzy opened her eyes and turned her head toward Maria. Seeing her sister tied up beside her, realization took hold. *This isn't a nightmare. It's real, and we're in deep shit.*

"So, the sleeping beauties are finally awake?" Billy asked from the doorway. "Frank and I was wonderin' how long it'd take you girls to recover from last night's party."

Looking in over Billy's shoulder, Frank added, "Yeah, we was thinkin' about startin' round two after we grab us some subs from the corner store."

"Want us to bring ya back anything?" Billy taunted. "Maybe a maxi pad for you, Blondie? You was bleedin' so much, Frankie and I had to go down the river this morning to wash our dicks."

"Maybe I'll take ya down later to clean yerself up some," Frank teased her.

"Only if you're a good girl, though," Billy said. "We'll be back soon, so don't go gettin' in any trouble."

"Can you get us some water?" Maria asked, her voice a scratchy whisper.

"No! We don't need anything from them," Izzy growled weakly.

"Oh yeah?" said Billy. "You sure was beggin' us for some-thin' last night."

"And will be again when we get back." Frank snickered and smacked Billy on the back.

"Water for Blondie, but none for the Bitch," Billy said, pointing his finger at Izzy. "See ya both real soon."

The men left the cabin, and Izzy looked with concern at her sister. "Maria, are you okay? Are you really bleeding that much?"

"Yeah, I guess so," Maria answered, grimacing as she strained to see her abdomen. "I hurt pretty bad, but I think I'll be okay. Unless I freeze to death, that is."

"I'm cold, too. Here, snuggle closer to me."

As sheets of rain pelted the windows, Maria and Izzy inched toward each other.

# SUNDAY AFTERNOON, DECEMBER 30, 1979

### FAYETTEVILLE, NORTH CAROLINA

C hief Wayne Roberts sat at his desk, worrying over the report in front of him. His neck and back ached, and he wanted a beer in a bad way. He was meant to be off today, what with all hands on deck for tomorrow night, but this incident at Jimmy's Joint was weighing on him. After the Steelers had routed the Dolphins, he'd kissed his wife good-bye and headed to the station. The radio crackled behind him, and he grabbed the mic. "Roberts here, come in."

"Chief, this is Rawlins," came the reply. "No luck so far finding Billy Ramone's truck. He's not at home, over at Frank Carter's or his sister's. Not sure if they're telling the truth, but everyone swears they haven't seen him or Frank since yesterday. I'm fixin' to get off in thirty. Want me to look anywhere else or come on in?"

"None of his family or friends have a clue where he or Frank could be holed up?" the chief asked.

"Nope. Everyone swears they don't know nothin'," Rawlins reported.

"Well, keep looking, Mickey. I just pulled a missing persons report off the wire with photos of two sisters matching the description of the girls seen at Jimmy's. Seems they were on their way to Florida and never made it. I expect we'll find them when and where we find Ramone and Carter."

"Will do, Chief. I could spare another hour or two if you're payin' overtime..."

"Already paying overtime tomorrow night, why not tonight too," the chief lamented. "I'll respond to this report, then head over to Jimmy's to show him these photos. Maybe cruise around a bit myself after that. Over and out."

# 13

# SUNDAY AFTERNOON, DECEMBER 30, 1979

### CAPE FEAR RIVER, HARNETT COUNTY, NORTH CAROLINA

True to his word, Frank untied Maria, winding a length of rope around her waist and pushing her, naked and shivering, down the rocky path. The wind-driven rain assaulted them, and when they reached the banks, the ice-cold river roiled around her ankles. Wavering when Frank ordered her to wade in deeper, he shoved her roughly and laughed as her head disappeared beneath the churning waters. Surfacing, she gasped and sputtered before scrabbling back toward Frank. She now stood unsteadily in knee-deep water, her arms wrapped tightly around her trembling body.

"Stop your blubbering, Blondie, and clean yerself up!" Frank ordered. Tossing her a rag, he added, "Use this."

Swallowing her tears, Maria quivered, "But—but—but I need soap."

"Well, you ain't gettin' none, so make do."

"But—"

"But fuckin' nothin'," he shouted over the howling wind.

Dipping the rag into the muddy water, she dabbed tentatively at her belly. "It's so cold," she complained.

Shoving his hands deeper into the pockets of his jacket, he scowled. "Well, the sooner you get all that blood off, the sooner we get back to the damn cabin."

With her teeth chattering so fiercely she feared they'd crack, Maria wiped the rag across her belly and down her thighs. After rinsing it out, she gently swabbed between her legs, grimacing as the rough cloth chafed her bruised and swollen labia.

Despite her efforts, the blood continued to trickle down her legs, mixing with the rain before whisking away in the current. Looking up, she addressed Frank, who stood entranced by her exposed body. "It won't stop."

"What?" he mumbled, shifting his focus from her breasts.

"I said, I'm still bleeding. I'm washing it off, but it's still coming out of me."

"You must be having your fuckin' period," he accused. "I fuckin' hate when girls're on the rag."

"It's not my period," Maria screamed, drops of water spraying from her shaking hair. "You messed me up inside."

"We didn't know you was a virgin, for Chrissakes," he spouted, as though her virginity could have stopped their assault.

"Well, I'm not anymore, am I?"

Anger inflamed his cheeks, and he bristled. "Shut up and finish so we can get out of this fuckin' rain."

When she'd done the best she could, she stepped from the water, quaking violently. Frank grabbed her elbow, propelling her up the path. Stepping on a sharp rock, she yelped, sinking to her knees.

"Get up," Frank snarled, grabbing under her arms. "You're all fuckin' dirty again."

Pulling the rag from his pocket, he bent to wipe the mud

from her legs. Seeing an opportunity, Maria raised a knee, smashing it into his chin. Frank's mouth slammed shut, and he closed his eyes against the wooziness. Maria spun to get away, but he held tightly to her tether. Cursing angrily, he jerked it, and her feet slipped from under her.

"Shoulda known this was a fuckin' bad idea," he huffed, smacking her across the face.

She sucked in a jagged breath and pleaded, "Just let me go, Frank. I'm no good bleeding like this. Let us both go, and we won't tell anyone. I promise."

"Yeah, right, like Billy would ever let that happen," Frank countered, bitterness seeping through his words. Yanking her arms behind her back, he pushed her toward the cabin.

It was silent when Frank all but dragged Maria through the door of the cabin. "We're back," he called out. He threw a dish towel at Maria and headed toward the bedroom.

Wrapping the skimpy towel around her shoulders, Maria followed, peering around him into the darkened room. "Izzy, I'm back," she called quietly.

Frank snapped on the light. Billy lay naked and spread-eagle on top of Izzy. Blood oozed from a fresh gash on her scalp, her eyes staring blankly at the ceiling.

Pushing past Frank, Maria rushed to the bed. With a backhanded smack to the side of Billy's head, she yelled, "Get off my sister, you animal!"

Startling awake, Billy grabbed her arm before she could strike again. "Did she just fuckin' hit me?" he asked incredulously, rearing up.

"Yeah, sorry, Billy," Frank answered, muscling Maria around the foot of the bed. "She got away from me."

"You cunt!" Billy seethed. "How dare you fuckin' hit me." As Frank pushed Maria onto the mattress, Billy grabbed her leg, biting down on her calf. A jolt of pain shot up her leg and into her groin.

As Frank secured her wrists, Billy wrenched apart her ankles, roping them to the metal footboard in a V formation. Straddling her waist, he slapped her hard before yanking her hair and stretching her neck away from her shoulders.

"I'll show you what happens to cunts who hit me," he threatened. As Maria twisted helplessly beneath him, Billy ordered, "Get me the knife, Frank!"

"No, Billy, please," Maria pleaded. "You don't need to do this."

"Shut up!" Billy demanded. As he ran the rusty blade along her jawline, Maria shrieked in pain, causing Frank to cover his ears and turn his back to the bed. Izzy lay silent, a steady stream of tears the only indication she was aware of the assault taking place beside her.

Pleased with himself, Billy jumped from the bed and warned, "There'll be more of that for both of you if you pull any more bullshit."

Punching Frank in the arm, he suggested, "How 'bout you and me go get somethin' to eat? I've worked up quite an appetite since breakfast."

"Sounds good. I'm starvin'," Frank replied, watching as Billy sauntered cockily from the room.

"Dammit, Blondie," Frank hissed, looking at her with disgust. "See what you made him do?" After swiping the towel across her face, he shoved it between her legs, then trudged behind Billy.

# 14

# SUNDAY EVENING, DECEMBER 30, 1979

## DOYLESTOWN, PENNSYLVANIA

The doorbell rang, stirring Tony from a restless nap. The muted TV illuminated the otherwise darkened room. Blinking, he noted the Rams and Cowboys were in a tight matchup. The doorbell chimed again, and he slapped his cheeks to wake himself up. Anna called his name from the second floor, and he boosted himself from the recliner and walked to the door.

Officer Johnson stood, hat in hand, on the front porch. "Sorry to disturb you, Mr. Thomas. May I come in?"

"Yes, yes, I was just dozing a bit. Come in. Anna," Tony called up the stairs, "Officer Johnson is here."

"I'll be right down," Anna replied.

"Is there any news?" Tony inquired.

"Maybe. Let's wait for Mrs. Thomas to join us, and I'll review what we know so far." As the two men walked into the kitchen, Johnson asked, "You haven't heard from the girls, have you?"

"No. I talked to our friends in Jacksonville a little over an hour ago, but nothing."

Anna entered the kitchen, quietly sitting at the table

beside Tony. Her hair had loosened from its chignon, and wispy tendrils trailed over the collar of her blouse. She smiled, but the police officer noted that the effort failed to reach her eyes, the lids puffy from crying.

"Mrs. Thomas, as I was saying to your husband—"

"Call me Tony, please."

"Yes, sir. As I was saying to Tony, we don't know much, but we have heard from a police chief in North Carolina. Fayetteville," he continued, looking at his notes. "It seems two young women matching the descriptions of your daughters were last seen at a bar where their car is alleged to have broken down."

"Dammit, Tony!" Anna scowled, her voice thick with anger. "I told you to take that car in for a tune-up before the girls left, but *no*, you had to do it yourself!"

Tony flinched with embarrassment. "Anna, calm down. Let's listen to what Officer Johnson has to say."

Squirming in his seat, the officer looked sympathetically at Anna. "No sense getting yourself so upset, Mrs. Thomas. It's water under the bridge, and getting angry won't help find Isabella and Maria."

Tony squeezed Anna's hand as Officer Johnson continued, "Anyway, it seems the car broke down, and the girls went into the bar to ask to use the phone. Two men inside offered to help, and then all four left the bar."

"Okay, so?" Tony prompted.

"Well, that's where the known story ends. Another man in the bar went to help not long after the girls walked out with the two men, but he somehow ended up in the hospital with a concussion and can't remember anything that happened."

"Where are our daughters now?" asked Anna, her voice catching in her throat.

"We don't know," the officer admitted, swallowing hard. "According to this report, a yellow 1971 Subaru with Pennsylvania tags—that's their car, right?"

"Yes, that's it," Tony quickly confirmed.

"Well, a car matching that description was found in the parking lot next to the man who'd been knocked unconscious. It's speculated that your daughters left the premises with the two men."

"What, exactly, does that mean?" Tony asked, his voice rising. "Do those men have our girls? Should we be down there, in Fayetteville, looking for them ourselves?"

"Sir, if I had any better information or advice, I'd give it to you. But as it stands now, I think we should let the Fayetteville police do their job. They have a BOLO out for the truck owned by one of the men, and while it hasn't been located, it will be soon. I'm sure of it."

"Thank you for that," Tony said, reaching out his hand. "Please let us know as soon as you learn more. In the meantime, I think we'll sit tight and say a few prayers."

"Little more you can do, but I'll say a few of my own," the officer replied, shaking Tony's hand. "Mrs. Thomas, trust me, your daughters will be found."

# 15

# MONDAY MORNING, DECEMBER 31, 1979

## ORLANDO, FLORIDA

Settling up at the receiving warehouse, Henry pocketed his check and pulled his weary body into the cab of his truck. The foreman hadn't been happy about getting in so early to unload the thirty pallets, but Henry hadn't been released from the hospital until late Sunday afternoon. There'd been no way to meet the original deadline, so he'd driven through the night and had been waiting outside the padlocked gate when the foreman had arrived before dawn.

Henry was exhausted, and his head and ribs throbbed. The discharge doctor had given him strict instructions to rest for the next several days, and turning right around to drive home to Virginia Beach was, he knew, not part of that prescription. What a bizarre few days he'd had, and he wondered again if those two girls had ever shown up. Well, it was none of his business, he concluded. He had his own worries. As he buckled himself into the driver's seat, a niggling guilt poked through his fatigue: if those girls were in trouble, he was to blame.

Wearily, Henry returned to the warehouse and asked to use the phone. He pulled Chief Roberts's card from his wallet and dialed the number. Roberts picked up on the first ring.

"Chief, Henry Long here."

"What can I do for you, Henry? Have you remembered anything that might help us find those girls?" Roberts asked.

"Well, you've answered my first question, Chief. I was hoping they'd turned up safe and sound by now."

"No such luck, Henry. We're all on overtime trying to find the men who likely took off with them. So far, no one's spotted them."

"Could you use my help?"

"No offense, Henry, but what can you do?" Chief Roberts asked in return.

"Well, I used to be a pretty good marine, and I feel some responsibility for the girls being in trouble."

"Honestly, Henry, with it being New Year's Eve, we're expecting quite a bit of activity around here tonight. If you really want to help out, maybe you could come by the station this afternoon to lend a hand monitoring the phones and radio. Where are you now?"

"Orlando, but I could be back in Fayetteville no later than, say, four o'clock," Henry calculated.

"That'd be great. See you then, Henry. And thanks." Chief Roberts signed off.

# 16

# MONDAY MORNING, DECEMBER 31, 1979

### CAPE FEAR RIVER, HARNETT COUNTY, NORTH CAROLINA

The day broke cold but sunny, with yesterday's storm having moved up the coast. Billy stretched out on the grungy couch as Frank added another log to the fire. Both men were naked, and Billy, proud of his physique and prowess, positioned himself like a porn star, one leg cocked against the back cushions and the other dangling over the front.

Snapping his fingers, he said, "Hey, Frank."

"Yeah?"

"What if we get one of those VHS recorders and film ourselves with the girls?"

"Uh, I dunno," Frank said, shrugging. "Don't they cost a lot?"

"We wouldn't buy one. Just rent it. Where d'ya think the nearest RadioShack is?"

"Probably back in town, but do ya wanna take a chance going back? I bet the cops are lookin' for us."

"Nah, you're right," Billy conceded. "Maybe we can ask that old guy at the market if he has one we can borrow. What's his name?"

"I think it's Otis. Like on *Andy Griffith*."

"What a fuckin' hick." Billy laughed. "Wouldn't that be a great way to rock in the New Year? Starring in our own porno."

Warming to the idea, Frank plopped down on the arm of the couch, his flabby belly jiggling as he spoke. "You can tape me doin' Blondie, and then I'll get you fuckin' her friend."

"That's just what I was thinkin'," Billy said excitedly, stroking his dick. "Remember when we sneaked into the Miracle Theater to watch *Behind the Green Door*?"

"Yeah, girls doin' girls," Frank recalled, smiling as his cock twitched to life. "Think we can get them to lick each other?"

"Hell yeah, they will!" Eyeing Frank's engorged cock, Billy teased, "Question is, Frankie, do *you* wanna lick *me*?"

"No way, man," Frank replied uncomfortably. "We ain't queers."

"Didn't say we are, but no one'll ever know. Come on, we might as well give it a whirl while the bitches are resting up for later." Leaning forward, he squeezed Frank's erect penis. When Frank moaned, Billy lay back, saying, "I know you want to, Frankie, I can tell."

Shifting to his knees, Frank took Billy's swollen shaft in his mouth. Grunting, Billy angled his head for a better view. "Suck harder, Frank, come on!" he begged, grabbing onto Frank's hair. Moments later, he cried out as he exploded in Frank's mouth. "Oh man, that was fucking amazing," he proclaimed.

Frank pushed himself away, hurrying to the sink. After wiping his mouth with a dish towel, he leaned over the back of the couch, kissing Billy full on the mouth.

"What the fuck was that for?" Billy recoiled and back-handed Frank across the face.

"Just messin' with you, Billy," Frank replied, looking hurt.

"Well, cut it out."

"All right, no kissing," Frank said, pouting. "But how 'bout you blow me now?"

"No fuckin' way," Billy rebuffed. "Just 'cause you're a fag doesn't mean I am."

"I'm—I'm not a fag!" Frank stuttered, his face reddening and fists clenching. Incensed, he grabbed his overalls from the hook by the fireplace and stormed out the door.

# 17

# MONDAY EVENING, DECEMBER 31, 1979

## FAYETTEVILLE, NORTH CAROLINA

F ayetteville was crazy. New Year's Eve had brought out all the usual revelers and an abundance of unusual ones. Before he'd headed out on patrol, Chief Roberts had commissioned Henry as an honorary deputy, asking that he assist his dispatcher, Deputy Mary Martin, in monitoring the phones and radio.

While Mary, a no-nonsense woman in her sixties with short gray hair and tortoise shell eyeglasses, manned the radio, Henry answered the phone. After taking a call, he'd pass the report on to Mary for dispatch. It seemed the phone had been ringing nonstop for the past hour, and as soon as Henry disconnected one call, another would come in, sometimes two at a time.

"Fayetteville Police," Henry answered for the umpteenth time. "What's the nature of your emergency?"

"I just seen a near-naked woman running along the banks of the Cape Fear!" the caller reported breathlessly.

As per the guidelines, Henry calmly asked, "Your name, sir, and where you're calling from?"

"What does my name have to do with anything?" the

caller replied. "This girl's only wearing a shirt, and a bloody one at that. You'd better send someone now!"

Working to maintain his composure, Henry continued, "Sir, where exactly did you see this girl?"

"I seen her when I crossed the Highway 217 bridge heading toward Linden. She was running south, just above the bridge."

"Just a moment, sir." Putting his hand over the mouth-piece, Henry asked, "Mary, where's the Highway 217 bridge near Linden?"

"Out of our jurisdiction," Mary replied in exasperation. Grabbing the phone from Henry, she spouted, "Sir, this is Deputy Mary Martin. It sounds like you're in Harnett County, not Cumberland or Fayetteville. Please hang up and call the Harnett County Sheriff's office."

As she went to hang up, Henry shouted, "Wait!" Putting the phone to his ear, he asked, "Sir, are you able to stay put until officers arrive?"

"Fuck, no!" the caller cursed. "I have a party to go to."

"Please, sir," Henry pleaded. "We've got two missing girls, and you may have just seen one of them."

"Whatever. I've done my good deed for the day." With that, the caller hung up.

# 18

## MONDAY EVENING, DECEMBER 31, 1979

### CAPE FEAR RIVER, HARNETT COUNTY, NORTH CAROLINA

I sabella was catatonic. After days of sadistic rape and abuse, with no food or water, she was barely breathing on the mattress beside Maria. While the two animals had granted Maria a sip of water every so often, at least until she'd smacked Billy the afternoon before, they'd withheld even that little mercy from Izzy as punishment for her "bad attitude." Maria now feared her sister wouldn't make it.

After smoking a joint on the front porch, Billy had popped his head in to announce that he and Frank were heading out to stock up on munchies and beer. He'd promised to return shortly for a good old New Year's celebration.

"We might even bring back somethin' to make the night real memorable," he'd hinted ominously.

Listening to the sound of spitting gravel as the truck drove away from the cabin, Maria concluded, *It's now or never*. Something had gone on between the two men earlier in the day, and although she couldn't fathom what it was, they'd been acting more crazed than ever, even toward each other. It was evident that Billy, and to a lesser degree, Frank, was becoming increasingly unhinged. She desperately needed to find a way to escape or risk dying.

She'd been working to loosen the ropes that tied her hands and feet to the metal bed, stretching them ever so slightly with every pull. Each tug had cut deeper into her raw and bloodied flesh, but the ropes seemed to be yielding just a bit.

Steeling herself against the agonizing pain, Maria wrapped her right hand around its tether, pulling as hard as she could. Crying out as the coarse twine cut deeper into her wrist, she begged, "Dear God, help me!" Drawing on whatever grit she had left, she yanked. Her hand slipped free of its bind.

Her arm had lost so much feeling, it took a few minutes before she was able to move it from where it had landed above her head. After shaking it to revive the blood flow, she reached up and pulled the rope loose from her left hand. Taking a moment to rest both arms, she hauled herself into a sitting position and freed her ankles. Her feet were numb and swollen, but unsure of how much time she had, she rolled onto her side, throwing her legs to the floor. Standing quickly, she swooned as her blood pressured dropped. Falling back to the bed, she gasped when the blood-soaked mattress squished beneath her.

Catching her breath, she waited until her thundering heart slowed before pulling herself up. Holding the footboard for support, she swayed unsteadily around the bed, recoiling when she stepped on the fillet knife Frank had heedlessly left on the floor. Picking it up, she freed Izzy's arms and legs from their binds, massaging each limb for a brief moment to revive the circulation.

Hastily searching the outer room, she found an unopened bottle of water on the counter and a grimy, moth-eaten blanket beside the couch. She returned to the bedroom and, while lifting Izzy's head, poured a trickle of water into her sister's mouth. After covering her with the blanket, she kissed her gently on the cheek.

"Izzy," she promised, "I'm going for help. You just lie here and breathe. Just keep breathing, and I'll be back real soon."

Maria stopped in the doorway, then returned to the bed to wrap the knife in Izzy's left hand. "Use this when they come back, Izzy," she ordered her sister, hoping to God she'd have the chance.

Hurrying now, Maria staggered for the front door. As she passed the smoldering fireplace, she noticed a flash of red in the wicker log bin. Peering closer, she recognized Izzy's flannel shirt. Pulling it around her beaten body, she walked out of the cabin and into the darkness.

# 19

# MONDAY NIGHT, DECEMBER 31, 1979

FAYETTEVILLE AND HARNETT COUNTIES, NORTH CAROLINA

After convincing Mary to radio Chief Roberts, Henry grabbed the mic, relaying his conversation with the anonymous caller.

"It's got to be one of the Thomas girls," he insisted. "Mary's on the phone with Harnett County now, but I think we should head up there, too."

"I agree," Chief Roberts stated. "I'm just down the road. I'll pick you up in five."

Henry met Roberts's patrol car in the station parking lot, jumped in the passenger seat, and buckled up. Flicking on the rooftop lights and engaging the siren, Chief Roberts tore onto 95 Business. Radioing in to the Harnett County dispatcher, he was patched through to the car en route to the scene, relaying his ETA and asking to be kept informed of all developments.

"Will do, sir," the patrol officer responded. "Sheriff Dunn is on his way, too."

"Good," Roberts replied. "Remember, there are two girls missing. Once we find this one, we'll need to move quickly to find the other."

"Yes, sir, understood."

Thirty minutes later, with siren wailing, Roberts and Henry arrived at the bridge. Three Harnett County patrol cars were parked haphazardly across the span, an array of lights flashing through the swaying treetops. After jumping from the vehicle, Henry rushed to the closest officer, who was directing a strong spotlight over the bridge's southwest railing.

"Have you found her?" he asked, out of breath.

Looking over his shoulder, the officer replied, "Who the hell are you?"

Coming up beside them, Roberts flashed his badge and said, "Chief Roberts, Fayetteville. He's with me."

"Yes, sir, we spoke by radio. We've got a team down there scouring the banks for the girl. They've found footprints, but not her. They've been calling out, but so far, no response."

"She might be hiding," suggested Henry. "Afraid the search team is really Ramone and Carter."

"Didn't think of that," the office conceded.

"Let me try calling out to her," Henry offered. "She might remember me from the bar. How do I get down?"

"There's a ladder at the end. There," the officer said, pointing. "Be careful, though, it's real slick from the rain. My sheriff nearly went down headfirst a bit ago."

Henry started down the ladder, followed closely by Chief Roberts. When they reached the bottom rung, the two men jumped the remaining few feet, rolling toward the water in ankle-deep mud.

"Shit," the chief swore, righting himself and plodding after Henry.

"Maria and Isabella, right?" Henry confirmed. "I wonder which one she is."

"Just holler for Miss Thomas," suggested Roberts. "Tell her who you are."

Henry called out into the trees overhead, "Miss Thomas...Miss Thomas...I'm Henry Long, the old man from the bar who wanted to help with your car."

He stopped to listen for a reply, then continued: "That asshole hit me good on the head, but I'm all right. I've come with the police to help you and your sister."

Quieting again, he and Roberts continued their trek until catching up with the search party. Introductions were made all around, and it was agreed that Henry and Chief Roberts would venture farther into the woods, where the girl might be hiding. Using tree roots to pull themselves up the bank, they reached the crest and looked around.

"I sure hope she went into the woods instead of the water," the chief whispered.

"We'll find her," Henry insisted, pulling out his pocket light as they hiked into the shadowy thicket. "Miss Thomas! Are you Isabella or Maria? It's me, Henry, from the bar. Chief Roberts and I have come to help you."

"Miss Thomas! I'm Police Chief Roberts from Fayetteville. Henry's right. We're here to help you and your sister. Please come out. You'll be safe with us."

Henry held a finger to his lips before pointing to a copse of mountain laurel off to their left. Moving quietly, he called softly, "Miss Thomas, your mom and dad are worried sick about you and your sister. They've been so afraid, and they need you home with them."

"Miss Thomas," the chief continued, "we've all been worried. Please come out so we can find your sister, too. Please help us find her, and you'll both be safe."

A rustle sounded from the underbrush, and Maria stepped into view. "I'm Maria," she choked out. Shining the light in her face, Henry watched as tears flowed down her dirt- and blood-streaked face. Rushing to her side, he dropped the flashlight, catching her as she collapsed into his outstretched arms.

"We've found her!" Chief Roberts shouted to the men below. "Bring a stretcher. She's injured."

As Henry held her, Maria sobbed uncontrollably, crying Izzy's name over and over. "Help her," she pleaded as they placed her on the stretcher, strapping her in tightly before lifting her up and over the bridge railing. Paramedics blanketed her in layers of warmth, giving her sips of water before placing the stretcher in the ambulance. Henry climbed in beside her and, while the EMT hooked up an IV line with fluids and a mild sedative, held her hand, repeating, "You're safe now, Maria, you're safe."

# 20

# MONDAY EVENING, DECEMBER 31, 1979

## CAPE FEAR RIVER, HARNETT COUNTY, NORTH CAROLINA

B illy, carrying a paper grocery sack, stumbled into the cabin, calling out in an exaggerated Desi Arnaz voice, "Lucy, I'm home!"

Giggling, Frank followed with a six-pack and a bottle of Jack Daniels, setting both on the counter. "What, no answer from Lucy and Ethel? Where are our girls?" he joked. He twisted open the whiskey bottle and took a deep swig as he headed into the bedroom. Flicking on the overhead light, he slurred, "What the fuck! Where's Blondie?"

"Whatcha say?" hiccupped Billy, drunkenly humming the theme song from *I Love Lucy* as he tore into a bag of nacho chips.

"Hey, Bitch." Frank loomed unsteadily over Izzy. "Where's Blondie?" Shaking her roughly, he yanked back the blanket.

Izzy, eyes widening, rolled abruptly to her right side, ignoring the searing pain in her dislocated shoulder. Catching Frank off guard, she shoved the knife deep into his upper thigh. As she forced the blade upward into his groin, whiskey erupted from his mouth, and the bottle crashed to the floor.

"Ahhh!" Frank gasped, panicking as he struggled to remove the knife. With his vision fading, the room gyrated around him. Managing a weak "Billy...," he collapsed to the floor, twitching spasmodically.

Rushing into the room, Billy howled, "What the fuck did ya do?" Dropping to his knees, he cradled Frank's head in his lap, pleading, "Frank, Frankie, hang on, buddy." Yanking the hilt of the knife, Billy heard a sickening slurp as warm blood spurted from the wound, forcing its way into his eyes and nose. Shrieking, he dropped the knife, raking his hands over his face. "No, no, no," he cried, scrabbling to his feet.

"You've gone and done it now, cunt!" he shrieked. Grabbing Izzy by the throat, he picked up the bloody knife and drove it straight into her belly. "That's for Frank!" As sobs overtook him, he staggered from the room, leaving the knife protruding from Izzy's abdomen.

Izzy heard Billy's muttering in the other room before the cabin door slammed shut. Outside, the truck engine revved before fading away. Strangely, she'd felt the knife's sharp penetration, but it hadn't really hurt. She'd done what Maria had told her to do, and now she was at peace. Taking a shallow breath, she smiled before slipping into unconsciousness.

# 21

# MONDAY NIGHT, DECEMBER 31, 1979

### DOYLESTOWN, PENNSYLVANIA

Tony and Anna Thomas, along with a few of their closest friends, sat in the kitchen, watching the small television atop the Amish baker's rack. Erin Moran and John Schneider exchanged flirtatious banter in the lead-up to the ball drop, but no one in the room really cared.

When the phone rang, Tony jumped, sloshing champagne across the table. "Hello?" he inquired nervously.

"Mr. Thomas?" came a man's voice.

"Yes, this is Anthony Thomas."

"Sir, this is Chief Wayne Roberts of the Fayetteville, North Carolina, police department. We've found Maria."

"Oh, my God, thank you!" Tony shouted into the receiver.

Anna rushed to his side. "They're safe?"

Tony held up his finger, imploring, "And Izzy?"

"Sir, Maria was alone when we found her. We're working with her now to learn Isabella's location."

"Can we talk to her? Is she okay? I mean, is she hurt?"

"As well as can be expected, sir," the chief assured him. "She's been through a lot, but we're taking good care of her.

The doctors are keeping her sedated, and they tell me it's best for you not to speak with her just now."

"We'll catch the next plane out of Philly," Tony began anxiously. "What's the closest airport to Fayetteville? How can we reach you when we arrive? What's the name of the hospital?"

"Sir, please slow down. I've asked the Doylestown PD to assist you in getting here. They'll be contacting you shortly."

"Okay, Chief, uh, Roberts, did you say? We'll wait to hear from the local police. Find Izzy, please. And tell Maria we're on our way." Hanging up, he held Anna tightly as their friends gathered around them.

# 22

# MONDAY NIGHT, DECEMBER 31, 1979

## FAYETTEVILLE, NORTH CAROLINA

T he ambulance had taken Maria, accompanied by Henry Long, to the Cape Fear Valley Hospital, where attending physicians had worked to clean and dress her wounds, which included ligature abrasions, deep contusions, a broken nose, cigarette burns, and slashes that appeared to have been inflicted with a sharp-edged blade. Her feet and hands were badly cut and bruised from running through the woods and along the river bank, and great care was taken to remove the embedded stones and splinters.

A female gynecologist, specializing in the care of sexual assault victims, had arrived with a rape kit and conducted vaginal and rectal exams and performed pregnancy and STD screenings. Her initial determination was that Maria's internal injuries would likely heal on their own. In any event, they would wait before considering the need for surgical intervention.

Chief Roberts stood at the foot of Maria's bed, as he had at Henry Long's just a few days earlier, with his notebook open. "Maria," he said gently, "I've just talked to your parents in Doylestown."

Maria rolled her head to the side, the tears overflowing as her shoulders shook.

"Calm down, honey," the chief consoled. "They'll be here tomorrow. Right now, I need you to help us find Izzy. Do you know who took you?"

Maria sniffled, sneering, "Frank and Billy."

"That's good, Maria. Any idea where they took you?"

"To a cabin near a river. They tied us up and hurt us. Bad."

"I know they did, Maria. I'm sorry about that," Roberts said, sitting in the bedside chair. "It's a big river, and we have men searching near where we found you, but do you have any idea how far or long you'd been running?"

"A long time," Maria said, coughing. "I was so cold, so tired. If you hadn't found me, I couldn't have gone much farther."

"Well, we did find you, Maria," Roberts said, rubbing her arm. "You're safe now. But we need to find Izzy. Did Billy or Frank say anything that might point us in the right direction? Did they mention the name of the cabin or who it might belong to?"

"Izzy, oh, my God, Izzy's still there," Maria sobbed. "You've got to find her. She's hurt real bad. I couldn't take her with me."

Fearing that Maria was spinning toward hysteria, Chief Roberts buzzed for the nurse.

"Yes?" came the crackling voice over the receiver.

"I think Miss Thomas needs another sedative," Roberts replied.

"No!" Maria shouted in panic. "I don't want to be sedated! I need to talk so you can find Izzy!"

"Okay, Maria," the chief assured her, then told the nurse, "Never mind."

Roberts turned back to Maria and said, "We'll continue talking, but you need to stay calm, for your own good and Izzy's. Now, think. Did Billy or Frank say anything about where the cabin is or who owns it?"

"I'm trying to remember," Maria said, taking a deep, calming breath. "They talked a lot, but I closed out their voices. Especially when, you know, they were hurting us."

"I'm sorry about that, Maria," Roberts said again, truly meaning it. "We'll catch them and make them pay for what they've done. Help me catch them, Maria, please. Help us find Izzy."

Covering her ears with her bandaged hands, Maria rocked her head back and forth, her blackened eyes closed. Chief Roberts waited.

"Bobby!" she said suddenly, opening her eyes. "They talked about somebody named Bobby. A couple times."

"Can you remember exactly what they said?" the chief pressed. "About this Bobby?"

Maria paused before saying, "The first time, we were still at the bar, in the parking lot. They said we'd have to wait for Bobby...Stod, or something like that, to fix our car, but it might not be until after New Year's."

Chief Roberts wrote furiously in his notebook. "And they mentioned Bobby again?"

"Yeah. Later, in the cabin, Billy said they'd been there before, I think last summer, fishing with Bobby. That's when Frank got the knife. I gave Izzy the knife before I ran away. Oh, my God, Izzy's still there."

"I know she is, Maria, but what you've told me is great. We're going to find her now." After squeezing her hand, he added, "Close your eyes, and I'll be right back."

Grabbing the deputy in the hallway, he ordered, "Radio Mickey Rawlins to find Bobby Stott. He's probably at Jimmy's Joint. Tell him to get the location of Bobby's fishing cabin. Tell him to contact Sheriff Dunn in Harnett County with the address. Now!"

"Yes, sir!" the deputy responded and ran toward the elevator.

Grinning as he returned to Maria's bedside, he assured her, "You did good, little girl. We'll find Izzy now. Go to sleep, and when you wake up, this will be all over for both of you."

Maria sighed deeply, closing her eyes. Chief Roberts watched over her until her breathing quieted. After wiping a tear from her cheek, he turned and headed out the door. Running into Henry coming up in the elevator, he said, "Stay with her. We've got a lead on Izzy."

"Will do, Chief. I'll keep her safe."

# 23

# EARLY TUESDAY MORNING, JANUARY 1, 1980

CAPE FEAR RIVER, HARNETT COUNTY, NORTH CAROLINA

I zzy faded in and out of consciousness. Some moments, she knew she was in the cabin and that she was hurt. At others, she was at the beach. Or was it a pool? Floating on water, drifting back and forth, back and forth. She so wanted to drink the water. She was thirstier than she'd ever been in her life. Her throat hurt, her shoulder hurt, her stomach hurt. Like the cramps she got during her period. Stabbing, pulsing pain, all the way through to her back.

A noise from outside startled her. *What was that*, she wondered. *Please don't let it be Billy. Frank? Where's Frank? Didn't I stab him like Maria told me to?*

The noise grew louder, and harsh lights flashed through the window. "No!" Izzy cried. She had to get away. Attempting to sit, she gasped as searing pain tore through her. "I'm toast," she mumbled, then giggled at the absurdity of the phrase. "Toast," she repeated, her head falling back to the mattress.

"Isabella?" came a booming voice from outside. "Isabella Thomas, are you in there?"

"Yes?" Izzy whispered, more a question than a statement.

*Billy ought to know I'm here*, she thought, giggling again at her ridiculous predicament.

"Ramone and Carter," the booming voice continued. "Surrender or you will be shot."

*Ramone and Carter*, Izzy thought. *Who's that?*

"Billy. Frank. Come out with your hands up!"

*Oh, I know them.* "Frank's dead," she tried answering in her own booming voice.

Minutes passed before she heard a crash at the cabin door, and a uniformed man, weapon drawn, burst into the bedroom.

"Isabella Thomas?" he asked, stepping over Frank's body as he rushed to the bed. He yelled behind him, "She's in here! She's in here! Get the medics now!"

"Izzy," Chief Roberts said softly. "You're safe. We're going to take good care of you."

"Frank's dead," Izzy said matter-of-factly. Searching Roberts's face, she asked, "Where's Maria?"

"Maria's safe, Izzy," he assured her. "You're both safe. Frank and Billy can't hurt you anymore."

What followed was lost to Izzy. She drifted in and out of consciousness as the EMTs hooked up an IV. They left the knife in her abdomen, not wanting to inflict further internal damage or blood loss. The surgeons would know better how to handle that. She awoke for a brief moment in the ambulance, wondering why no one would turn off the damn lights and sirens so she could sleep.

## 24

# THURSDAY MORNING, JANUARY 24, 1980

FAYETTEVILLE, NORTH CAROLINA

Anna Thomas pushed Isabella's wheelchair through the revolving door of the hospital and into the bright sunshine of the crisp and cool day. As she shielded her eyes from the glare, Tony pulled the rental sedan to a stop in front of them. From the back seat, Maria struggled to open the door. "I've got it, honey," Tony told her, unbuckling his seat belt. "Why don't you slide over so Izzy can sit on that side."

"Okay," Maria sighed, smoothing her skirt around her as best she could. She'd been released from the hospital six days earlier while Izzy had remained behind, first in the ICU and then in a step-down ward. Maria and her parents had been staying at a nearby extended-stay motel, which, though far from ideal, had two full-size beds, a rock-hard sleeper sofa, a small kitchenette, and a decent bathroom.

Since her release, Maria had spent most of her time propped against a headboard or the arm of the sofa, watching the old black-and-white TV across the room. Her parents hadn't wanted her to watch the news, but when they left each day to visit Izzy, she'd limp over to the armoire and turn the knob round and round until she found a news channel covering their abduction.

Tony and Anna helped Izzy out of the wheelchair and into the back seat. When Tony pulled the seat belt across her hips, she cried out in pain. "Dad," she managed breathlessly, "it hurts too bad. I'll be fine without it. Just give me my pillow."

"Here it is, honey," Anna said solicitously, wiping the beads of perspiration from Izzy's forehead. "Hold this tightly, and take shallow breaths like the nurse showed you."

Izzy laid her head back against the seat, closing her eyes. "Hi, Maria. How're you?"

"Better than you, it seems," Maria replied, reaching out to take her sister's hand.

"Yeah, seems so," Izzy said, exhaling. "Mom, can I have a pain pill?"

"Not yet, Isabella. We haven't even left the parking lot. If you take one now, you'll overdose before we make it home."

"If only," Izzy muttered under her breath and then angrily ordered, "Then let's get the hell out of here. Now!"

"Jeez, Izzy," Maria said, squeezing her sister's hand. "Cut her a break. We've all been scared to death we'd lose you."

"Yeah, yeah, blah, blah, blah," Izzy replied, pulling her hand away.

"Whatever," Maria retorted, turning her head to stare out the window.

"Okay, girls," Tony said with more enthusiasm than he felt. "We're off for home. Just lay your heads back, go to sleep, and we'll be there before you know it." Reaching across the seat, he gave Anna's thigh a squeeze. She smiled weakly and swiped a tear from her eye. The past three weeks had taken their toll on the entire family. She wanted them all home again. Now. Closing her own eyes, she reflected on all they'd been through since getting the call that Maria had been found.

# 25

# TUESDAY MORNING, JANUARY 1, 1980

## FAYETTEVILLE, NORTH CAROLINA

By the time Tony and Anna had reached Cape Fear Valley Hospital, they were exhausted and on edge. The young uniform who'd picked them up at the airport hadn't known, or had simply refused to tell them, anything about the girls. The last they'd heard before boarding the plane in Philadelphia was that both girls had been found and were receiving medical care. Beyond that, nothing. Tony remained strong despite his fears, but Anna found it hard to control her thoughts and emotions. What had her girls been through? How badly were they hurt, or worse, had they been raped? Her knee bounced anxiously, her hands shaking uncontrollably.

As the officer escorted them through the emergency entrance, Anna's eyes darted back and forth, irrationally hoping to catch sight of the girls. When they approached the admittance desk, the uniform flashed his badge, explaining, "This is Mr. and Mrs. Thomas, parents of the two young women brought in last night."

"Isabella and Maria Thomas," Tony added quickly.

Looking at her clipboard, the nurse stated, "Just a

moment, folks, while I page the doctor." Gesturing toward the rows of plastic chairs to her left, she suggested, "Please have a seat over there."

Glancing at the ID badge hanging from her neck, Tony said with exasperation, "All due respect, Nurse Watkins, but we've been sitting for hours. If you don't mind, we'd like to be taken to our daughters now."

"Sir, I understand," Nurse Watkins stated authoritatively, "but you're not going anywhere until the doctor comes for you. Now, please do your wife a favor, and find her a place to sit."

Tony glanced at Anna, who was drenched in sweat and teetering slightly. "Anna?" he asked with concern.

"I think I'm going to faint, Ton...," she managed, before collapsing to the floor.

The uniformed officer caught her just before her head hit the linoleum. Looking up at Nurse Watkins, he demanded with his own air of authority, "Excuse me, Nurse Watkins, but we'll take a wheelchair for Mrs. Thomas, and please insist that the doctor get down here stat."

Without hesitation, she paged, "Doctor Remis to emergency, Doctor Remis to emergency," then added, "Stat."

Ten minutes later, Tony and Anna stood at the foot of Izzy's bed in the ICU. She looked like a mere child under the sheet, her body pale and smaller than when they'd last seen her just days earlier. An oxygen cannula wrapped around her head and rested under her nose, which was splinted and bandaged. Both eyes were swollen shut, and blood-tinged gauze covered her entire head, scalp to chin. Intravenous tubes administered fluids into her left arm, which was strapped to the bed rail. Her right arm, with its dislocated shoulder, was bound tightly to her body.

"She's a strong woman," Dr. Remis offered. He was a

stout man with thick black eyeglasses. Not quite what Anna was used to seeing on her soap, *The Doctors*, every afternoon. "We revived her once in Emergency as we worked to remove the knife. She lost a considerable volume of blood, but she pulled through."

"The knife? Just what the hell did they do to her?" demanded Tony.

"Yes, please tell us," begged Anna, leaning over the railing to kiss Izzy lightly on her cheek.

Leading them into the corridor, Dr. Remis said, "I'll get into the details after you've seen both girls, but in the simplest terms, Isabella sustained a stab wound through her abdominal wall. Once we removed the knife and opened her up, we found it necessary to remove approximately twelve inches of damaged bowel."

"Oh, my God!" Anna cried.

"Mrs. Thomas, I know the details are difficult to hear, but rest assured your daughters are receiving the very best possible treatment. Now, Isabella will likely sleep for several more hours, so why don't I take you to Maria, and then we'll talk privately in my office."

After taking the elevator up to the next floor, Dr. Remis led Tony and Anna through a maze of brightly lit hallways before pausing outside a closed door. "We're keeping her sedated," he whispered, "due to her high degree of agitation."

"She's safe now, so why is she so agitated?" inquired Tony, holding tightly to Anna's hand.

"She's upset about her sister. We've explained that she's safe and here in the hospital, too, but she doesn't seem to trust what we're telling her. Once we feel she's strong enough, we'll take her to see Isabella, but for now, we want her calm."

Hearing the door, Maria's eyes fluttered open. As her parents entered the room, she broke into keening sobs. Anna rushed to her bedside, and after Dr. Remis dropped the security railing, she gingerly enveloped Maria in her arms. "There, there, baby," she soothed. "Daddy and I are here now. You're safe, you're safe."

Leaning over the opposite railing, Tony gently kissed his daughter's forehead, tears trickling unabashedly down his face. "Maria, honey, Daddy and Mommy are here. Izzy's here, too. We're all together, and you're safe."

"Izzy?" Maria asked, gulping back the sobs. "Where's Izzy? Why can't I see her?"

"She's okay, baby," Anna soothed. "We just saw her. She's downstairs being cared for, just like you."

At the instruction of Dr. Remis, a nurse injected a clear liquid into one of the IV tubes hanging from the stand behind Maria's bed. As Tony and Anna continued to comfort Maria, her breathing calmed and her eyes closed. Watching her now, they noticed the bandages wrapped around her hands, the swollen nose and split lip, the bruising around her eyes. A line of stitches ran the length of her right jawline. She, too, appeared gaunt and tinier than when she'd left home only four days earlier.

"She'll sleep now," Dr. Remis said, checking Maria's pulse. "Let's head over to my office."

Anna kissed her daughter's cheeks, then pulled away. "We'll be back soon, Maria," she whispered.

Reeling from what they'd seen and heard, Anna and Tony followed Dr. Remis out of the room. As the door closed behind them, Anna grabbed the sleeve of Dr. Remis's white lab coat. "What in God's name did those men do to them?"

"Anna, honey," Tony said, noticing the concerned looks

of the nurses at their station, "let's wait until we have some privacy."

"Mrs. Thomas," the doctor said, "I believe Chief Roberts is waiting for us in my office. Please come with me, and we'll fill you in on everything we know."

---

AN HOUR LATER, Anna and Tony walked out of Dr. Remis's office, dismay and horror clouding their faces. They had learned the gruesome details of their daughters' abduction and where and how they'd sustained their many injuries. Chief Roberts had also given them his best determination as to how one kidnapper, Frank Carter, had been killed. As for the second man, he'd admitted that Billy Ramone had yet to be captured, but that the full force of Carolina law was on his trail.

"Might I suggest that one of you sit with Isabella in ICU and the other with Maria. You can then trade off at some point," the doctor said.

"Good idea," agreed the chief. "And just so you know, I've taken the liberty of booking you into a hotel nearby. I'll have one of my officers pick you up at, say, six to take you there. You'll be comfortable and close by."

"Thank you both," Tony said, extending his hand to each man in turn. "We appreciate all you've done for Izzy and Maria. Please let us know when you've caught this Billy Ramone. We won't rest until he's in custody and our girls are home with us."

"I understand perfectly, Mr. Thomas. My men and I won't rest either, I assure you." With a nod to the doctor, Chief Roberts turned and strode down the corridor.

"How 'bout I have a candy striper show you to our cafeteria. It's my professional opinion that you should get something to eat before returning to the girls' rooms. You won't be doing them any good if you don't take care of yourselves first."

"I suppose you're right," Tony agreed, looking at Anna.

"I don't think I could eat a thing," Anna said, but as she pressed a hand to her abdomen, she admitted, "But maybe a cup of soup would give me a bit of strength."

# 26

# TUESDAY EVENING, JANUARY 1, 1980

### FLORENCE, SOUTH CAROLINA

Billy lay on the stained sheets covering the ratty mattress in the fleabag motel, the television glowing quietly on the dresser at his feet. He'd tried to sleep after checking in at dawn, but the vision of Frank's bloody body jerked him awake whenever he'd drifted off. He now stared at the screen in front of him, seeing, but not really watching, the Rose Bowl game.

*How had things gone so terribly wrong*, he asked himself once again. *How did those cunts get themselves untied? Where had Blondie gone, and how had the Bitch been able to stab Frankie? She was dead now*, he thought, grinning. Grabbing a beer from the nightstand, he hoisted it in the air, toasting, "Here's to you, Frank Carter. I hope I did good by you when I stabbed that skinny cunt!"

After downing the beer, Billy threw the empty can at the mirror over the dresser, hitting it dead center and barely missing the TV screen. "Fuck them!" he shouted, a loud knock countering from the room next door. "Fuck you, too!" he hollered at the wall.

Pulling himself off the bed, he walked into the grimy

bathroom to relieve himself. His stomach growled as he zipped up, and he realized he hadn't eaten anything in twenty-four hours. Grabbing his jacket off the floor, he stormed from the room, slamming the door behind him.

Pausing at the motel exit, Billy glanced right, then left, hoping to spot a fast food joint to grab a bite to eat. Spying a Hardee's a few blocks away, he headed in that direction. Pulling into the drive-through lane, he leaned over to open the glove box, where he'd stashed his wallet. Just as he grabbed it, a crunching thud stopped his truck dead in its tracks.

"Fuck me," Billy cussed, straightening in the seat. A doughy man sporting a too-tight Members Only jacket was exiting the car ahead of him, the rear bumper of the shiny new Olds 88 now smashed against Billy's front bumper.

As the red-faced driver approached, pointing his finger at Billy, Billy swore under his breath, "Not tonight, asshole." Quickly reversing the truck, he hit the gas, swerving out of the drive-through lane and back onto the highway. Looking in his rearview mirror, he watched the fat man run into the road and flip the bird in Billy's direction. "Ooh, that scares me," Billy said, laughing as the truck accelerated away from the restaurant.

A mile farther on, Billy pulled into a McDonald's, backing the truck into a spot at the rear of the building. *Might as well eat inside*, he reasoned. *No chance of hitting another asshole that way.* After placing his order for two Big Macs, large fries, and a Coke, Billy sat in a booth facing the restaurant's side entrance. Two bites into his second sandwich, he watched as a cop car turned into the lot. The cruiser moved slowly around the building as Billy clenched his rectum and held his breath. *No need to panic*, he assured himself. *Cop's just grabbing himself some dinner.*

Five minutes passed, and Billy bagged the remains of his fries and casually walked outside. Peering around the corner of the building, he saw the cruiser idling directly in front of his truck. The cop, flashlight in hand, was bending over the crumpled front bumper. As the cop straightened, he spoke into his shoulder mic. Billy couldn't hear what he'd said, but he knew he was in trouble.

"Not tonight, asshole," Billy swore again, smiling at his newly minted mantra. Slipping into the men's room, he closed the door, leaving a narrow gap to peek through. After another minute, he watched the cop stride by and enter the building. Cracking open the door, Billy peered out. Seeing the coast was clear, he lowered his head and walked quickly to his truck.

Hunkering down, he edged open the door and pulled himself into the driver's seat. Billy turned the key in the ignition, and the engine roared to life. Shifting into gear and flooring the accelerator, he rammed the truck into the police cruiser, spinning its front end just enough to maneuver around it. As he careened through the lot, Billy screamed, "Get the fuck outta my way!" at a couple who'd just left the restaurant. Speeding away from the McDonald's, he considered returning to his motel room, but when the large green road sign for I-95 appeared ahead, he veered up the ramp, merging with a thousand other vehicles heading south toward Georgia.

# 27

# WEDNESDAY MORNING, JANUARY 2, 1980

## FAYETTEVILLE, NORTH CAROLINA

C hief Roberts pushed through the door, smiling at Mary Martin, who stood at the makeshift coffee bar in the station's small lobby. "Mornin', Mary."

"Mornin', Chief," she replied, handing him a steaming mug. "Get any sleep?"

"Some," he replied. "You?"

"A bit. Got a wire here might interest you."

"Yeah? Only good news this morning, Mary," he said, frowning into his cup.

"Can't say if it's good or bad. You decide," she said, handing him the flimsy sheet of paper.

Glancing it over, Roberts took the three steps into his office, slamming the door behind him. He picked up his phone and dialed the number shown at the top of the wire. The call was picked up on the fourth ring.

"Florence County Sheriff's office," came the voice on the other end of the line.

"Chief Roberts here, from Fayetteville. Got a wire from your sheriff this morning. Is he available?"

"Yes, sir, please hold the line."

"Chief Roberts?" came the deep Southern drawl. "Sheriff Amos here. For your information, your boy Ramone might've been in my county last night. Seems he was spotted in Florence, where he slammed his vehicle into an Olds 88 in the Hardee's drive-through lane. A brand-spanking new Olds 88, I might add. He then fled the scene, and it is suspected that he drove to a nearby McDonald's, where he escaped after ramming his truck into one of my cruisers."

"Busy boy, isn't he?" Roberts replied.

"Seems so. Busy and hungry, I'd say," the sheriff noted.

"You certain it was Ramone?"

"Green Ford F100 pickup with North Carolina tags? Expired, I might add."

"Expired tags are the least of our worries with that boy," the chief stated simply.

"Got that, Chief. We believe he's headed south on 95 and have issued a BOLO to that effect. He'll be stopped sooner or later."

"Sooner'd be my preference. He's a loose and dangerous cannon. Don't want any other innocent folks hurt, or worse."

"Keep you advised if we hear anything else, but I suspect he's left Florence County, and maybe even South Carolina, far behind him."

"You might be right, Sheriff, you might be right." With that, Chief Roberts disconnected the call. "Mary!" he bellowed.

"Chief?" she asked, opening the door.

"Get me the number for the FBI. Goddamn Billy Ramone has gone and crossed the state line. He'll have more than Carolina police chasing down his sorry ass now."

# 28

# WEDNESDAY AFTERNOON, JANUARY 2, 1980

### FAYETTEVILLE, NORTH CAROLINA

Izzy wasn't doing so well. During the early morning hours, she'd spiked a fever high enough to call Anna and Tony back to the hospital not long after they'd fallen into a fitful sleep.

"Infection in her bowel, we suspect," the doctor on duty had advised them. "We'll take her back into surgery to reopen the incision and clean out any infected tissue."

"How quickly can that be done?" Tony had asked the man.

"We've scheduled the OR for eight a.m. Dr. Remis will be by to talk with you beforehand. In the meantime, we've upped her antibiotics. Sorry to have awakened you, but I knew you'd want to be here."

"No, you were right to call us. Thank you," Tony had assured him.

Anna had stood at Izzy's bedside, stroking her arm gently. "She's so hot. Can I get a cool washcloth to wipe her down a bit?"

"Of course, I'll have the nurse bring you one."

"Has she woken at all tonight?" Tony had asked.

"No," the doctor had replied, checking the chart. "We noted the fever begin to rise at two this morning, and it spiked to a hundred and four by three."

It was now late afternoon, several hours since Izzy had been wheeled from the OR. Dr. Remis had assured Tony and Anna that she was doing as well as could be expected, but it had been necessary to remove an additional three inches of infected intestine. Izzy lay pale and delicate under the thin sheet while tubes dripped and monitors beeped in a cacophony behind her bed.

When the privacy curtain opened, Anna started from her doze in the chair beside the bed.

"Sorry to wake you, Mrs. Thomas. I'm Dr. Jasper. Dr. Remis asked me to check in with Isabella this afternoon. How's she doing?"

"I'm not sure," Anna stated. "She's been whimpering off and on, but shouldn't she be awake by now?"

"We might try to rouse her once we get her vitals. Often-times patients suffering from a traumatic experience find it hard to wake up. It's a means of protecting themselves from the reality of what's taken place."

"I know I'd have rather slept through this ordeal myself," Anna admitted sadly.

"Here's our nurse now," the tall, lanky doctor said as a petite young woman entered the cubicle.

"Just gonna take Miss Isabella's vitals," the nurse explained with a sweet Southern twang. As she wrapped the black band around Izzy's left arm, Anna noticed the veins visible beneath her daughter's fair skin. A moment later, the nurse looked up, stating, "Pressure's still a bit low, ninety over fifty."

Dr. Jasper spoke up. "We've been giving her transfusions of packed red blood cells since she was brought in, but we've added white cells to the mix to help her fight the infection."

"Temp's a hundred and one. Not good, but down from earlier," the nurse added, pulling the beeping thermometer from Izzy's mouth.

"Still high," Dr. Jasper said, "but heading in the right direction. With the antibiotics and fluids she's getting, her stats should improve a little every day."

"So can we wake her?" Anna asked hopefully. "I really want her to know I'm here."

"Try calling her name. If she doesn't stir, we'll give her an assist with a little ammonia inhalant."

"Ammonia? Isn't that toxic?"

"Just smelling salts, Mrs. Thomas. No need to be concerned."

Leaning in close, Anna whispered, "Isabella, it's time to wake up. Mommy's here with you, and I need you to wake up." Izzy didn't stir, and Anna repeated, "Isabella, wake up. Mommy wants to see your beautiful blue eyes."

Stepping to the bed, the nurse snapped a small glass vial and waved it under Izzy's nose. Izzy nostrils flared, and her left hand, still strapped to the railing, flinched as if to swat away the offensive odor.

Anna pleaded. "Open your eyes, Isabella."

Izzy's eyes fluttered but remained closed.

"Isabella, honey, you're safe. You're in the hospital, and Mommy's here with you. Daddy's upstairs with Maria. Please wake up."

Anna watched as Izzy strained to open her eyes. After several attempts, her lids parted, her eyes darting right to left. Seeing Anna, she whispered, "Mom?"

"Yes, baby. I'm here."

Izzy's face contorted. "What happened to me?" she

asked, her voice weak and scratchy as tears spilled onto her cheeks. Running her tongue over her chapped lips, she added, "Where am I?"

"In the hospital, honey," Anna replied, stroking her arm.

Dr. Jasper stepped to the bed and gently placed his hand over Izzy's. "Isabella, I'm Dr. Jasper. You've been hurt, but we're taking good care of you."

"My stomach hurts," she grimaced, pressing her bruised eyelids together. "Why does it hurt so much?"

"We'll talk about that after you've rested some more," Anna said, kissing Izzy's forehead and gently wiping the tears from her battered face.

"Can I have some water?" Izzy asked, and Anna looked quizzically at the doctor.

"Sure, but we'll go slow with that. Don't want to upset your belly any more than it already is."

Slurping on a few precious ice chips, Izzy sighed and whispered, "So tired."

Smiling, Anna said, "I know, baby, you sleep. You'll feel a whole lot better when you wake up."

# WEDNESDAY & THURSDAY, JANUARY 2 & 3, 1980

### HUGUENOT MEMORIAL PARK, JACKSONVILLE, FLORIDA

B illy had always wanted to live at the beach. Ever since he'd gone to Caswell Beach with Frank's family when he'd been eight, he'd dreamed of living in a cottage by the ocean, swimming whenever he felt like it and fishing for his dinner. *Why not*, he asked himself now. *I'll just hunker down here until the heat's off, and then I'll find me that cottage. Shame that Frankie can't be here, too. He'd love this place.*

Billy looked through his windshield to the deserted stretch of beach in front of the truck, waves rolling gently toward the sand. He pulled off his boots and socks, jumped from the cab, and rolled up the legs of his overalls. *It'd feel good to dive right in*, he thought, strolling to the edge of the water. It was so damn cold, though, and he didn't have a change of clothes. He could kick himself for leaving his new duffel behind in that motel room. He'd spent almost twenty dollars on clothes at that Kmart in Florence, twenty dollars he sure as hell didn't have to waste. He figured he had about ninety left, which included the bills he'd found in the girls' purses in his truck's cargo box. He'd need to get cash soon, and he cursed himself for not snatching the money from

Frank's wallet before he'd left the cabin. Too wired to grab some shut-eye despite having driven through the night, Billy set out to explore the beach and surrounding park.

Hours later, as the moon rose over the water, Billy returned to the truck. *Gotta get me some sleep tonight*, he thought. *A man's no good without his rest.* He lay across the front seat, closing his eyes. His body was exhausted, but his mind refused to shut down. *What the hell have I gotten myself into*, he wondered as the events of the last twenty-four hours played out in his head.

Figuring he had run far enough to not be recognized, Billy had stopped for gas just south of Savannah. While waiting to pay, he'd picked up a brochure on Florida beaches. Seeing the photo of this one, with cars parked right on the sand, he'd followed the directions here.

He'd arrived in early morning, hours before the gates would open, so he'd found himself a diner down the road and grabbed a big breakfast. As he sat at the counter eating, he listened to the wail of country music playing on a radio somewhere behind the swinging door. He and Frank had loved singing along with Waylon and Willy to "Mamas Don't Let Your Babies Grow Up to Be Cowboys." Damn, those were good times. He shook his head, blinking back an unbidden tear. When the waitress had asked if he wanted more coffee, he'd said glumly, "What I want, you don't have." She'd smiled and slipped the ticket under his saucer.

Remembering those runny eggs and grits now, his stomach rumbled, and he rolled over to quiet the hunger. If he left the park to grab something to eat, he wouldn't be able to return until the gates reopened in the morning. He wasn't even sure he was allowed on the beach this late, and at this point, he craved sleep more than food. He contemplated lighting up the joint tucked above the sun visor, but the munchies were the last thing he needed. Shivering against the cold, Billy pulled his knees to his chest and rocked himself, something he'd taken to doing all those many nights ago whenever his dad had unleashed his rage on him.

---

A THUNDEROUS BLAST from a container ship as it rounded the jetty startled Billy from his nightmare. Frank had been knocking on the truck window, begging Billy to let him in. Blood oozed through his fingers and dripped down the window. Billy attempted to open the door, but it was locked, and he couldn't find the release. Frank's cries of pain and desperation split the night. Just as Billy had turned in the seat to crawl out the rear window, the ship's horn had sounded.

Lurching up, Billy anxiously scanned the area. Frank was nowhere to be seen. A dense fog had moved in overnight, and although he could hear the lapping waves, he couldn't see the water through the murky light of dawn. He ran his fingers through his greasy hair and spun the rearview mirror to look at himself. Bloodshot eyes underscored with dark smudges stared back at him. His stubble, though blotchy as always, was thicker than he'd ever let it get before. An angry zit flared on the tip of his nose, and he leaned forward to examine it more closely. "A real looker this morning, Billy Boy," he observed, popping the pimple between his index fingers.

Realizing his need to pee, Billy opened the truck door and dropped into water up to his shins. "Shit," he cursed, watching as the wake sloshed over the truck's door ledge. Fearing unknown sea creatures, and not knowing if the tide was coming in or going out, Billy looked toward the dunes and waded in that direction. After relieving himself in the grasses, he removed his overalls, laying them flat on the ground. Stretching out, his back against the sandy rise, he shivered in the clammy morning air. Sand chafed the back of his thighs, and he bent his knees to brush it off. *Maybe I should rethink this beach-living dream*, he thought. "You're an idiot, Billy Boy," he muttered. "A real fuckin' brain surgeon."

# 30

# THURSDAY MORNING, JANUARY 3, 1980

## FAYETTEVILLE, NORTH CAROLINA

Maria rolled onto her side, wincing. There was no getting comfortable in this damn hospital bed. Her body ached everywhere, and she could feel that she'd bled through the pad the nurse had secured between her legs hours earlier. If she cared, she'd press the call button, but she didn't care. Not anymore. She'd been poked, prodded, invaded in every manner possible over the last two days. Humiliation at first, then resignation. After what she'd gone through in the cabin, how could she complain when clean, caring doctors and nurses touched her.

"Good morning," greeted the way-too-cheerful nurse. "I'm Holly, and I'll be your day nurse."

"Hey," Maria said grudgingly. It wasn't Holly's fault she was in such a bad mood. As she watched Holly erase the night nurse's name from the chalkboard on the wall, she tried to think of something positive to say. Nothing came to her.

"I understand from the doctor's notes that you might be taking a little wheelchair visit to your sister today."

"Really?" Maria asked, smiling hopefully. Finally, she

was getting out of this bed for a reason other than a trip to the bathroom or radiology. "How's Izzy doing?"

"I'm not sure, but she must be well enough for a visit."

"Dad said she had another surgery yesterday. Something about an infection?"

"Can't really say," Holly offered, skirting the issue. "How do *you* feel this morning?"

Squirming, Maria counted off her ailments. "Everything hurts. I have ridiculous cramps. My hands and feet ache. My head is pounding, and I can't breathe through my nose. And to top it off, I've bled through four pads in the last twelve hours. I need another, by the way."

"Anything else?" Holly asked, concern shadowing her pleasant smile.

"Can I get something to drink other than water? Coffee, maybe?"

"I'll ask the doctor when he comes by. I'm sorry you're in so much discomfort, but can you tell me, on a scale of one to ten, what's your overall pain level?"

"Ten," Maria said without hesitation.

"A ten," Holly repeated, writing on the clipboard. "I'll see if I can speed up your next dose of morphine. And I'll be back to change your pad in a minute."

"Thanks, Holly. Sorry you have to do that."

"Not to worry, Maria," Holly assured her. "We've got this."

# 31

# SATURDAY MORNING, JANUARY 5, 1980

### HUGUENOT MEMORIAL PARK, JACKSONVILLE, FLORIDA

B illy knew he should have left the park before the weekend rolled around, but after spending hours digging his tires out of the sand two days earlier, he'd chosen to move the truck to an adjacent campground and lay low there. For a short while, the remote location had seemed the perfect spot to do just that. Until this morning, that is, when he'd been awakened by a boisterous group of scouts singing "This Land Is Your Land" as they trundled, two-by-two, into the campsite.

"Fuck," Billy mumbled, scrambling into a seated position. He'd slept like hell and was in no mood for any form of cheer. Frank had appeared in another dream, this time with his face in Billy's crotch. He could swear he'd heard Frank's slurping as he sucked Billy off, and after climaxing, he'd awakened, mortified. Lying in uneasy silence until sunrise, he'd fallen into a fitful sleep as the horizon revealed itself in shades of gold and pink.

"Hey, you!" shouted a man wearing the same silly getup as the boys. "You, in the truck."

*Is he talking to me?* Billy wondered.

"You're not allowed here. This is Outdoor Adventure Saturday, and you need to leave, or I'll call the park ranger." The man walked up to the truck, pounding on the driver's-side window. He was a pudgy dude with ruddy cheeks, reminding Billy of the evening his mom had playfully brushed her rouge across his cheeks. She'd been getting ready for choir practice—that is, until his dad had walked in at just that moment. Without a word, he'd stomped over and punched his wife in the back of the head, driving her nose into the top of the vanity. Makeup jars and perfume bottles crashed to the floor as Billy ran to his room, hiding under the bed until he'd fallen asleep there. That had been the last time he'd seen his mom. When he'd walked down to the kitchen the next morning, his dad told him she hadn't come home from church and had probably run off with a boyfriend.

*Who is this dick*, Billy thought now, rolling down the window. "Hey, man, chill out. I'm on a little adventure of my own here."

"Well, you'll just have to take your adventure somewhere else. These boys will be setting up their tents in this area, and you can't be here."

"Okay, okay, no need to be a douche about it. I'll leave in a little while."

The man leaned through the truck window, and his spittle struck Billy's face as he threatened, "Leave now or, mark my word, you'll be in big trouble, buddy."

Billy threw open the door, and the troop leader jumped back, stumbling over a mound of oyster shells and falling to the ground. Billy, pointing his finger at the man, leapt from the truck. "Don't *buddy* me, you fag, or you'll be the one who's sorry."

Fearing Billy's rage, the man scrambled backward. Finding his footing, he yelled to the boys, who stood mesmerized twenty feet away. "Scouts Macy and Jackson, go back to the gate and tell the ranger we need him here. Run!"

As the two boys separated from the troop, running in the direction they'd just come, Billy seethed. "I said I'm leaving, fucker! Don't be threatening me."

Reaching into the cab, Billy grabbed the wooden paddle he'd fashioned from a downed tree limb and used to dig his truck out of the sand. Taking one long step, he swung the paddle full force into the troop leader's head. The man collapsed to the ground. With the man out cold, Billy kicked him in the ribs and stomped on his crotch. Waving the limb in the boys' direction, he watched them scatter, screaming as they ran in all directions.

"Fuck, fuck, fuck!" Billy cursed, jumping into the truck. When the engine caught, he drove full speed out of the campsite, aiming for the park entrance. Seeing the two boys who'd gone for help, Billy swerved in their direction, forcing them to somersault into the roadside brush. As the truck approached the gate, the ranger stepped into the road, holding out his arm for Billy to stop. Billy's foot never eased off the gas, and the man was forced to jump through the office door to save himself.

As the truck sped from view, the ranger picked up the phone and punched in the numbers for the sheriff's office. He'd noted the truck's make and model and the North Carolina license plate, and he relayed the same. As he disconnected the call, two out-of-breath scouts appeared in the doorway. "Mr. James needs help back at camp. That man in the truck was yelling at him," one boy managed in between gulps of air.

"And I think he hurt Mr. James," added the other.

Lifting the phone again, the ranger redialed the sheriff's office, this time requesting an ambulance to the park.

# 32

# SATURDAY MORNING, JANUARY 5, 1980

## DARIEN, GEORGIA

Retracing his route out of Jacksonville, Billy chose to avoid I-95 and instead headed north on Business 17, figuring he'd blend in better with the local traffic. For the past hour, his mind had been plotting where he'd go next. Thinking he ought to stay in the South to avoid any bad winter weather, he wondered if Alabama or Mississippi might be good places to disappear. Sighting a Shell station at an upcoming exit, Billy pulled off the highway. He'd fill up here and grab a map to strategize his course.

He walked into the office, paid the attendant ten dollars for gas, and asked if he could buy a map.

"Sure," the freckled young kid said. "That'll be two fifty more."

Billy threw down three dollars, told the kid to keep the change, and grabbed a map from the rack beside the register. "Got a men's room I can use?" he asked.

"Yep, 'round the back," the boy replied, pointing his thumb over his right shoulder. "Here's the key. Bring it back when you're done."

"Whatcha think I'm gonna do with it?" Billy growled, grabbing the key.

"It's what I'm supposed to tell you. Don't mean no disrespect, sir."

Billy exhaled a derisive "Shit," and strode from the office. Finished in the restroom, he was buckling his shoulder straps as he pushed through the office door. "Hey, kid!" he called out when he didn't see the boy behind the counter. "Here's your fuckin' key." Throwing the key ring at the back wall, he pumped a fist in the air when it hit a framed photo of a Pop Warner football team, shattering the glass. "Fuck you, you fuckin' hick," he muttered and headed out to the pump.

As Billy walked toward his truck, the sun reflected off its windshield, momentarily blinding him. Putting his hand up to shield his eyes, strobing red lights stopped him dead in his tracks. Looking around, he counted three police vehicles blockading his truck. In a moment of panic, he dropped to a crouch behind a stack of tires.

"Billy Ramone, come out with your hands up," a voice boomed.

Billy's thoughts jumbled through his head. "Fuck this bullshit!" he swore.

"Billy Ramone, you are surrounded. Stand with your hands in the air!"

With no weapon to defend himself and no chance of getting to his truck, Billy took off around the side of the building.

"Stop!" came a thundering voice, and he heard footsteps pounding behind him.

At the treeline behind the station, he dithered for a split second too long. A bullet slammed into the back of his right knee, sending him sprawling headfirst into a pine tree.

Attempting to right himself, his leg buckled, and he crumpled to the ground. As he lay on his belly panting, a burly sheriff's deputy straddled his back.

The deputy grabbed each wrist to lock on the steel cuffs, reciting, "Billy Ramone, you are under arrest for the kidnapping, rape, and attempted murder of two women in the state of North Carolina."

As Billy struggled beneath him, the deputy continued, "You have the right to remain silent. Anything you say can and will be used against you in a court of law."

"Fuck you!" Billy spat. "You should be arresting them for killing my best friend!"

As the officer completed the Miranda warning, the pain in Billy's knee finally registered. "You shot me?" he screamed at the cop. "You fuckin' shot me. I'll fuckin' kill you, you bastard!"

"An ambulance is on the way," the officer stated calmly. "When your leg is patched, you'll be taken to the county jail while you await extradition to North Carolina. You're the one who's fucked, Ramone."

# 33

# SATURDAY AFTERNOON, JANUARY 5, 1980

### FAYETTEVILLE, NORTH CAROLINA

Chief Roberts sat at his desk, reconciling his expenses from the past week. Expenses that had far exceeded his budget for all of December and certainly surpassed the January estimate. When Janie, his weekend desk sergeant, stuck her head in the door, he shook his head in irritation.

"Sorry to interrupt, Chief, but there's a Sheriff Brown on the phone for you."

"Yeah, where's he from?" Roberts growled.

"I believe he said McIntosh County, Georgia," Janie replied.

"Go ahead and put him through."

"Chief Roberts," he stated gruffly, picking up the call. "What can I do for you, Sheriff?"

"Well, Roberts, you'll be happy to hear we've got one William Ramone in custody, as we speak."

"No shit!" the chief exclaimed. "That's the best news I've heard all week."

"Thought you'd feel that way, Chief. Need you to wire the extradition papers as soon as you can get 'em to us. We don't want this slime bag stinkin' up our jail any longer than absolutely necessary."

"Be happy to. I'll call our DA after we hang up. Give me your contact information."

When the chief disconnected the call, he shouted, "Hallelujah! Janie, get in here!"

Janie rushed into the office, a look of concern clouding her face. The chief stepped from behind his desk and picked her up, twirling her through the air. Flustered when he put her down, she blushed, asking, "What's gotten into you, Chief?"

"They caught the bastard, Janie. Ramone's off the street. Get me Jim Paulson on the phone now. We've got to bring Ramone back to Fayetteville as soon as possible."

"Will do, Chief. Congratulations!"

After speaking with the DA, Chief Roberts placed a call to the hospital, asking the operator to page Dr. Remis. When Remis picked up, the chief relayed the good news, requesting the doctor to arrange another meeting with the Thomases. After agreeing on a time, he leaned back in his chair, hoisting his boots atop the desk. "Thank you, Lord," he prayed and picked the phone up to call his wife.

---

AN HOUR LATER, Chief Roberts sat with Anna and Tony Thomas in the office of Dr. Remis. "So," he continued, "we'll be bringing Ramone back to Cumberland County for trial. With all the evidence against him, we should get his case on the docket fairly quickly."

"Will the girls have to testify?" Anna asked fearfully. "They've both been through so much. I don't want them to suffer any more."

"Mrs. Thomas," Dr. Remis cut in, "I won't allow Maria or Isabella to do anything until they're fully recovered. And I certainly won't permit any activity that will set back that recovery, regardless of what the police chief or district attorney may want."

"And I feel the same way," the chief agreed. "But the girls will have to testify at some point. If they aren't ready to do so by the time of the trial, and I admit I want the trial to be sooner rather than later, the judge might allow the prosecutor to present written testimony."

"Frankly," Tony spoke up angrily, "when I see that bastard, I'm not sure I'll be able to stop myself from killing him!"

"Tony, calm down," Anna soothed. "You'll do no such thing. We want *him* in prison, not you."

Tony stood to pace the office, clenching his fists and breathing deeply. "You're right, but"—he stopped to pound the desk—"I will not allow Izzy or Maria to go through anything that causes them one single iota of pain."

"Understood, Mr. Thomas," the chief concurred. "Let me handle it. Knowing Ramone's financial situation, he'll be assigned a public defender, and he or she's not likely to push for a subpoena. Accepting the girls' depositions will take much less effort than cross-examining them."

"So we're all in agreement with this?" asked Dr. Remis. "Neither Isabella nor Maria will testify at trial unless and until they are completely healed. If not, they will be permitted to provide written testimony only."

"Agreed," the chief said, standing to say his good-byes. Taking Anna's hand, he pulled her close for a quick embrace. "Let me know when they're well enough for visitors. I'd love to see them, and I know a few others who would as well."

"We'll let them know," Anna answered.

# 34

# THURSDAY EVENING, JANUARY 24, 1980

## DOYLESTOWN, PENNSYLVANIA

It had been a long, grueling drive from Fayetteville to Doylestown. They'd stopped several times to stretch their legs and use the bathroom. While Maria's appetite had returned somewhat, and she managed to keep down smaller meals, Izzy's damaged intestines wouldn't allow her to eat anything solid. Vanilla milkshakes were the only thing that appealed to her, so Tony had made a point to stop at a Dairy Queen and a McDonald's as they headed north on I-95.

The house was quiet now, the girls safely in bed upstairs. Tony and Anna sat in the family room, watching the late news, the volume a low hum. After the first commercial break, the anchor reported on the girls' return home that day and continued the segment with an update on Billy Ramone's arrest and pending trial.

"Why are they talking about this here?" Anna asked in dismay. "Can't we catch a break from the nightmare in our own home?"

"It's news," Tony assessed simply. "I'm afraid there'll be reporters on our doorstep tomorrow."

"Well, I'm not answering the door or the phone until this

all dies down!" Anna exclaimed. "This is our home, not a public square."

"I'll call Officer Johnson in the morning and ask for police presence to keep both reporters and the curious off the property," Tony said.

"That's a good idea. Once he gets here, I'll run to the Acme to stock up. We should plan to stay home for a while."

"We'll call Dr. Oates, too, to schedule a house visit. The girls shouldn't need to go into his office for their checkups," he added.

Standing, Anna stretched to relax the knot between her shoulders. "I'm exhausted, Tony. Let's go to bed."

"You go on ahead, Anna. I'll be up in a little while."

"Okay," she said, kissing the top of his head. "Don't stay up too late."

Hearing their bedroom door close, Tony walked through the silent house, peering out each window and checking all locks. *I'll call a security company tomorrow*, he thought. *I should have been doing more to protect this family all along.* Sitting at the piano, he covered his face with his hands and wept. *Dear God*, he prayed, *keep us all safe, now and forever.*

# 35

# MONDAY MORNING, MARCH 17, 1980

### FAYETTEVILLE, NORTH CAROLINA

*S t. Patrick's Day*, brooded Tony as his thoughts returned to last year's celebration with friends at the Irish tavern in Chestnut Hill. Recalling the many pints they'd enjoyed, Guinness for him and Harp for Anna, he hung his head at the stark contrast between then and now. This year, he and Anna sat in the first row of the Cumberland County Courthouse. In front of them, District Attorney James Paulson, who'd insisted on trying the case of *North Carolina v. William J. Ramone* himself, sat with two assistant prosecutors.

Anna and Tony had left Izzy and Maria home with Tony's brother and sister-in-law. Sal and Janice had driven to Doylestown from their home in Dayton, Ohio, insisting they'd do anything to make things easier for the family.

Izzy and Maria had been deposed two weeks earlier in the Bucks County Courthouse after Paulson and Billy's court-appointed attorney, Artie Lawler, had flown to Pennsylvania. Their in-person testimony would not be required at trial, but Anna and Tony had been adamant about being there to see Billy Ramone convicted and put away. In a meeting the day before, the DA had told them that the trial would be a quick one. "Shouldn't take more than a week, even with cross," he'd assured them.

Looking across the austere courtroom, Tony chilled when his eyes settled on Billy Ramone hunched beside his attorney. He'd been escorted in moments before, limping in his orange jumpsuit, hands and feet shackled. The steel handcuffs were now secured to a hook screwed into the table in front of him. Gone was the tough guy who had so hurt his girls. As Tony scrutinized the scrawny, beaten-down man, he shuddered with vehemence and anger. Anna, refusing herself to look at Billy, held tightly to Tony's hand, focusing her attention on a plaque of Lady Justice hanging behind the judge's bench.

Since Maria and Izzy wouldn't be testifying in person, their depositions, as read aloud by the court reporter, would be entered into testimony. The prosecution would then proceed by calling a number of witnesses, with Artie Lawler being given the opportunity to cross-examine each. The public defender could then call his own witnesses, if he had any, but they'd most likely be character witnesses only. What, really, could be said in Billy's defense?

As the bailiff called, "All rise," the Honorable Albert B. Rogers ascended the bench, calling for order. He was an imposing man in his late sixties, and his mane of thick white hair fell just below his collar, a trait his wife of forty-two years teased was a reflection of his strength and virility, like Samson. Too many sedentary hours in the courtroom, however, had transformed his formerly fit physique into its current grandfatherly manifestation. A jurist in Cumberland County for over a quarter century, he was known as a tough but fair man, slow to either condemn or absolve until all the facts had been brought to light.

"Let us begin, ladies and gentlemen, with opening statements. Mr. Paulson, please proceed."

As the district attorney stood and walked toward the jury, a hush fell over the room. Jim Paulson was commanding in his hand-tailored charcoal suit, crisp pink shirt, and black-and-gray paisley tie. He stood quietly for a moment, looking each juror in the eye.

"Ladies and gentlemen of the jury, thank you for your time and service today. As you know, we are here to examine the facts surrounding events that took place between Saturday, December 29, 1979, and Saturday, January 5, 1980. A period of one week only, but a lifetime of terror for two young women heading to Florida for fun in the sun with friends."

Pausing briefly to appraise Billy, he continued, "During a short but fateful stopover in this town, *our* town, they were, against their will, abducted, held captive, sexually assaulted, and left for dead by the defendant, Mr. William J. Ramone. You will hear testimony from many witnesses, including the victims themselves in the form of their depositions. Too traumatized, physically and emotionally, by the injuries inflicted upon them by the defendant and his coconspirator, their physicians have not released them to appear in court this week."

As the jury listened with rapt attention, Billy sat beside his attorney, his eyes boring holes through the table. Despite her best effort to avoid looking at him, Anna dared a glance. Seeing the man who had so hurt her babies, a physical pain pierced her heart, and she swallowed hard to keep down the bile.

"Witness testimony will show how the defendant injured a brave Good Samaritan, threw the girls into his truck, drove them to a remote cabin on the Cape Fear River, and raped and tortured them over a period of three horrifying nights. And finally, you will learn of their escape and rescue. How, despite the worst of evil intentions by Mr. Ramone, their strength and fierce will to live enabled them to do just that. To live."

With that dramatic finish, Jim Paulson returned to his seat, reaching back to take Anna's and Tony's hands in his own.

"You're up, Mr. Lawler," the judge stated.

Artie Lawler, looking sheepish and nervous in his too-tight, powder-blue seersucker suit, stood and faced the jury. Taking a deep breath that ballooned his already fleshy cheeks, he exhaled histrionically.

"Ladies and gentlemen of the jury, thank you for performing your civic duty here today. Let me begin by saying that, despite the district attorney's attempts to blame my client for the unfortunate series of events, I ask that you keep an open mind as you listen to all the testimony. While it is true that Mr. Ramone did, in fact, participate in the spiriting away of the two women, you will learn that he did so under duress. That Frank Carter—his *coconspirator*, I believe the DA called him—threatened Mr. Ramone with grave bodily injury if he refused to go along with the kidnapping and what transpired thereafter. Billy Ramone, himself, is a victim here."

A hum went through the courtroom as Lawler continued, "While Mr. Carter is unable to be here, it will be shown that Billy Ramone is not the evil man the prosecution will paint him out to be. We will prove that he is a good man forced to perform evil deeds. A good man who grew up in horrid conditions. A good man whose father beat him and whose mother vanished before she could prevent more of those beatings."

Before concluding, Artie smiled conspiratorially at a matronly juror in a frumpy brown jumper who had frowned and shaken her head sadly as he spoke those last words. "You may not believe this just yet, but I implore you to pay close attention to all testimony. Do not make up your minds about Billy Ramone until all the facts have been laid bare, not just those the prosecution wishes you to know. Thank you."

Leaning, Tony hissed in Anna's ear, "That's bullshit! There's no way he was an unwitting victim."

Turning back, the DA placed a finger to his lips before standing and addressing the judge. "Your Honor, the State calls for the testimony of the victims, Isabella Anna Thomas and Maria Alice Thomas, to be read into evidence."

"Agreed. Will the court reporter please proceed?"

As the depositions were delivered in the dispassionate voice of the female court reporter, Anna thought of the victim impact statements Isabella and Maria had prepared for the sentencing phase of the trial. Unlike depositions, which are fact-based responses to specific questions, victim statements are intended to be raw and emotional.

When Anna had asked the girls if she could read their statements, Izzy had refused. "No way, Mom!" she'd huffed, placing her statement in the pre-addressed, postage-paid envelope provided by the DA.

Maria, on the other hand, had photocopied her statement, giving the copy to her mother. That evening, while Tony surfed TV channels, Anna had pleaded a headache, escaping to the privacy of their bedroom. Sitting on the edge of the soaking tub, tears clouding her vision, she had read her daughter's heart-wrenching words.

*To whom it may concern,*

*My name is Maria Alice Thomas, and I was kidnapped, held*

hostage, and repeatedly raped by Billy Ramone and Frank Carter. I am now, and always will be, a damaged woman. What they did to me, and to my sister, Isabella, was worse than any person should have to endure.

Before we were abducted, I was shy, but strong. A decent college student with a few good friends. Not exactly innocent, I was still a virgin, which can't be said about a lot of girls my age. At twenty years old, yes, I'd never had sex. I was planning to wait until I fell in love, really in love, with the man I would marry. Most of my friends had been sleeping with guys since high school, and although I was curious about what it would be like, I wanted to wait for Mr. Right. How stupid and naïve was I?

What they, Billy and Frank, did to me nearly killed me. Inside and out, body and soul. Yes, it was sex, but it wasn't remotely love. In fact, it was just the opposite. It was hate. Instead of making love, they made <u>hate</u> to me. Beating me, badgering my body internally and externally. How could what they did to me ever be considered an act of love and reverence?

My scars are deep. Internally, I bled from my uterus, vagina, and rectum for weeks after I was found. I was dehydrated and malnourished. I experienced kidney and bladder infections. Multiple concussions. The doctors still don't know all the internal injuries I might have suffered.

Externally, I endured a broken nose, a split lip, two cracked teeth, black eyes, bleeding ears, burn marks across my breasts and abdomen, and knife slices along my jawbone and other, private, places.

After I escaped, I damaged my feet and hands as I ran through the woods and along the river. When found, I was in shock and suffering from hypothermia.

I still have nightmares and wake up shaking, crying, and calling for my mom. My dad. My sister. And for God. Why didn't He stop them?

*I am angry with everyone and no one at the same time.*

*I blame myself, Izzy, everyone, and no one.*

*I don't know if I'll ever be able to trust anyone enough to make new friends or meet and fall in love with the man I'll want to marry.*

*I am a damaged woman. Billy Ramone should be made to pay for what he and Frank Carter did to me. Frank's dead, and I thank Izzy for that every day. The filthy, evil beast that was Frank Carter will never be on top of, inside of, another woman. Please make certain that Billy Ramone never is either.*

*Thank you for your consideration,*

*Maria Thomas*

*March 11, 1980*

# MONDAY MORNING, MARCH 17, 1980

### FAYETTEVILLE, NORTH CAROLINA

S haking herself from the memory of Maria's haunting words, Anna listened as the court reporter droned through the last of Isabella's deposition and began reading Maria's. When finished, she gave copies to the judge and sat down, poising her hands over her steno keyboard.

"Will the prosecution call its first witness," ordered Judge Rogers.

Standing, Jim Paulson replied, "Your Honor, the prosecution calls James Marcus to the stand."

Jimmy Marcus, with a fresh cut and shave and wearing an ill-fitting brown suit, strode to the bar, placed his right hand on the Bible, and swore to tell the truth. Over the next few minutes, the DA took Jimmy through the events of Saturday, December 29, starting with the girls' entering the bar and ending with Henry Long's being carried away in an ambulance. There were no surprises in his testimony, but when Paulson asked if he'd ever suspected that Ramone and Carter were capable of such heinous crimes, Artie Lawler objected loudly.

"Your Honor, Mr. Marcus is a barkeep who serves beer and liquor. He's not a psychic or a psychiatrist."

"Mr. Paulson, defense is correct there. Please move on."

"Your Honor, as a bartender who has known and served the defendant for years, Mr. Marcus has a unique perspective into the way Mr. Ramone thinks."

"Okay, I'll allow Mr. Marcus to answer. But let's move on from there, please."

"Yes, Your Honor," he agreed, turning back to Jimmy. "Mr. Marcus, shall I repeat my question?"

"No, I'm good. Billy and Frank were reckless boys who liked beer and girls. When they drank too much, which was pretty typical, they both had real mean streaks. I once saw Billy break a cue stick over the head of a dude he accused of hustling him. Frank jumped into the fray, which, again, was pretty typical, and it took four guys to pull them off the poor bastard. He spent a week in the hospital."

"So, to answer my question, you can see them kidnapping, raping, and attempting to murder the Thomas sisters?"

"If they were pissed enough, I guess so. And if nobody was there to stop them, they'd keep at it til they grew bored."

"No further questions, Your Honor."

"Mr. Lawler?"

Artie stood, glancing at his notes. "Mr. Marcus, exactly how much did you serve Ramone and Carter on the day in question? Before they left the bar with the Thomas sisters?"

Jimmy reached into his pocket and pulled out a small rectangle of paper. "According to this bill here, which I saved because I never got paid, Billy and Frank drank thirty-nine dollars' worth of beer, excluding tax and tip."

"And exactly how many beers can someone buy for thirty-nine dollars?" Lawler followed.

"On a Saturday afternoon, you can get twenty American beers or twelve European beers."

As chuckles arose in the gallery, Lawler pressed on, "And what kind of beer were Billy and Frank drinking on that particular Saturday?"

"Well, here's the thing," Jimmy answered. "Those boys thought they were drinking Heinekens, but I was pouring 'em Buds. After their first draw, they wouldn't have known a fine ale from a bottle of cat piss."

When the courtroom erupted in laughter, Judge Rogers pounded his gavel. "That'll be enough," he ordered, "or I'll empty this room."

The laughter died down, and Artie continued, "So you admit to charging them more than they owed? How do you justify that, Mr. Marcus?"

The DA rose from his seat and stated, "Objection, Your Honor."

"Sustained," Judge Rogers intoned. "Mr. Lawler, as the witness was never paid for the beer he did or did not serve, your point is moot. It does seem to me, however, that *caveat emptor* might apply here. In any event, I suggest you move on."

Reddening, Artie turned back to Jimmy. "So if my math is correct, and you were charging my client and Mr. Carter for Heinekens, that'd be six beers apiece. Was that enough to get them so intoxicated that they made the unfortunate decision to kidnap the two women?"

Jimmy pondered a moment before replying. "Maybe. Maybe not. I'm not sure if my bar was their first stop of the day, so I can't say if they'd been drinking somewheres else or what else they might have been using."

Looking confused, Artie asked, "What do you mean by that, Mr. Marcus?"

Pinching his thumb and forefinger together, Jimmy placed them to his lips and inhaled deeply. Artie shook his head, conceding, "Nothing further, Your Honor."

After Jimmy stepped down, the prosecutor called Henry Long to the stand. Although Henry's memory of events in the bar parking lot was still fuzzy, he'd stayed in touch with Chief Roberts over the past two months and wanted to make sure the jury heard his take on Billy Ramone. A few weeks earlier, he'd even written a lovely letter to Izzy and Maria.

Once sworn in, Henry sat in the witness chair and looked encouragingly in the direction of Anna and Tony. "Mr. Long, can you take us through the events of Saturday, December 29, after you arrived at Jimmy's Joint?"

Henry gave a succinct, detailed report of entering the bar, avoiding the men already seated, ordering his dinner, and watching the two girls enter the building. When Paulson asked his recollection of the women leaving the bar with the men, Henry's reply of "I thought those two yahoos were up to no damn good, with trouble on their minds if I'd ever seen it" had Lawler jumping to his feet.

"Your objection is overruled, Mr. Lawler. The district attorney's question asks for the witness to recollect. In my estimation, his recollection is, in fact, quite eloquent." Even a few of the jurors snickered.

"Mr. Long, a few more questions and you can step down," the DA said. "Has your memory of the events in the parking lot improved?"

"Sorry, Mr. Paulson, but no. As hard as I've tried to remember, I can't. All I know is that I was knocked out cold —by a wooden stake, they tell me—and I woke up with my face in the gravel."

"I'm sorry to hear that, Mr. Long. Let's move ahead to New Year's Eve, if you will. Please describe for the jury how you came to be part of the search party looking for Maria Thomas. And while you're at it, give us your description of Maria's physical appearance and state of mind when you found her."

"To answer your first question, I was helping out at the police station and took a call from a man saying he'd seen a girl running along the Cape Fear River. After that, you couldn't stop me from helping find her."

"And to my second request asking you to describe Maria?"

Henry sighed deeply, a look of profound sadness creasing his forehead. "A sad sight, that little girl was. Blood covered her legs and matted down her pretty blond hair. She was real scared, too. Hid behind bushes until the chief and I convinced her it was safe to come out."

"Did she say anything to you?"

"Cried a lot and pleaded for us to find her sister."

"Nothing about Mr. Ramone or Mr. Carter?"

"No, sir, she just wanted us to find Izzy. Seemed she was more concerned about Izzy being left behind in the cabin than she was about herself."

"Thank you, Mr. Long. That'll be all. Mr. Lawler, he's all yours."

The public defender stood, shuffled a few papers, and stated, "The defense declines to cross this witness."

Next up was Otis Dean, the owner of the Cape Fear Corner Market, where Billy and Frank had gotten provisions while at the cabin. He was in his seventies, with thinning hair and a runny nose that he blew repeatedly into a yellowing handkerchief. His testimony included a matter-of-fact description of the purchases made—"subs, beer and whiskey mostly"—how they'd paid—"cash"—and what he heard them say—"lots of laughin', not much else."

"Nothing else you might've forgotten that could be important in this case?" the DA prompted.

Mr. Dean shook his head, then settled his gaze on Billy. "Oh, wait just a second! Come to think of it, there was a couple things I found a bit odd, if you will."

"Care to expound on that, sir?"

Flushing across his nose and cheeks, he lowered his voice, whispering, "They bought a box of sanitary napkins. You know, the kind women use during their monthlies."

Smiling, Paulson replied, "That's very helpful, Mr. Dean. Thank you. Did either of the men say anything when buying the napkins?"

"Can't remember the exact words, but I know the big, goofy-looking guy, not the one sitting there," he pointed at Billy, "said something like, 'All that blood grosses me out!'"

"You said there were two things? What's the second?"

"The last time I seen 'em, on New Year's Eve, they asked if I had one of those new camcorders I could loan 'em."

"And did you?"

"No, sir, I don't own one, so they was outta luck."

"What did they say to that, Mr. Dean?"

"That one, there," he pointed again at Billy, "looked real disappointed and said, 'Shit.'"

"Thank you, Mr. Dean. That'll be all, Your Honor."

As the DA returned to his seat, Artie Lawler stood, advising the judge that he declined to cross this witness as well.

"Mr. Lawler, if I were you, I'd...," the judge began. "Oh, never mind. I'm hungry. Let's break for lunch. We'll reconvene in an hour."

# 37

# MONDAY AFTERNOON, MARCH 17, 1980

## FAYETTEVILLE, NORTH CAROLINA

On the side steps of the courthouse, the DA, Chief Roberts, Henry Long, and the Thomases stood in a tight circle.

"Appears to be going in our favor," Paulson offered. "Maybe this'll be over sooner than Friday."

"We hope so," Tony replied. "Anna and I don't want to be away from the girls for too long."

"How are they doing?" Henry asked quietly.

"Well, Maria's healed completely, at least physically," Anna said, "but Isabella's still suffering from the bowel resection and the infection that followed. She's lost too much weight, and we're a bit concerned she's lost her desire to ever eat again."

"Sorry to hear that," the chief said, frowning. "Putting this behind them once and for all should help, don't you think?"

"That's what we're hoping," Tony agreed.

"Billy's lawyer's pathetic," Henry scowled. "Thank goodness for that."

"Not much to defend against, if you ask me," Tony noted.

"You're right there. Too bad we had to go to the expense of a trial to begin with. Billy should've just pled guilty and gone straight to Central," the chief continued.

"Central?" questioned Tony.

"Maximum security prison outside of Raleigh. That's where he'll be sent, hopefully for the rest of his days."

"Will the sentencing take place immediately?" asked Anna, looking to the DA.

"Depends on how the judge feels once the verdict's handed down. Sometimes he's known to accept the jury's recommendation, other times he'll ruminate awhile, read the victim impact statements."

"Jury's in our corner, though, right, Mr. Paulson?" asked Henry.

"I've been watching them," Tony interjected. "The young blonde wiped away a tear when you testified how you'd found Maria by the river."

"But then there's that woman in brown who clearly felt sorry for Ramone when his damn attorney boohooed about how pitiful his upbringing was," the chief recalled. "Anyone up for a cheeseburger? I'm buying."

"Not me," the DA said. "Meeting with my team before we head back in."

"Okay, we'll see you there. I've got to put something in my stomach before you call me to the stand."

# 38

# MONDAY AFTERNOON, MARCH 17, 1980

## FAYETTEVILLE, NORTH CAROLINA

Chief Wayne Roberts was sworn in right after lunch. As an expert at testifying in front of judge and jury, he presented an imposing figure in his dress blues. Unlike the earlier witnesses, he was quite comfortable on the stand, from which he could stare down at the defendant. If only Billy Ramone would shift his focus from the table in front of him. Since he didn't, Roberts chose to make the public defender as uncomfortable as possible. While he looked at the DA when asked a question and to the jury with his answers, his eyes always returned to bore through Artie Lawler.

As the DA questioned him, the chief mesmerized the entire room with his recollection of the harrowing hours and days following Izzy and Maria's abduction. How the search had stalled when it seemed as though Ramone, Carter, and the Thomas girls had disappeared into thin air. And how, on New Year's Eve, the fortuitous call came in to the station about the girl seen running along the banks of the Cape Fear in Harnett County.

"Great work, Chief," Paulson lauded, an hour into the

testimony. "Your dedication and determination prevented anything worse from happening to the Thomas sisters. Not that what they'd already gone through wasn't absolutely horrific. It was, and that's why we're all here. But the fact that Maria escaped their clutches, that you found her, and that she led you to the cabin and Isabella, all before those two degenerates could kill them both, which they were surely wanting to do, makes me proud you're Fayetteville's police chief."

Artie Lawler, appearing somewhat rejuvenated after the lunch break, jumped to his feet. "Objection, Your Honor. The District Attorney is certainly overplaying it. Not only is he doing quite a bit of bootlicking, his assertions as to what my client wanted to do are mere speculation, not fact."

"Mr. Lawler, I'm proud of you," the judge said, chortling. "Thought you were going to let the DA get away with his little tribute. Motion sustained."

Grinning, the DA said, "No further questions, Your Honor. Artie, now's your shot."

Pleased with himself, Lawler swept to the witness stand, fawning, "Chief Roberts, let me begin by saying thank you for your service to this fine city."

"You're welcome, Artie," the chief replied, amusement playing across his brow.

"You just stated that, up until the anonymous call on New Year's Eve, you were at a complete loss as to where the girls were, or even if they were with Ramone and Carter?"

"A loss as to where they were, yes, but I was absolutely positive they were with Ramone and Carter."

"And it was that out-of-the-blue call from a man who refused to give his name, refused even to wait for the police, that led you to the missing girls?"

"That's right. Mind you, Maria actually enabled us to locate Izzy when she recalled Bobby Stott's name."

As if he'd just been reminded of his next question, Artie tapped his temple. "Speaking of Bobby Stott, Chief, let's go back to how you learned the cabin's location."

Shrugging, Roberts said, "As I explained, we found Maria up in Harnett County, and after she'd been brought to the hospital here in Fayetteville, I was able to talk with her. During that conversation, she remembered hearing the defendant mention Stott. I then recalled that he'd built a fishing cabin up on the Cape Fear somewhere, and I put two and two together."

"Amazing, Chief," Artie flattered. "But, um, did Mr. Stott give you permission to search his cabin?"

"As a matter of fact, Artie, he did. After we tracked him down at Jimmy's Joint—remember, it was New Year's Eve, and folks were out partying—he gave us directions to his cabin, authorizing us to search it."

"Hmm." Artie hesitated, trying to regain the upper hand. "Do you know if Mr. Stott had given my client permission to use his cabin?"

"It seems Bobby had invited Ramone and Carter up to fish last summer, so then, yes. But not in December."

"If they didn't have approval to use the cabin in December, then how'd they get in?"

"According to Mr. Stott, who you could always call to the stand, you know, save me the breath...," the chief said with frustration, "it was no secret that he kept a spare key in a tackle box under the front porch."

Standing, Jim Paulson addressed the judge. "Your Honor, is there a point to Mr. Lawler's line of questioning? If so, please ask that he enlighten us all, as I'm at a loss to see how any of this is a cross of my direct line of questioning."

"I was thinking the same thing, Mr. Paulson. Move along, Mr. Lawler."

"My point, Your Honor," Artie offered triumphantly, "is that Bobby Stott might have been the anonymous caller who reported seeing Miss Thomas. He could have gone to the cabin that night, discovered the girls, freed them, and then called it in."

"Huh?" the chief responded, his mouth agape. "That doesn't even make sense. If he'd found the girls, why wouldn't he have just released them and taken them to the hospital? And let's not forget that the girls would likely have mentioned if that had been the case."

Artie's face fell, and he fumbled with his stack of papers before speculating, "Maybe he was too afraid to admit that the girls had been held in his cabin?"

The DA stood again. "Your Honor, is there a single intelligent thought there, let alone a question? What I'm hearing is nonsensical conjecture, pure and simple."

"Agreed. Chief Roberts, you may respond to the PD's speculation, if you so choose, but if not, Mr. Lawler, wrap this up."

"I'll gladly address his idiotic thought process." Roberts scowled. "When we found Stott at Jimmy's, where he'd been since dinner, he was more than willing to cooperate with us. He gave us his key to the cabin, for God's sake."

Flushing, Lawler continued, "One more question, Chief. Was Maria Thomas sedated when you interrogated her at the hospital? Was she placed under oath before answering your questions?"

"I did *not* interrogate Miss Thomas at the hospital. When we *spoke*, Maria was quite awake. As a matter of fact, she was so determined to find her sister that she refused sedation until after our conversation. As for being under oath, why was that even necessary at the time? You heard her sworn statement this morning, or have you already forgotten that?"

"There's no need to get snippy with me," Lawler sniveled. "I have no further questions, Your Honor."

# 39

# MONDAY AFTERNOON, MARCH 17, 1980

## FAYETTEVILLE, NORTH CAROLINA

Over the next two hours, the prosecution called five additional witnesses: the sheriff of Florence County, South Carolina; the park ranger from the Huguenot Memorial Park in Jacksonville, Florida; the Boy Scout leader of Troop 9898, Jacksonville, Florida; and the arresting deputy from McIntosh County, Georgia. Since only the McIntosh County officer had anything of value to add to the charges concerning the Thomas sisters, the first four were questioned and dispatched quickly.

"Officer Vance, thank you for coming today to testify," DA Paulson began, addressing the officer from Georgia.

"Honored to be here, sir."

"In the interest of brevity," the DA said, looking at his watch, "your arrest report has been entered into evidence, so I'd like to focus specifically on what the defendant said after you detained him behind the gas station in Darien. What do you recall Mr. Ramone saying?"

"Sir, I was in the process of reciting the Miranda warning when Mr. Ramone said, and I quote, 'Fuck you! You should be arresting them for killing my best friend.'"

"Officer Vance, I may be stretching here, but if Frank Carter were, in fact, Ramone's best friend, this would dispute the defense's assertion that Billy Ramone is a victim who'd been intimidated and coerced by Frank Carter to participate in the crimes, doesn't it?"

"Common sense would say so," Vance answered, looking directly at Lawler.

"Thank you, Officer Vance. Your Honor, the prosecution rests."

"Mr. Lawler," the judge said, "I'm sure you can't wait to cross this witness, but it's dinner time, and your cross can wait. We'll reconvene at nine o'clock tomorrow morning. Let's try to wrap up earlier than today, please." After banging his gavel, the bailiff called for everyone to stand, and the judge left the courtroom.

As the jury filed out, what started as a dull murmur quickly rose to shouts as spectators and reporters called out questions to Billy and the attorneys on both sides. As the court officers worked to corral everyone from the room, Billy was escorted out by two sheriff's deputies. He never looked up.

Artie Lawler gathered his papers and, glancing angrily at the prosecution's table, strode over. "Paulson," he spat indignantly, "just because you're the DA doesn't mean you or your witnesses can demean me and undermine my authority. I am an officer of this court, just like you!"

"You are?" asked Paulson, lowering his voice so as not to be overheard. "Well then, if I were you, Artie, I'd ask myself why I feel so demeaned and undermined. If you're honest with yourself, or just smart enough to figure it out, you'd realize it's because you're an idiot. Not only do I know it, but today everyone in this courtroom figured it out. Sorry I have to be the one to tell you."

"I swear to God, Paulson," Artie threatened, his face getting splotchier with every word, "if you so much as look cross-eyed in my direction tomorrow, I'll report your behavior to the state bar."

"Game on, Artie," the DA said and laughed. Lawler turned and harrumphed out of the room.

# 40

# TUESDAY MORNING, MARCH 18, 1980

## FAYETTEVILLE, NORTH CAROLINA

At 9:15 a.m., Judge Rogers looked down from the bench at Artie Lawler. "Mr. Lawler, do you wish to cross-examine Deputy Vance at this time?"

"Yes, Your Honor, I do," stated Artie, looking more disheveled than he had the day before. Today he was dressed in a tan polyester suit so worn that the lining of his jacket hung below the hem line. Dark sweat stains were already showing under his arms, and a sheen of sweat glistened atop his balding head.

"Mr. Vance, please return to the stand. And remember, sir, you are still under oath this morning."

As Deputy Vance waited for the public defender to sort through his notes, he looked confident, calm, and well rested, in stark contrast to Lawler who, as he approached the stand, startled when an assistant prosecutor knocked a folder onto the floor. Turning to glare at the DA, who simply shrugged his shoulders, Artie tripped on an errant shoelace. As he squatted to tie it, the papers he was holding skidded across the floor. Kindly, the court reporter stepped away from her keyboard to help him gather them.

"Are you ready now, Mr. Lawler?" the judge asked, looking pointedly at his watch.

"Yes, Your Honor, sorry about that."

"Thank goodness. I will tolerate no further delays."

"Deputy Vance," Artie began, "you stated yesterday that, after advising the defendant of the grounds for his arrest, he shouted something before you had read him his Miranda rights. Am I correct?"

"No, you are not. I had started to Mirandize the defendant, when he said, and again I quote, 'Fuck you! You should be arresting them for killing my best friend.'"

"Okay, Officer, but since Mr. Ramone spoke those words prior to being read his entire Miranda rights, shouldn't his words have been withheld from your testimony?"

"Again, no. As I had already advised Mr. Ramone that anything he said could and would be used against him in a court of law, and as I did not compel him to say anything, nor did I question or interrogate him in any way, everything he did say, of his own accord, is permissible testimony."

"Could it be said that Mr. Ramone was under legitimate duress when he spoke those words? Had he not, after all, just been shot in the leg?"

"Yes, Ramone was shot as he attempted to elude arrest. He had been sought as an armed and dangerous criminal, and we took all necessary measures to take him into custody, thus protecting the public from further harm. The fact remains that he spoke those words, and I have testified under oath to that effect. It's up to the jury to decide what it all means in terms of his guilt or innocence."

Dismayed, Artie glanced at the papers in hand, shaking his head. "Nothing more for this witness, Your Honor."

"Very well, then," Judge Rogers stated. "The witness may

step down. If the defense is prepared to call any witnesses, Mr. Lawler, please do so without delay."

# 41

# TUESDAY MORNING, MARCH 18, 1980

FAYETTEVILLE, NORTH CAROLINA

A rtie looked around the gallery, searching. With a smile, he turned to the bench. "Your Honor, defense calls Mary Rose Carter to the stand."

A short, dumpy woman in her late twenties, with a sallow complexion and dark, over-permed hair, rose from her seat in the gallery and walked through the gate. She wore an ill-fitting dress of pink and yellow flowers, a black shawl thrown over her shoulders. Approaching the bench, she glanced at Billy, who was sitting as before with his head down.

After being sworn in, Mary Rose sat rigidly, her hands clutching a wad of tissues in her lap. When Artie addressed her, she appeared to be on the verge of tears.

"Miss Carter, thank you for your testimony today. This can't be easy for you. Tell the jury, please, who you are."

"I'm Frank Carter's big sister, Mary Rose."

"So sorry for your loss, Miss Carter. Would you please tell us why you're here today?"

"Because I wanted to tell everyone what good boys Frank and Billy are. Or were," she corrected.

"But they allegedly committed heinous crimes, Miss Carter. How can you defend them in this courtroom today, knowing that?"

"Because they had an awful time growing up. My folks at least tried with Frank. And he had me to come to when he needed, but Billy didn't have no one but Frank. His daddy, Buck Ramone, was a mean old cur. Always drunk and beatin' on Billy. He even beat on Frank when he'd done something wrong, or when he just felt like it."

"Didn't your parents object to Mr. Ramone hitting their son?"

"Frank would never rat on Billy or his pa. I knew, though, and one day I saw Mr. Buck at the Piggly Wiggly, and I told him to keep his mitts off Frank."

"And what did he say to that?"

Looking embarrassed, she whispered, "He told me to keep my fat ass out of his business or he'd teach me a lesson or two. After that, I'd just patch Frank and Billy up and keep my mouth shut."

"What's the worst beating Billy or Frank took from Mr. Ramone? Can you remember any specific incidents?"

Mary Rose wiped her eyes and looked directly at Billy. "Billy," she said, beginning to weep in earnest, "you know better than me. Why don't you get up here and tell everyone?" Billy raised his head slightly but dropped it before meeting her eyes.

"Miss Carter," Judge Rogers cut in, "if you need a moment, let us know."

"No, I'm good," she replied, then blew her nose loudly. "One time, when the boys were in high school, Mr. Buck beat Billy and Frank so bad I had to take them to the emergency room."

"Describe your brother's injuries, please."

"Don't know all the medical terms, but he couldn't see or talk real good after. I remember the doctor saying he had a concussion, and he needed lots of stitches in his head. His eye was always droopy afterwards, and sometimes he could be real stupid about things."

"What about Billy's injuries?"

"His face was cut up real bad, and his arm was kinda useless for a long time after."

"Why wasn't Buck Ramone arrested after that beating?" Artie asked, throwing up his arms. "If Frank and Billy were treated at the hospital, the police must have been notified."

"They both swore they'd fallen off their skateboards riding down a hill out by Sandy Run Creek. Wasn't no one to say different."

"Miss Carter, do you think the injuries sustained by Billy and Frank, at the hands of Mr. Ramone, were to blame for any of the crimes Billy is being tried for now?"

After taking a sip of water, Mary Rose answered, "Absolutely. If you coulda seen those two boys when they were little. They were so cute and cuddly. What Mr. Ramone did to them, he should be on trial here, not Billy. And he should be blamed for Frank dyin', too."

Smiling, Artie turned to the jury, bowed a bit and said, "Thank you, Miss Carter. Judge, I have no further questions for this witness."

As Mary Rose struggled to stand, the judge said, "Miss Carter, please remain seated. Mr. Paulson, would you like to question the witness?"

"Yes, Your Honor, I would. Thank you." Rising from his seat, looking as polished as ever, the DA walked to the bench and smiled compassionately at the witness.

"Miss Carter, may I call you Mary Rose?"

"Sure," she said, smiling shyly.

"Mary Rose, then. I have a quick question about Billy's father, Buck Ramone, while he's still fresh on our minds. The court hasn't heard testimony as to how he died. Do you know?"

Mary Rose shrugged, her watery eyes on Billy. "Mr. Buck got real drunk one night and took a header down the cellar steps."

"Is that so? And when was this?"

"Don't know exactly. Not long before the boys graduated high school, if I remember right."

Paulson paused to look first at Billy, then at the jury, before continuing. "And do you know where Billy was the night his father took that fateful plunge down the basement stairs?"

"Can't say as I ever knew, but he and Frank must've been around somewhere."

"Why do you say that?"

"Because they're the ones who found Mr. Buck's body."

"Interesting," the DA commented with a nod. "And while we're on the topic of Billy's parents, do you know what happened to Irma Ramone, Billy's mother?"

Artie Lawler jumped to his feet. "That calls for speculation, Your Honor."

"Not if Miss Carter knows, Your Honor," Paulson stated.

Addressing Mary Rose, the judge asked, "Miss Carter, are you in a position to answer Mr. Paulson's question?"

"Not sure that I am. Nobody really knows, I guess. She just up and disappeared one night when Billy was little. Didn't show up for choir practice at the church, and no one seen or heard from her again."

Paulson pressed on. "Wasn't their some talk that Buck Ramone killed his wife and buried her body somewhere?"

"Yeah, I guess we heard that rumor, too. But it was never proved."

As Mary Rose shifted uncomfortably in her chair, the DA walked over to the the prosecution's table and picked up a clipboard. "Okay, let's move on, shall we? Before the incidents detailed in this courtroom, the events that took place around New Year's, had Billy or Frank been in any sort of legal trouble?"

Artie Lawson was apoplectic as he jumped from his seat. "Objection, Your Honor! That calls for the revelation of prior crimes. As the defendant has not taken the stand, this line of questioning is impermissible."

Looking back at the PD with a smirk, Paulson spoke to the judge, "Your Honor, shall I explain to Mr. Lawler how, by calling Miss Carter to the stand, he has chosen to make Mr. Ramone's character an issue in this trial and thus has opened the door for a discussion of his prior crimes and convictions?"

"I believe you've just done so, Mr. Paulson," the judge said dryly as Artie sank into his chair. "Overruled, Mr. Lawler. You may answer the question, Miss Carter."

"Do I have to?" she asked the judge.

"Yes, Miss Carter, you do," he replied, nodding.

Twisting the tissues in her lap, Mary Rose swallowed hard. "Both Frank and Billy got into lots of trouble after high school. And some during, too."

"Such as?" Paulson prompted.

"Don't you have copies of their record?" she asked, stalling.

"I do, Miss Carter," Paulson said, smiling as he held out his clipboard, "but I'd like you to tell the court yourself. I can clarify the details if need be."

"Well," Mary Rose started. "One of the worst was when Frank and Billy broke into Doc Horton's office and stole a bunch of pills."

"That would have involved," Paulson read from the clipboard, "charges of breaking and entering, malicious destruction, theft of a controlled substance, distribution of a controlled substance, and unauthorized use of a controlled substance. All felonies."

"Yeah, I guess."

"Anything else?"

Averting her eyes, she added, "Um, they really liked the ladies, and I know they'd sometimes go down to Hay Street to pick up hookers. I think Billy mighta beat one up once when she told him he stank."

"That would have been when Mr. Ramone was charged with solicitation and felony assault," the DA read, looking directly at Billy and Artie, their heads hung low. "Go on, please, Miss Carter."

"Ummm, I can't think of much else. Maybe speedin' a couple times?"

"By my count," Paulson said, running his finger down the sheet of paper, "Mr. Ramone was ticketed five times for speeding, with driving under the influence a factor in three of those incidents."

"Maybe."

"It's a shame, don't you think, Mary Rose, that neither Frank nor Billy went to jail on any of these earlier charges. Or, for that matter, for the unfortunate billiard incident detailed yesterday by Jimmy Marcus. If they had, maybe we wouldn't be here today. Maybe Frank would be alive."

"They were just boys being boys," Mary Rose protested defensively. She dabbed at a tear trickling down her cheek.

"Unfortunately, Mary Rose, with each of their earlier arrests, Frank and Billy pled down to lesser crimes and were released after paying only minor fines and court fees, several of which, I believe, were covered by you. Isn't that correct?"

"Yeah, but why'd they get off so easy if you're saying they should've been locked up?"

"I can't answer that, Mary Rose. But your assertion that your brother Frank and Billy Ramone were good boys before they kidnapped and raped the Thomas sisters does not hold true. There was an escalation to their crimes, and each time they got off easy, as you have observed, their exploits became increasingly violent."

"Your Honor, is there a question there?" Artie Lawler asked, not bothering to stand.

"Mr. Paulson? Do you have any more questions for this witness?"

"Just one, Your Honor," the DA said. He gestured in the direction of Billy and Artie Lawler, then continued. "Mary Rose, do you believe the defense attorney's claim that Frank was the instigator of all crimes committed against the Thomas sisters? That Billy was threatened with grave bodily harm if he didn't go along with Frank's plans?"

Mary Rose shook her head vehemently, her eyes projecting daggers at Artie and Billy. "That's an outright lie! Frank worshipped Billy. He was the one who always went along with whatever Billy wanted, not the other way around!"

"That's what I thought," the DA said quietly. "Nothing further, Your Honor." Tucking the clipboard under his arm, he returned to his seat.

Looking somewhat rattled, Judge Rogers dismissed

Mary Rose. As the bailiff helped her from the witness stand, the judge sipped from his glass of water before addressing the court. "At this time, I'd like to call a brief recess so we can all grab a snack and catch our breath. We'll reconvene for closing arguments in thirty minutes sharp."

# 42

# TUESDAY AFTERNOON, MARCH 18, 1980

## FAYETTEVILLE, NORTH CAROLINA

"Ladies and gentlemen of the jury," Jim Paulson began his closing argument, "as the testimony has clearly shown, the defendant, William J. Ramone, and his accomplice, Frank Carter, deceased, did knowingly, willingly, and with malice of intent, abduct, falsely imprison, sexually assault, and attempt to murder Isabella and Maria Thomas. Had it not been for Maria's brave escape on the thirty-first of December, it is reasonable to assume that Mr. Ramone and Mr. Carter would have succeeded in killing both women. Yet after Maria's escape, Isabella, in her desperately weakened physical and emotional state, managed instead to fatally stab Mr. Carter. In self-defense, might I remind you. In so doing, Isabella, herself, sustained a life-threatening stab wound."

Listening to the horrific account once again, Anna dropped her face into her hands. Tony hugged her to his side, never taking his eyes off the jury as the DA continued.

"In an effort to satisfy their wanton lust and rage, and what amounted to an out-of-control need to inflict grave bodily pain and injury, the two men carried out their heinous crimes with no thought or care as to the impact their actions would have on Isabella and Maria, the Thomas family, and, frankly, society at large.

"Let me repeat that, ladies and gentlemen. As you deliberate upon the verdict you will hand down and, should you find the defendant guilty, on the punishment you will recommend, I ask that you bear in mind the irreversible damage Billy Ramone and Frank Carter inflicted upon these women, their family, the city of Fayetteville, Cumberland and Harnett Counties, and the great states of North Carolina, South Carolina, Florida, Georgia, and Pennsylvania, where the Thomas family resides.

"While Frank Carter cannot accept his sentence here on earth, and mind you, I hope he's being duly punished in the afterlife, I ask you to sentence Billy Ramone to his full term *plus* the sentence Frank Carter would have incurred had death not let him off so easily.

"Ladies and gentlemen, I again thank you for your time and service to this great court. It has been my pleasure to have served beside you. On behalf of Isabella and Maria Thomas, and their parents sitting right here"—Paulson gestured in Anna and Tony's direction—"I wish you Divine guidance with your deliberations. Thank you."

With that, the district attorney nodded to the judge and returned to his seat.

"Mr. Lawler," the judge said, "you're up."

Artie, gulping visibly, pushed back his chair. Beside him, Billy fidgeted restlessly with the cuffs around his wrists. "Ladies and gentlemen of the jury," Artie began, "while what you've heard in this courtroom over the past two days may sound bad, you must remind yourselves of what we've learned of Mr. Ramone's life before he chose the misguided path that led to his being here. The path that ultimately led to Frank Carter's untimely death."

*Untimely*, Anna thought, fuming beside Tony. *Artie Lawler is a despicable man. If Billy weren't such a degenerate human being, someone might actually feel sorry for him. But he deserves whatever punishment is meted out, and I, for one, won't lose any sleep over his poor legal representation.*

"Furthermore, I ask you to consider how Billy Ramone has suffered already. Firstly, at the hands of his father, Buck Ramone. Then with the loss of his mother at such a tender age, and more recently, the death of his best friend, Frank Carter. Even though I maintain that Frank Carter was the instigator of all crimes against the Thomas sisters, Billy loved Frank, and it was that love that prevented him from walking away before things spiraled out of control. And let's not forget that Mr. Ramone was shot in the leg, a wound he suffers from still, and likely always will."

# 43

# TUESDAY AFTERNOON, MARCH 18, 1980

### FAYETTEVILLE, NORTH CAROLINA

After babbling a few moments longer, Artie Lawler returned to the defense table as Judge Rogers began his final instructions to the jury. After the judge had retired to his chambers, Anna and Tony watched as the jury filed out and Billy was led from the room. As they stood to leave, the DA turned to ask that they stay put a moment longer. After conferring quietly with one of his prosecutors, he sat on the bench beside them. "I think deliberations will take only a few hours, at most. We could have our verdict before five today."

"Should we stay here or return to the hotel?" Tony asked.

"We'll have an hour to return once the judge learns there's a verdict," Paulson replied. "Why don't I have a deputy take you back to the hotel. He can hang in the lobby until we notify him to bring you back."

"Thank you, that's much appreciated," Anna replied.

In a corner booth in the hotel restaurant, Anna and Tony ordered sandwiches and talked quietly. When the waitress brought their meals, tuna on rye for Tony and a grilled ham and cheese for Anna, they thanked her before bowing their heads for grace.

*If nothing else*, Anna thought to herself, *our marriage has become stronger because of this tragedy. If only Isabella and Maria's relationship can survive.* Ever since they'd brought the girls home, Izzy had become increasingly despondent. She refused to leave her bedroom most days, and when she did join the family downstairs, she sniped at Maria and her parents alike. Although Dr. Oates continued to indicate that the girls were healing physically, and Maria's pre-abduction disposition was resurfacing, Izzy seemed mired in a dark funk, lacking an appetite for food or comfort of any kind.

Thinking aloud, Anna said, "Once this trial is over, maybe we should make an appointment with a counselor for Isabella. She doesn't seem to be getting better like she should."

"Give her time, Anna. It's been less than three months, after all."

"I know, Tony, but Maria seems to be rebounding from the whole ordeal. Or at least she's coping better. I just don't want Isabella suffering needlessly if we can make things better for her."

"I suppose," Tony agreed. "Let's worry about that once we get home, okay?"

Anna and Tony requested that the meal be charged to their room, then they stepped into the lobby. Seeing them, the deputy who'd driven them to the hotel rushed over. "Verdict's in," he stated. "We should head back to the courthouse."

# 44

# TUESDAY AFTERNOON, MARCH 18, 1980

FAYETTEVILLE, NORTH CAROLINA

I n the charged courtroom, conversations buzzed as Anna and Tony took their seats. Billy Ramone was escorted back to the defense table, looking more haggard and despondent than earlier that morning. It occurred to Anna that he had to know what was coming down on him. *Suffer, you wicked man*, she thought, before silently asking God to forgive her ill intentions.

The jury filed in next, blank expressions on their faces.

"All rise," called the bailiff as Judge Rogers ascended the bench, then gaveled for silence.

"Has the jury reached a unanimous decision?" he asked the foreman.

The stately gentleman with gray tufts of hair and rimless eyeglasses stood. "We have, Your Honor."

"Will the defendant please rise," instructed the bailiff, and Billy stood unsteadily.

"What say you?" the judge asked.

Clearing his throat, the foreman stated, "Your Honor, before I begin, I would be remiss if I didn't point out that each individual count actually addresses two separate charges, one for each victim."

"I appreciate that clarification, sir. Thank you and please proceed."

The foreman glanced quickly at Billy before refocusing his attention on the paper in his hands. "On the charge of kidnapping in the first degree, we find the defendant guilty."

A cheer rose from the gallery, and the judge again gaveled for silence. "I'll have order in this court," he demanded, and the ruckus slowly petered out. Billy and Artie dropped their heads.

"Continue." The judge nodded to the foreman.

"On the charge of false imprisonment, we find the defendant guilty. On the charge of rape in the first degree, we find the defendant guilty. On the charge of inflicting mayhem and gross bodily injury, we find the defendant guilty. And finally"—the juror paused—"on the charge of attempted murder, we find the defendant guilty."

Again, the gallery erupted with cheers. The judge allowed a moment to pass before calling for order.

"Have you a recommendation on sentencing?"

"We do, Your Honor."

"May I see it?" the judge asked. The bailiff retrieved the folded sheet of paper, handing it to the judge.

After reading, the judge looked directly at Billy. "Mr. Ramone, the jury has recommended a sentence that I find to be fair and just given the crimes for which you have now been convicted. I would, however, like to take this evening to read the victim impact statements before rendering my final decision. We will reconvene tomorrow morning at ten sharp."

While the prosecution celebrated, Billy huddled with his attorney before being led from the courtroom. Artie

Lawler then walked over to Anna and Tony, waiting impatiently until they noticed him. "Mr. Lawler," Tony said, "is there something you want?"

Hearing Tony, Jim Paulson looked back, growling, "Artie, what the hell do you want?"

Ignoring the DA, Artie handed a crumpled piece of paper to Tony. "My client asked that I pass this on to you. I haven't read it and take no responsibility for what it might say." He turned abruptly and walked away.

"Let me see that," the DA demanded. Reading the note, he cursed, "What the hell?"

"What is it, Jim?" Anna asked.

"Here, read it before I have the bailiff deliver it to the judge. Rogers needs to see this before he imposes his sentence."

*Tell those cunts I'm coming for them. No matter how long it takes.*

"Oh, my God!" cried Anna, covering her mouth with her hand.

"I hope he dies in prison, so help me God," Tony swore.

"If I can do anything to ensure that, Tony, I will," Paulson promised, and he walked up to the bailiff.

# 45

# TUESDAY EVENING, MARCH 18, 1980

FAYETTEVILLE, NORTH CAROLINA

J udge Rogers draped his robe over the valet, pulled the leather chair from beneath his desk, and sat down, his head in his hands. Although the trial had been short, he was exhausted, wanting nothing more than to head home to the warmth of his wife and a generous tumbler of Dewar's 12.

Hearing a strident knock on the door, he sighed deeply, ordering, "Come in."

His bailiff stuck his head in. "Your Honor, the DA asked that I give this to you," he explained.

"What is it?"

"Apparently Artie Lawler just handed it to Mr. and Mrs. Thomas."

Unfolding the wrinkled sheet of paper, the judge read the scrawled words.

"Am I to assume this was written by Ramone?"

"Seems so, according to what Lawler told the Thomases."

"Thank you. Please lock the door when you leave."

"Yes, Your Honor."

Leaning back in his chair, the judge closed his eyes. This trial had disturbed him from the start. Disturbed him for many reasons that went far beyond the crimes committed. He chastised himself, again, for not having recused himself from the get-go because of his prior dealings with Billy Ramone. He'd been one of the judges, mind you, just one of them, who had let Billy and Frank Carter off with mere wrist slaps. He'd justified those earlier light sentences because he'd known the two friends had been dealt a rough hand growing up. Hell, he'd even had dealings with Billy's dad, Buck, long before Billy'd gotten himself in trouble.

Listening to Mary Rose Carter's testimony today, specifically when she'd asked the DA why Billy and Frank had been let off so easy for their earlier transgressions, the judge had been overcome with a deep sense of regret and remorse. Regret for not locking those boys up when he'd had the chance, and remorse for what they'd ended up doing to the Thomas sisters.

Shaking his head in shame, he ran a letter opener under the flap of the envelope containing Maria Thomas's impact statement. When he'd finished reading it, he slipped Isabella Thomas's statement from its envelope.

*To whom it may concern:*

*My name is Isabella Anna Thomas, and I am twenty-one years old. This past December (1979), as my younger sister, Maria, and I were driving to Florida, my car broke down in Fayetteville, North Carolina. When we looked for help at a local bar (we'd broken down in front of the bar—we hadn't stopped there to drink!), we were kidnapped by two men, Billy Ramone and Frank Carter.*

*Billy and Frank took us to a cabin in the woods, which I later learned was along the Cape Fear River in Harnett County, North Carolina.*

*I know I've testified already (to a Mr. Paulson and Mr. Lawler at the Bucks County Courthouse) about everything that happened to us (Maria and me) at that cabin, so I won't go over everything again in this letter. I just wanted you to know that Maria and I didn't do anything to deserve what happened to us. Even though I blame myself for everything.*

*You see, it was my car that broke down. Maria's my little sister, and I should have made sure she was safe, even if it meant I alone was kidnapped, raped, and nearly killed.*

*I am guilty of not being careful, of not being attentive, of not watching my surroundings, of not taking care of Maria. If my mom and dad drummed anything into my head from the time I got my learner's permit, it was that I had to be aware, 100 percent of the time, of everything that was going on around me. I used to think they expected me to have a head that could spin around on my shoulders, but after we were taken, I understood what they'd really been trying to instill in me. I had to understand that there are people "out there" who would sooner kill me, kill Maria, then not. I assume they tried to drill this unpleasant tidbit into Maria, too. In any event, it was my responsibility, as the older sister, to make sure those people "out there" didn't hurt her.*

*Maria saved my life when she left the cabin to get help. I should have been the one to get help. Mind you, I killed Frank, that inhuman monster, but it was Maria who put the knife in my hand and told me to do it. I am a failure at being a big sister, and I don't deserve to be alive.*

*The memories of and injuries from what Billy and Frank did to me will never go away. I still can't sleep without nightmares. I can't eat without wanting to throw up. Even my favorite foods, which Mom keeps making in the hopes I'll get my appetite back, taste bad. Or is it that they taste too good, and I don't deserve* them? I'm not sure if I'm just punishing myself by pushing away everything I used to love.

I think I need to talk to a psychiatrist, but how embarrassing is that? Every morning I get up and tell myself to "get over it." I lecture myself every waking minute to pick myself up, dust myself off, get on with my life. But I can't seem to do it on my own. And I'll be damned if I'm going to ask my parents for help. I can't even stand to have them look at me with their eyes full of pity.

And I'll never be able to ask Maria for help. Ever again. I think I'll move far, far away.

Please put Billy Ramone in prison forever and ever and ever. It's too late for me and Maria, but you can't let him hurt anyone else like he hurt us. Regardless of whether they are 100 percent aware of their surroundings or not.

Thank you for listening,
Isabella Anna Thomas
March 10, 1980


JUDGE ROGERS DROPPED the letter to the desk and opened the top right drawer, shuffling around until he found the green plastic bottle. Isabella's words had reignited the sharp belly pains he knew to be an ulcer. His doctor had as much as told him that if he didn't reduce his stress level, get some exercise, and eat healthier, he'd end up in the hospital with a bleeding ulcer or heart attack. "Your choice," the doc had said.

Chewing four of the antacid tablets, he pulled out his legal pad and began writing. Twenty minutes later, after scratching out a few lines and adding a few others, he reread what he'd written, smiling sadly.

Although it was certainly too late to right his earlier wrongs, he'd make damn sure that the Thomas sisters knew he had read their heart-wrenching words, had truly listened to their pleas. He wished he could tell them what remarkable young women they were. Both of them. Perhaps he'd write them personal letters once the trial was over. In any event, he knew what he had to do tomorrow.

# WEDNESDAY MORNING, MARCH 19, 1980

## FAYETTEVILLE, NORTH CAROLINA

"All rise," called the bailiff as Judge Rogers entered the courtroom and sat down. He looked tired still, the bags under his eyes darker than they were the day before.

Looking around the room, the judge cleared his throat and began. "Ladies and gentlemen, the past sixteen hours have been quite distressing for me. After dismissing y'all yesterday afternoon, I retired to my chambers to read the letters from the Thomas sisters and to contemplate the jury's recommended sentence. No sooner had I removed my robe, my bailiff knocked on the door to deliver this."

Waving the note in front of him, murmurs arose throughout the room. "I'll explain what this is in a moment, but I wish to address the defendant now. Mr. Ramone, stand and look at me."

Artie nudged Billy, who appeared not to be paying the least bit of attention. "Billy, stand up!" he urged.

Billy stood, but his eyes remained on the table.

"I ordered you to look at me, Mr. Ramone!" the judge bellowed, and Billy's head jerked up. Red flared across Judge

Rogers's cheeks, and he took a sip of water before speaking again.

"Never in my twenty-eight years on the bench have I encountered a man, criminal or otherwise, with so little regard for others. Someone so intent on ruining everything and everyone in his wake. You may have escaped legal punishment for your previous crimes, and I am to blame for some of that, but your blatant contempt and disdain for this court of law, and for those you have hurt, stops here and now."

Ignoring the courtroom buzz, the judge continued, "Ladies and gentlemen, Isabella and Maria Thomas wrote heart-wrenching impact statements. They have asked that I keep their words confidential, and I will honor their request. Suffice it to say, had the jury read them, they likely would have added many years to their proposed sentence. I will do that for them, but not because of the moving statements. Rather, I am enhancing the jury's recommended fifty years—"

Shouts erupted in the room, and Billy dropped his head while Artie simply shook his.

"Order," the judge gaveled. "Mr. Ramone, you will look at me."

Billy looked up, a single tear sliding down his cheek.

"And shed no tear for yourself, young man. I will not tolerate your sniveling in my courtroom!"

Taking a moment to calm himself, Judge Rogers continued, "As I was saying, I am enhancing the jury's recommended fifty-year sentence because of this"—he shook the paper—"the note Mr. Ramone wrote to Mr. and Mrs. Thomas that was, fortunately, turned over to me. Pardon me if you find the words offensive."

As the judge read the threat, exclamations of disbelief and outrage filled the gallery. This time, the judge allowed the disruption to quiet on its own.

"Pretty damn upsetting, isn't it? Threatening the Thomas sisters for doing nothing but staying alive. Well, Mr. Ramone, I hereby sentence you to life in prison, which in the state of North Carolina is eighty years, not fifty. Eighty years with no chance of parole or early release."

Cheers sounded from the crowd. Anna and Tony hugged each other before reaching over the railing to do the same to Jim Paulson and his assistant prosecutors.

"Thank you, thank you," Anna told them.

"You will be forever in our gratitude," Tony added.

"Just doing our job," the DA said, grinning. "Billy Ramone won't be getting out of prison unless he lives to be a centenarian!"

"Thank God for that," Henry added, coming up behind them. Anna hugged him as well, and then Chief Roberts when he walked up.

"I believe a celebration's in order. Who'd like to join me back at the station for a bottle or two of champagne? I've been holding a couple since New Year's Eve, when I was a little too busy to pop them." the chief said, smiling.

"As much as we'd love to join everyone," Tony said, "I think Anna and I will be heading for home tonight."

"We want to get back to the girls as soon as we can," added Anna. "They're in good hands with Tony's brother and his wife, but we need to be there for them."

"We understand perfectly," the chief said. "Please drive safely and give those beautiful girls hugs from all of us."

"Absolutely," chimed in Henry. "If I'm ever in Pennsylvania, I'll take time to stop in to see you all."

"That would be lovely," Anna enthused.

"Thank you all again, so much," Tony finished. Grabbing Anna's hand, they walked from the courthouse.

# PART II

*The past is never where you think you left it.*
—Katherine Anne Porter

# 47

## MONDAY MORNING, AUGUST 6, 2018

### SOUTHPORT, NORTH CAROLINA

M aria grumbled and rolled over in bed. Stretching her legs, she rotated her ankles five times in each direction. Taking a deep, cleansing breath, she threw her legs over the side of the mattress. Reaching her arms above her, she bent to each side, bringing her hands down in namaste.

She wished she felt like getting on the floor to do more poses, but last night's one-too-many Southern Comforts had her feeling queasy, and the pounding behind her eyes threatened to mushroom into a full-blown headache. Again. "I've got to quit that shit," she muttered, heading to the bathroom. Smarty Pants, her rescue cat, jumped down from the chair by the window, meowing as if to say, "About time, Mom."

"I know, I know, Smarty," Maria answered her. "Give me a minute, and I'll feed you."

An hour later, feeling slightly better after two cups of coffee, pecan praline this morning, Maria laced up her sneakers for a walk into town. *At least I can sweat out the residual alcohol*, she thought as she placed her phone in her pocket, locked the door behind her, and carefully navigated the front steps.

Heading down Clarendon Street, Maria focused on her breathing while she glanced around her, taking in the beauty of the live oaks draped with Spanish moss. She stopped to snap a photo of one particularly impressive tree, the resurrection ferns blanketing its network of massive branches.

Her Fitbit vibrated on her wrist, and checking it, she saw a text from an unknown caller. *It can wait til I get home*, she thought, continuing her trek toward the Yacht Basin. She toyed with the idea of having an early lunch in town, but as she glanced up at a stained-glass window of Friendship Baptist Church, a wave of nausea assailed her. Bending at the waist, she muttered an unholy "Hell!" When the queasiness subsided, she turned back to sit on a bench in the park across the street.

As she watched two young children laughing on the merry-go-round, their young mothers chatting nearby, Maria's heart ached for the children she'd never had. As tears threatened to spill onto her cheeks, she angrily rubbed her eyes, scolding herself for being so melodramatic. "Get over yourself, Maria," she muttered. Standing, she headed in the direction of home.

Stripping off her sweaty clothes, Maria stepped into the shower, adjusting the temperature to as hot as she could stand. The steaming water poured mercifully from the rainfall head, and she let it wash over her until a dense fog clouded the stall. Once again, she chastised herself for getting drunk the night before. It was way out of control this time, she admitted. *I've got to get control of my life instead of letting it spin wildly out of control.*

After washing her hair and shaving her legs, Maria

turned the water on cold for a few tortuous seconds before turning it off all together. After squeegeeing the stall, she stepped out onto the air foam mat, wrapping her body in a lush bath blanket. Slipping on her flip-flops, she sat at her vanity, flicking on the lighted makeup mirror. As she examined her now-magnified wrinkles and pores, her phone vibrated, and she remembered the earlier text. Glancing at the unknown number, she swiped open the text:

*Maria, this is Wayne Roberts. Not sure if you remember me from Fayetteville? Got your cell from your mom. I must speak with you. Please call as soon as possible.*

*Why in God's name does he need to talk to me*, she asked herself. With no intention of returning his call, Maria slipped on her robe, dropping the phone in its pocket.

# 48

# MONDAY AFTERNOON, AUGUST 6, 2018

## SOUTHPORT, NORTH CAROLINA

Later that afternoon, Maria dialed her mom's number in Arizona. Anna and Tony Thomas had retired to Phoenix in 1995, and sadly Tony had passed away from a heart attack in 2006. Anna had lived alone out there ever since, traveling back to Bucks County every October to visit Tony's grave. Maria visited her mom over Thanksgiving or Christmas, staying for both holidays only once, the year Mike had left her.

Her mom's voicemail picked up, and Maria left a message: "Hey, Mom, it's Maria. Just checking in. Call me when you have a minute."

In an effort to distract herself, Maria opened her iPad to check her Instagram feed. Not one to post much, really, she lived vicariously through the posts of her friends and their children. Her thoughts went back to Chief Roberts's message, and she wondered why he wanted to talk to her. *Let him call me*, she thought, typing Mike Smythe into the search box. Scrolling through the long list, she looked closely at each profile photo to see if her Mike had opened an account yet. No, her Mike hadn't.

Her Mike hadn't been hers for over eight years now. He'd left in 2010, May 4th to be exact. Said he'd had enough of her drinking, her nightmares, her inability to pull herself together. Pitiful. They'd been happy once, when they'd first married in 1996. She'd been thirty-six by then, older than most first-time brides. Older than Mike by four years, even, but after meeting on a flight from Chicago to Wilmington, they'd fallen head over heels in love.

Mike was a promising heart surgeon then, working with a growing practice in Chicago, and heading to North Carolina to open a branch on the East Coast. His senior partner, Richard Flanigan, owned a vacation home on the Outer Banks, and thus they'd selected Wilmington for their second location. Mike would head it up, and Rick would see patients when vacationing nearby, allowing Mike to take some time off of his own.

Maria had been a freelance writer, returning home after interviewing interior designers at the Merchandise Mart for an article she'd been commissioned to write. She and Mike had spent the entire flight talking and had met for dinner that evening. A year later, with the Wilmington office of Flanigan and Smythe, PA, open and running smoothly, they'd married in a simple but beautiful ceremony on Carolina Beach. Honeymooning in St. Lucia, they'd discussed how soon to start a family—next spring; how many children to have—four, two boys and two girls, of course; and where they'd finally settle down.

Maria had been living in a small condo near Wilmington's riverfront, but Mike wanted a big house, a true "low country" house, he'd said. They'd settled on Southport, a beautiful seaside village at the juncture of the Atlantic Ocean, the Cape Fear River, and the Intracoastal Waterway.

Maria had thrown herself into married life. She'd

cooked and she'd cleaned, relishing every aspect of being Mrs. Michael Smythe. Thirteen years and three miscarriages later, with more arguments under their belts than she cared to remember, Mike had found himself a younger, fertile woman to replace her. He'd learned she was fertile when she'd conveniently become pregnant six months into their affair.

Fertile. How Maria hated that word. Her infertility hadn't been her fault, the doctors had assured her. The physical trauma she'd suffered all those years ago had left her with too much scar tissue to sustain a fertilized egg. One more memory, one more toxic fallout from 1979. She hadn't told Mike about 1979 at all until the doctors had determined why she wasn't able to carry a child to term. He'd been livid that she'd withheld that major detail of her life. Her parents hadn't told him either, he fumed. Because she had asked them not to, she'd explained. Water under the bridge now.

Opening the freezer, Maria pulled out a ready-made meal, one of those high-protein, gluten-free variety that allowed her to think she was still adhering to a healthy diet. Punching in the recommended five minutes on the microwave keypad, she looked longingly at the bottle of merlot on the counter. "No!" she chastised herself, grabbing the bottle and emptying it down the drain. She retrieved an empty box from the garage and took it to the bar, packing up two unopened bottles of Southern Comfort, three bottles of Kendall-Jackson Chardonnay, her favorite summertime beverage, and two unopened bottles of merlot. Returning to the garage, she hoisted the box high on a shelf, shoving it behind containers of Christmas decorations. Decorations she hadn't put out since December 2009.

Waiting for the microwave to beep, Maria spooned food

into Smarty's bowl, poured herself a glass of sparkling water over ice, and asked Google to play Rod Stewart. After placing the heated meal on the table, she bowed her head, praying quietly, "Thank you, Jesus, for helping me through this day. It's not over, though, so please stay with me."

# 49

## TUESDAY MORNING, AUGUST 7, 2018

### SOUTHPORT, NORTH CAROLINA

M aria awoke early, feeling refreshed despite not having fallen asleep until past midnight. Optimistic after one night's sobriety, she immediately changed into her walking attire. While the water in the Keurig heated, she filled Smarty's bowls with fresh food and water. "There you go, good girl," she said, stroking the cat's back. With coffee cup in hand, she grabbed her iPad and headed out to a front porch rocker. *Life really is good*, she reflected, watching as two children from across the street boarded a bus bound for summer camp. Waving to their mother, she smiled, making a mental note to invite her neighbor over for tea one afternoon soon.

Lacing up her sneakers a while later, Maria was startled by a knock at the front door. *Who in the world*, she wondered. Looking through the door's glass panel, she observed a tall man in a black shirt, tie, and slacks, campaign hat in hand. Opening the door, she looked up at the man, asking, "What can I help you with, officer?"

"Miss Smythe?" he inquired.

"Yes, I'm Maria Smythe," she replied. "Is something wrong?"

"Ma'am, I've come at the behest of retired Fayetteville Police Chief Wayne Roberts, who has been trying, unsuccessfully, to reach you."

"Why?" Maria asked bluntly.

"Why what, ma'am? Why did I come, or why is Chief Roberts trying to reach you?"

"Both, I suppose. Please come in, Officer...?" Maria prompted.

"Sheriff Franklin, ma'am. John Franklin," he responded, nodding.

Following her into the living room, he took a moment to assess her features, a practice he'd been perfecting since his days at the academy. He noted Maria's small stature and graceful gait, like a ballerina, perhaps. Her shoulder-length blond hair was pulled back in a low ponytail, likely for the walk she'd been about to take, and her beautiful blue eyes, accented by soft lines, were makeup-free. As she motioned for him to take a seat on the sofa, her smile was radiant and welcoming, albeit a bit nervous.

"Did Chief Roberts tell you why he's been trying to reach me?" Maria asked, sitting in a chair to his left. When she crossed her legs, he noted how toned they were. Although he knew from his quick research she was fifty-eight, she appeared ten years younger.

"Not in great detail, but he did say it has something to do with the release of a felon from Central Prison. He wants to discuss the need for you to protect yourself," he said, hoping that his scrutiny hadn't been as obvious as it now seemed.

"Why should I need to protect myself? If the prisoner being released is who I think it is, then it's been nearly forty years since he was put away," Maria stated, somewhat flustered by the revelation that Billy Ramone was being released.

"Ma'am, that's why Chief Roberts is so eager to speak with you," Franklin replied, getting back on track with his reason for being there. "And why he asked me to intercede. He'd like us to call him together, a conference call, if you will, so that we can both be made aware of the situation. I suggest we head to my office to make that call."

"I really don't have time for this," Maria objected. "Chief Roberts is obviously overreacting, and—"

"Miss Smythe, I've taken the liberty of looking into your past a bit. I know what you and your sister went through back in 1979. While I wasn't in law enforcement then, neither Chief Roberts nor I would want anything, shall we say, unfortunate to happen to you now."

Shaken, Maria dropped her head. "No, you're right. I'm just being stubborn. Shall I follow you to the station?"

"Why don't you ride with me? I'll bring you back once we're finished talking to Chief Roberts."

During the twenty-minute drive to the Brunswick County Sheriff's office, Franklin asked Maria to tell him about herself and her routine. "Just to give me an advance idea on how best to protect you," he explained.

"I still think this is all overkill, no pun intended," she stated.

"Reserve your judgment until we speak with the chief," the sheriff suggested. "If you feel the same afterward, then we'll decide what steps, if any, should be taken."

"Fair enough," she agreed. "Let me see. I don't work full time, so I have a lot of free time. I like to practice yoga, sometimes at the dock in town, I walk or bike everywhere I can, and I shop and read. When I do work, it's usually from home. I'm an interior design blogger, so I only need access to my MacBook to do my job. You see, not very interesting."

"Okay, so when you walk and bike, where do you go?" the sheriff asked, silently acknowledging how her legs stayed so lean.

"In and around town," she replied. "No set path, I just meander wherever my feet or pedals take me. When I tire, I turn around and head back home."

"Hmm," he pondered. "We may have to tweak that nonroutine a bit. Do you head out at the same time each day?"

"No," Maria said. "If I wake feeling up to it, I'll set out early. Or if it's going to be a hot day, or a rainy one. You pretty much nailed it when you referred to it as my nonroutine. But isn't it better, or safer, if I don't follow a routine? Someone watching me could learn my routine and take advantage of that knowledge."

"True," the sheriff agreed, smiling. "But if there's no predictability to your activities, it also makes it difficult for someone to protect you."

"I could call you before leaving the house. I always carry my cell phone when I'm out," Maria offered.

"Not workable when I, or more likely one of my deputies, is across the county on other business," he explained. "We'll have to think on this one." Switching topics, he asked, "Do you have a security system in your home?"

"Yes, and I almost always turn it on," Marie said, reddening as she remembered she hadn't set the alarm when they'd just left the house. "I set it to 'stay' mode so it's not triggered by my cat, Smarty Pants."

"Smarty Pants? You've resorted to name-calling already?"

"No, my cat's name is Smarty Pants," Maria said, laughing. "She's a rescue. I've had her four years. I talk to her instead of myself, and she keeps me sane."

"Good to know," the sheriff noted. "Is she strictly indoors, or do you let her out?"

"Inside only. Too many critters outside," she said. "Sometimes she'll sit on the front porch with me, but that's as far as she goes."

"Do you sit on your porch often?" he asked.

"Of course. It's a big reason we bought the house to begin with. I love my front porch!" Maria said emphatically.

"You said 'when we bought the house,'" the sheriff began. "Who's we?"

"My ex-husband, Dr. Michael Smythe, presently residing with his current wife in Landfall," she explained. "We've been divorced nearly eight years."

"Okay," he stated simply. "Children?"

Swallowing hard, Maria replied, "No. Part of the reason my ex found himself a second wife."

"I'm sorry if these questions are painful, Miss Smythe," the sheriff said softly. "What about friends, clients, a housekeeper? Anyone we should consider in our security plans?"

"Well, of course I have friends and clients," she responded. "No one I regularly invite to my home, though. And no housekeeper either. Smarty and I don't make much of a mess."

"Well, here we are," the sheriff said, pulling into the county police parking lot.

# 50

# TUESDAY AFTERNOON, AUGUST 7, 2018

### BOLIVIA, NORTH CAROLINA

Once inside, Sheriff Franklin led Maria through the security checkpoint and down a short hallway to a small conference room. It held a table with four reasonably comfortable chairs and a credenza on which sat a coffee pot and several mismatched mugs. A whiteboard hung on one wall, while a darkened window covered the length of the opposite wall. A speaker phone sat in the center of the table.

"Have a seat," the sheriff said, pulling out a chair. "Coffee?"

"No, thanks. Is that a two-way mirror?" Maria inquired, pointing to the darkened window.

"As a matter of fact, it is. There's an interrogation room on the other side. Thought we'd be more comfortable in here, though. Let me see if I can get Chief Roberts on the phone."

The former Fayetteville police chief answered on the second ring. "Hello, Roberts here."

"Chief, this is John Franklin. I have Maria Smythe with me," he said from his chair on the other side of the table.

"Thanks for calling me back, John," the chief began. "Hello, Maria. It's been a long time."

"Yes, it has, Chief Roberts," Maria replied. "Can't say as I've missed you."

"No, I don't suppose you have, Maria. How've you been?" he asked, sincerity evident in his voice, which quavered more than she remembered.

"Well, thank you. And you?"

"As good as an old man can be, I suppose. I'm sure you're wondering what this is all about," he stated.

"Billy Ramone's being released?" she guessed.

"Billy Ramone's *been* released," he corrected. "About six weeks ago. Wasn't made aware of it myself until a few days ago when he failed to show for his weekly probation meeting. He's gone missing, and I'm afraid there's a good chance he's trying to find you."

"Why do you think that, Chief?" she asked. "After forty years, he certainly doesn't want revenge, does he? I'm not the one who killed Frank. Izzy stabbed him, not me."

"I've also spoken to Isabella about this," he said, surprising Maria. "She's on board with the need for extra security, and I'm trusting you will be, too."

"You've talked to Izzy? Recently?" Maria asked incredulously. "I didn't think she spoke to anyone who was involved —good or bad—in what happened to us."

"Yes, I got her number from your mother and called her yesterday. When you hear what I have to tell you, you'll understand," the chief explained.

"Does Mom know about this?" Maria asked, hoping he hadn't needlessly worried her.

"No. I simply told her I'd been thinking about you two and wanted to check in. She thought it was a wonderful idea," he said.

"So tell me what you told Izzy."

"Okay. Billy Ramone was released on June 24th." A phlegmy cough sounded over the line before the chief resumed. "Sorry about that. Doc calls it a smoker's cough, but I never smoked. Must've got it from my folks who were hooked on unfiltered Newports their entire lives. Where was I?"

"Ramone was released on June 24th," Sheriff Franklin reminded him.

"So Billy gets out and settles into a halfway house outside Raleigh. Finds himself a job cleaning garage floors at a nearby Jiffy Lube, and, for all intents and purposes, he's abiding by the terms of his release."

Pausing again, he cleared his throat. "Let me grab a bottle of water. Mouth's so dry on the god-awful inhaler my doc prescribed. Be right back."

While he was away from the phone, Sheriff Franklin asked Maria, "You okay? Can I get you a bottle of water?"

"Sure, thanks," she replied.

"I'm back," came the chief's voice. "So anyway, Billy was—"

"Wait, Chief. Sheriff Franklin is out of the room for a minute. Maybe we should wait for him to hear the rest of this."

"Sure. So, Maria, tell me. How has your life been since we last saw each other?" he asked kindly.

"Good with the bad. You know how it is. I'm healthy. That's what counts, right?" she said, smiling as Sheriff Franklin set the water bottle in front of her.

"I'm back," the sheriff stated. "Go ahead, Chief."

"In any event, Billy didn't show for his last probation appointment. The judge issued a bench warrant for his arrest—they were going to drag his sorry ass back to Central

—but no one's been able to find him. Of course, detectives talked to his cell mate and fellow detainees, and lo and behold, his last cell mate squawked. His name is Victor Hernandez, aged thirty-two, serving a twenty-year sentence for aggravated assault. He bashed his mother-in-law's head in with a hot steam iron, one she happened to be using at the time. Anyway, this Hernandez says that Billy told him he was, and I quote, 'going to find the bitches who took his life away.'"

"Do you think he's telling the truth, Chief?" Sheriff Franklin asked. "Hernandez, I mean."

"Being the cynic, I am," Chief Roberts replied, "I asked the same question. The warden had promised Hernandez extra time in the gym if he cooperated with the detectives, so who's to say? He knew a lot of the details of your case, Maria. Yours and Izzy's first names, what you looked like back then, things like that. Hernandez said Billy tried to find where you both were living, but he didn't have your current names. He told Hernandez that he knew a guy on the outside who'd be able to track you down. Not sure who that guy is, but the detectives on the case are slowly reviewing all Ramone's correspondence and computer activity since he learned he was getting out."

"Wow," Maria commented. "Bizarre how this is all coming back after nearly forty years. I foolishly believed I'd never have to worry about Billy Ramone again."

"Me too, dear," agreed Chief Roberts. "There's something else you should be aware of."

"What?" Maria asked hesitantly.

"Before Billy went away, back in 1980, he threatened to come for you and Isabella."

"Come for us? How?"

"On the day he was convicted, he had his lowlife

attorney deliver a note he'd written to your folks. They turned it over to the judge, who went on to hand down Billy's life sentence."

"I know about the life sentence, Chief, so why was he released?"

"I asked the same question, Maria. I don't have all the details, but it had something to do with North Carolina's new structured sentencing guidelines. In any event, with the help of Sheriff Franklin and his officers there, you'll be safe. Just make sure to do what he tells you—okay?"

"Thanks, Chief. I will. And you're sure Izzy's okay? I haven't talked to her in a long time, you know. She kind of ran away from the family after the trial. I guess I was too much of a reminder for her."

"Your mom filled me in on a little of that, Maria," he stated. "If you ask me, maybe you could be the one to take that first step toward rekindling your relationship. Izzy's still a little bitter about everything, it seems. Her injuries were significant, and she suffers from them still, did you know?"

"I didn't know," she conceded, then continued somewhat angrily, "but I still suffer from my injuries, too. You may not know this, but what Billy and Frank did to us left me sterile. I've never been able to have children. At least Izzy was. She has three. And a husband who didn't leave her because she was used goods."

"I didn't know that, Maria," the chief responded sadly. "I'm sorry you've suffered so much, and I apologize if I've offended you. Please forgive me."

Softening, she said, "No, I'm sorry, Chief. Your apology isn't necessary. Maybe it is time that Izzy and I talked."

"Be safe, Maria. And John, take good care of her, will you?" Roberts asked.

"I certainly will, Chief," he replied. "Thanks for

contacting me. I won't let you down. What do you say we talk in a day or two unless there are any urgent updates?"

"Roger that," the chief agreed. "Until then, take care—both of you."

"Good-bye, Chief," Maria said, slumping into the chair.

# 51

# TUESDAY AFTERNOON, AUGUST 7, 2018

## SOUTHPORT, NORTH CAROLINA

Sheriff Franklin drove Maria home in silence, a deputy trailing them. Once there, he and the deputy walked the perimeter of her property, observing and photographing all potential hiding spots and points of entry. Inside the house, they checked the window and door locks, testing the security contacts as they went along. Smarty Pants, resenting their intrusion, meowed loudly from her perch by the rear French doors.

After releasing the deputy with instructions to write up a summary of their findings, Sheriff Franklin sat at the kitchen table with Maria. She poured them each a glass of iced tea and laid out a plate of store-bought cookies. Taking a bite of one, he commented, "This is tasty. Haven't had a Chips Ahoy in forever."

"Always were one of my favorites," Maria said. "I keep them in the freezer, or I'd eat the entire package in one sitting."

"I can't believe that," he said, looking her over admiringly. "It's obvious you take good care of yourself."

"Thanks for noticing," she said, blushing, "but not nearly as well as I should."

"Okay then," he replied with a little laugh. "Getting back to business, we'll get back to you with a specific security protocol. In the meantime, I'd like you to stay inside for the rest of the day. When I leave, lock and bolt your doors and set the alarm. Turn on all outdoor lighting, but keep indoor lighting to a minimum. Close your shutters and blinds and all doors to rooms you don't use or won't be using tonight. Your study, for example."

"Why close the inside doors?" she asked curiously.

"Because if someone were to access one of those rooms through a window, a closed interior door presents a second barrier and a second opportunity for you to hear them. Plus, it's safer in the event of a fire."

"But every window in my house, including those on the second floor, are armed," she told him.

"Alarms can be disarmed," he stated matter-of-factly. "Do you have a backup battery system?"

"I'm not certain," she admitted. "I'll check with my security company."

"That's a good idea, and it wouldn't hurt to get them out here to give your system an overall audit," he said. "Also, keep your phone and charger by your bedside. I didn't see any weapons lying about, but do you own a gun?"

"Yep. Want to see it?" she asked proudly.

"Yes, I do," he replied. "I assume you know how to load and use it? Aim to shoot and shoot to kill, right?"

"I'm certified, if that's what you're asking," she replied, heading toward the bedroom to retrieve her Sig Sauer P238. "Enrolled in a class at the nearby range not long after my husband left."

Once he'd inspected her pistol, made certain his cell

number was programmed into her phone, and rechecked all the first-floor window and door locks, he said his good-byes. Maria stood on the porch until he'd pulled from the driveway. After heading back inside, she locked the front door and keyed on the alarm.

The cat wound through her legs, purring, and Maria reached down to pick her up. "Just you and me tonight, Smarty. Like always. How about some dinner?" She walked into the kitchen, then stopped and shook her head. She set the cat down, returned to the foyer, and flicked on the outside porch lights.

---

OUTSIDE, as the sun dipped below the horizon, a dark, older-model sedan pulled slowly down the street. Stopping in front of the neighboring house, the driver, invisible behind the tinted windows, smiled to himself. He'd driven by the bitch's house earlier, but when he'd noticed the two patrol cars parked in her driveway, he'd backed into a nearby side street until they'd left.

*So, this is where you've been living while I was stuck behind bars*, he thought. He took in the cheery yellow siding, wrap-around porch with its rockers, and the well-landscaped lawn and gardens. "Fuck her," he said aloud. "I'll fucking show her what hell is like!" When the outdoor lights on her porch came on, he quickly drove away, plotting how best to make his near forty-year dream a reality.

After returning to his room at the fleabag motel out on Route 17, Billy turned on the tiny TV. The local cable station was reporting on the upcoming tropical storm. Although a defined eye had not yet formed, the weather babe warning everyone to monitor its path and wind speeds.

"Nothin' like a hurricane to make things interesting." Billy laughed.

Plopping on the bed, he bolted up when his photo flashed on the screen. Turning up the volume, he listened as another woman reported, "Authorities have issued an all-points bulletin for a recently paroled convict, one William J. Ramone. Ramone was released from Raleigh's Central Prison in June, where he'd served nearly forty years of a life sentence for the kidnapping and rape of two young Pennsylvania women. Last week, Ramone failed to show for his weekly parole appointment. He is believed to still be in North Carolina and is considered armed and dangerous. Anyone seeing Ramone is advised not to confront him, but to call their local police or 911."

"Shit!" Billy muttered. He grabbed the backpack from the three-legged chair in the corner and stuffed in his few belongings, then stormed from the room. After throwing the bag onto the back seat of the old car, he drove south for several miles until he spotted a deserted shopping center, its broken windows and gaping doorways yawning hauntingly in the dark. As he drove through the parking lot, his tires crunched over dried-out brush and discarded trash. Parking beside a rusted-out dumpster at the back of the building, he flinched when he spotted the naked female mannequin trapped beneath its lid, her upper body twisted as if in agony. *Not the most welcoming place to spend the night*, he surmised, *but better than a prison cot*. He'd find somewhere else to crash tomorrow.

# 52

# WEDNESDAY MORNING, AUGUST 8, 2018

## SOUTHPORT, NORTH CAROLINA

The phone rang at 7:45 a.m., waking Maria from a crazy dream about a girl she'd known in college who was, in the dream, fixing dinner in Maria's kitchen. Grabbing her phone from the nightstand, she squinted to see who was calling, but without her readers, the screen stayed fuzzy. Swiping, she answered as chipperly as she could muster, "Hello?"

"Did I wake you, Maria?"

"Hi, Mom. You're up early. And yes, you woke me, but you also saved me from a ridiculous dream about Bonnie Peters. Remember her? My roommate from college?"

"That tall girl from Allentown?" her mom asked. "Yes, I remember her and her snooty ways."

"She was cooking dinner in my kitchen until you woke me," Maria informed her mother.

"Glad to have helped get rid of her," Anna said, playing along. "Sorry I missed your call yesterday. I was having lunch with my mah-jongg club."

"Have fun?" Maria asked.

"As always. So many laughs."

"Mom, I talked with Chief Roberts from Fayetteville yesterday. He said you gave him my number."

"Yes, I gave him yours and Izzy's. I said it was a good idea to check in with you both. Other than that nasty cough, he seems good, don't you think? A dear man, as I recall."

"Yeah, I don't remember him all that much, but he's getting old like all of us. Mom, he said he'd already talked with Izzy and that maybe I should call her, too."

"Might be a good idea, Maria," her mother suggested. "It's been too long, and like you just admitted, no one's getting any younger here. It'd be a shame to let too much more time pass before you and your sister make amends."

"What amends do I need to make, Mom?" she asked exasperatedly.

"Maybe none, but there are other reasons to talk to each other. Like life, for example. Life today, not life in 1979. For goodness' sake, Maria, Izzy's a grandmother now," her mom said. "You haven't even met her daughters, my grand-children!"

"I'll think about it, Mom. How are you feeling? Your back any better since you went to the chiropractor?"

"A little, I think. I have water aerobics in a little while. That always helps with my sciatica. Give your sister a call, Maria. Make an old lady happy, will you?"

"Yeah, Mom, I will. I promise. Love you."

"Love you too, second daughter. Love you too."

# 53

# WEDNESDAY AFTERNOON, AUGUST 8, 2018

## SOUTHPORT, NORTH CAROLINA

M aria dropped into the porch rocker, exhausted and sweaty from her walk. Ninety-three degrees with 100 percent humidity, the meteorologist had threatened this morning. The patrol car that had been tailing her for the past ninety minutes pulled into her drive, its driver then cutting the engine. A moment later, the phone in her pocket rang, and recognizing Sheriff Franklin's number, she answered, "Sheriff, how nice of you to check in."

"Miss Smythe, hello. Thanks for calling in earlier to let us know you were heading out for a walk. Sorry I wasn't around to take your call, but I trust Officer White was available to accompany you?"

"Yes, he was, thanks," Maria answered. "I guess he was nearby—surprise, surprise—since he was at my door within five minutes of my call. Followed me all through town and back. But you already know that, right?"

"I do, and I've instructed him to sit in your driveway until I get there in about an hour. I trust you're okay with that?"

"And if I'm not?" Maria teased.

"Too bad. I have the report on our security plan and an update from Central on Billy Ramone's current stats, in terms of appearance, I mean. Scares me just lookin' at his photo," the sheriff admitted.

"That can't be good," she said. "I'll jump in the shower and be ready when you get here. See you soon."

Fifty-nine minutes later, Maria opened the door for Sheriff Franklin, who was carrying a leather valise. He was a very good-looking man, she admitted to herself. Maybe a few years younger than she, and quite fit. His dirty-blond hair was cropped short in what Maria thought was a "military fade." The cut accented his classically defined nose, giving him an air of competence and authority. In subtle contrast, however, his eyes, a rich hazel with glints of blue, suggested a deep sadness as though he were, below the steely surface, heavy with grief.

"Hi," she said simply. "Care for tea and Chips Ahoy?"

"Tea, yes, but no cookies for me today." He grinned, patting his belly. "I can't let this girlish figure go to pot."

Maria looked at his belly and rolled her eyes. "I'm sure there's a washboard under that shirt, so I truly don't think you have anything to worry about."

"Not yet, but there would be if I ate cookies at your table every day."

"Perish the thought, but your loss. Iced tea only coming up."

Bringing a pitcher of tea and two glasses to the table, Maria noted the documents the sheriff had spread out in front of him. "What's all this?"

"A very thorough review of your security, as it stands now, and our recommendations for improving it," he said, sliding a photo in her direction. "But before we go over that, here's Billy Ramone today."

Maria looked down at a dangerously vicious man who appeared to be scowling at the camera with eyelids narrowed to menacing slits. He sported a long goatee, and the hair on his head was shorn so close that a tattoo of a large spiderweb, inked from ear to ear, was visible on his scalp. *Ouch*, she thought, shuddering as she noticed the snake slithering through razor wire wrapped around his throat. "Those tattoos must have hurt like hell."

"He has some on his hands, too," the sheriff commented, placing two additional photos in front of her. One showed a watch with missing hands wrapped around his right wrist. The other, of his left hand, focused on five purplish-black dots between his thumb and forefinger, the letters E, W, M, N inked on four digits.

"What do these all mean?" she asked, trying to reconcile this man with the Billy Ramone who'd abducted her. "He looks completely different today."

"I imagine so," the sheriff agreed. "Not that I knew him then, but thirty-eight plus years in a maximum security prison will definitely harden a man. As for the meaning behind the tattoos, only Ramone knows for sure, but if you're truly interested, you can read all about prison tats on the internet."

Shaking her head, she pointed out, "Billy was evil back then, or he'd never have done what he did. But this photo makes him look like the devil himself. Only missing the horns here."

"So now we know what he looks like," the sheriff said, pulling the photos back and placing them in a manila folder. "Unfortunately, we don't know what he's driving. He was loaned a car by the owner of the Jiffy Lube where he worked, but he left it behind when he disappeared."

"That can't be good. I might have seen his car and not even known it."

"No, it's not good, but we've come up with this plan for your increased security," he said, opening the binder in front of him.

An hour later, Maria was more nervous than she'd been when she'd first learned Ramone was hunting her down. Despite thinking she'd been safe in her home, alone these past eight years, Sheriff Franklin had just finished telling her there was so much more to be done to protect her.

"Shouldn't I just leave for a while?" she suggested. "Until you find him? I mean, it's almost like I'll be living in a prison cell now instead of him. How is that fair?"

"No one said it's fair, Miss Smythe," the sheriff stated. "Without knowing where he is or when he might find you, we believe our plan is the best—and safest—way to move forward. Do you agree with what I've outlined here?"

"Do I have a choice?" she asked, deflated. "And please, call me Maria."

"Maria, you can certainly waive your right to protection, but I really don't think you want to do that. Do you?"

"No, it's just that I'm so used to my freedom. I relish being able to come and go as I please, and now that bastard wants to take it away from me again!"

"I understand your frustration," the sheriff said, "and I hope he's found before long so that you don't get too restless. But try to think of this as a mini vacation, a staycation. We'll bring everything you need to your door. You and Smarty will be waited on hand and foot until you're again free to move about town as if none of this happened."

"I guess I can dust off my elliptical for the next few days," she conceded. "And if you're offering to deliver my food and necessities, I want lots of fresh seafood, eggs, and veggies, including avocados, a couple cases of Deer Park sparkling water—orange and lime, please—the best virgin olive oil you can buy, some really good balsamic vinegar, apples, grapes, bananas. And more pecan praline single-serve cups—lots of them. Oh, and peppermint tea."

"Anything else?" He chuckled while writing down her wish list in his small notebook.

"No, that should do it—for today, anyway." Smarty Pants jumped up on the table, meowing. "Umm, we can't forget her. Blue Buffalo canned food for indoor cats. She eats a can a day. Iams dry food for indoor cats, and Arm and Hammer kitty litter—the twenty-eight-pound box, please."

"I suppose I should get started on this list," he said, gathering up the papers and placing them in his briefcase. "Lock the door behind me, set the alarm, and I'll make sure to call when I'm on my way back."

"You're going to buy all that yourself?" she asked doubtingly, grabbing her purse from the hook by the laundry door. "Let me get you some money."

"No need to pay me, Maria," he said, refusing the cash. "I'll charge it back to the department. And yes, I'll be going myself. While I could send Officer White, I'd have to explain it all beforehand. My going to the market will save us all time. Be back in an hour."

# 54

# WEDNESDAY EVENING, AUGUST 8, 2018

## SOUTHPORT, NORTH CAROLINA

With the groceries put away, Maria sat at her kitchen table, contemplating her call to Izzy. The sheriff—John, he'd asked her to call him—had left about an hour ago. Another deputy now sat out front in his cruiser, a key detail of her round-the-clock surveillance.

She picked up the phone and opened her contacts list. It had been so long since she'd spoken to Izzy, she no longer remembered the number. *When did I talk to her last*, she wondered. *It must have been after Mike walked out. Was I in Phoenix with Mom at the time? Yes, that's right*, she remembered. She'd talked with her that Christmas. Izzy had been sympathetic when Maria had told her about the separation, but not so much that she'd checked back with her anytime since.

"Here goes nothing," she muttered, tapping the phone icon by Izzy's name.

Izzy picked up on the fourth ring, as though she'd had to think about it first. "Maria? What a lovely surprise."

"Izzy, it's good to hear your voice," Maria struggled to say.

"I guess you're calling about Billy Ramone?" Izzy asked. "Chief Roberts said he was going to call you."

"Yeah, we spoke yesterday. I'm now under twenty-four-seven police protection."

"Me, too. Jack is fit to be tied, but since he's free to come and go as he pleases, I don't know why he's making such a fuss. I'm the one stuck inside all day."

"I know how you feel. How are you, Izzy? And Jack, the girls? Mom tells me you're a grandmother. Congratulations!"

"Feeling a bit old these days, but other than that, I'm good. Jack's looking to retire next year."

"Good for him. Are you working?" Maria asked.

"No, not since 2012, when the builder I was with went under. I stay busy, though, with tennis and the house. You?"

"Freelancing a bit, and I write a weekly design blog. Mike was generous enough when he left to give me the house and an annual stipend that keeps me in hair color and nail polish. I'm able to maintain a fairly comfortable lifestyle, working only when I want."

"The least he could do. Maria, I'm so sorry I haven't been in touch. It's just…"

"We're both at fault, Izzy. You didn't call me, but I didn't call you either. Why is that?"

"Too many painful memories, I guess," Izzy suggested.

"And now they've all been brought roaring back with Billy's release. Why isn't a life sentence just that?" Maria asked rhetorically.

"If only," Izzy agreed. "Talking with you makes me think we should be together now, just like we were then."

"That'd be nice, Izzy, but we're on opposite coasts. At least if Billy finds one of us, the other'll be safe."

"Don't say that! He's not going to find either of us. And even if he does, the police will protect us and re-arrest him."

"Did you see his photo?" Maria asked.

"Oh, my God, yes. He's certainly not the stud he once thought he was." Izzy laughed.

"Not hardly. Do you have nightmares, Izzy?"

"Sometimes," she admitted. "Usually, it's when Jack's out of town. Or when I've had a spicy dinner. I don't know how you do it, Maria. Living alone."

"Until yesterday, I thought I was doing great. I miss having someone in my life, you know. I really loved Mike, and I loved being married. On some level, I wouldn't mind doing it again. But I'm content living alone. I have a cat to keep me company."

"Are you ever scared?"

"Every once in a while," Maria conceded. "But my house has a security system, and I keep a gun close by."

"Really? A gun? I think owning one would terrify me."

"Not if you know how to shoot," Maria refuted. "I'm fully trained, certified, and licensed to carry here in North Carolina. Although I hope to never need to shoot anyone, I'm ready if it comes down to it."

"Jack has a shotgun in the closet at his office downtown. Ever since the Rodney King riots. I could ask him to teach me how to use it."

Looking to change the course of the conversation, Maria said, "So tell me about your family."

"Are you sure?" Izzy asked.

"Why wouldn't I be?"

"I don't know. I thought maybe because you don't have children of your own..."

"Or a husband?" Maria questioned, irritation coming through in her tone.

"Maybe I haven't called you because I didn't want to stick my foot in my mouth, like just now," Izzy retorted.

Calming herself, Maria insisted, "Let's start again. Tell me about your family, Izzy."

# 55

# WEDNESDAY EVENING, AUGUST 8, 2018

### SOUTHPORT, NORTH CAROLINA

F orty-five minutes later, Maria set the phone down on its charging station. Despite the bumpy start, their conversation had been heartwarming, and she'd learned all about Izzy's three daughters, Marybeth, Amy, and Nicole, and her new grandson, Henry. It turns out Henry was named after the truck driver who'd come to their aid outside that Fayetteville bar. Just last year, Izzy had told her daughters what had happened in 1979 and had shared with them the letter Henry Long had written her after the kidnapping. Marybeth had been so moved, she'd convinced her husband they needed to name their first son after her mom's Good Samaritan.

Before saying good-bye, the sisters had promised to talk again soon, especially throughout their mutual staycations. After turning out the kitchen light, Maria opened the refrigerator to grab a bottle of water. Glancing at the microwave, she saw that it was only 8:30. *Too early to sleep*, she thought, *but I'll read for a while*.

"Come on, Smarty," she called. "Let's get settled in for the night." Walking through the house, she double-checked the locks, shut the interior doors, and locked herself in her bedroom.

She'd brought in Smarty's litter box earlier, placing it and her water and food bowls on the bathroom floor. "This'll be fun, won't it, pretty girl?" she asked the cat. Smarty jumped up on the foot of the bed, proceeding to knead the faux fur throw as was her bedtime ritual. "Make yourself comfortable."

After changing into her nightgown, Maria washed her face and brushed her teeth. As she applied her night cream, a shiver traveled down her spine. "What's that all about?" she asked herself. Looking into the mirror, she sensed, more than saw, movement outside the window behind her. Slapping off the light switch, she ran back into the bedroom, grabbing her phone from the nightstand. Opening her recent calls, she pressed the number for John Franklin. He picked up immediately.

"Maria, what's up?"

"John, there's someone outside my bathroom window," she whispered breathlessly.

"It could be Deputy Rouse. Stay put, and I'll call him now. Be back to you in a minute."

Moments later, John came back on the line. "Rouse has been in his vehicle, but I've asked him to walk around your house. You should see his flashlight as he gets to the backyard. Stay on the line with me—okay?"

"I'm not going anywhere."

"Have your gun?" he asked.

"At my side," she answered. "There's his flashlight now."

"Good. Maria, don't take this the wrong way, but is it possible your imagination got the better of you?"

"I don't think so," she said, dropping her head. "It's as if I felt someone more than saw them. My intuition's pretty good, and I got a chill just before I saw the movement."

"I'll send a second uniform to assist Rouse," John said. "One to stay in your driveway, and one to walk the perimeter throughout the night. If there was someone out there, he won't be coming back tonight."

"Thanks, John. I'll sleep better knowing there're two deputies keeping an eye out."

"Me, too, Maria," he said, surprising them both. "I'll come by as soon as I get my kids off to camp in the morning."

"Kids? You didn't tell me you have children."

"Two," he replied, a smile in his voice. "Jackie's eight, and Sam's six."

"Wow," Maria said, somewhat disappointed. "How long have you been married?"

"Jenny and I were married for ten years."

"Were?"

"Jenny passed away last spring," John explained quietly. "Breast cancer."

"John, I'm so sorry. I didn't know. And now you're raising the children on your own?"

"Not alone, exactly. My mom gets them off the bus a couple afternoons a week, and Jenny's mom picks them up the other days."

"You've got a full plate, John," Maria acknowledged. "I'm sorry to be taking up so much of your time."

"Not to worry, Maria. You are in no way a burden. Anyway, let me go now so I can assign that second deputy. Rest easy, okay?"

"I'll try. And someday, when this is all over," she said, "I'd like to meet your children."

"That would be nice. I'll look forward to it. Good night, Maria."

"Good night, John."

———

BILLY RAMONE LAUGHED to himself as he got back to his car. He'd parked two blocks over from the bitch's house and had walked through alleys and backyards, approaching her window from the rear. *That sorry cop is no match for my stealth*, he told himself. And how fun that she'd seen him outside her window. He'd wanted to knock to let her know he was watching, but seeing her look directly at him in the mirror had been a real rush.

She didn't look half-bad now. Older, sure, but her body was still mighty fine beneath that sheer nightgown. After years of sweaty, grunting sex with other men in the darkness of his cellblock, he couldn't knock a few wrinkles or gray hair. *She knows I've found her*, he thought. *It's just a matter of time before I crush her again with my enormous cock. This time, though, she won't live to enjoy it as many times as before.*

His thoughts went back to that long-ago time in the cabin. He and Frank had been having such a blast before it all came crashing down. He remembered the weed, the beer, the whiskey, and the sex. Incredible sex, as much as they wanted, and then some. He stirred at the thought of fucking the Bitch while Frank banged Blondie right beside him. Sometimes, they'd gone at it so hard, he'd thought the bed would crash to the floor.

Unzipping his fly, Billy reached into his jeans, releasing his rock-hard erection. Memories of the cabin always gave him a woody, and he closed his eyes, reliving those days. It took barely a minute to jerk himself off, and he shuddered with pleasure behind the tinted windows. "You still do it for me, Blondie," he said aloud, wiping himself off with his shirttail.

Billy started the car and slowly pulled out onto the deserted street. He wanted to drive by her house again, but he knew he couldn't take the chance at being seen. He was sure she'd called the cops after seeing him outside her window. He'd have to figure out how to get rid of that deputy. *I've come this far*, he thought, *I'm not going to let anything get in my way. The bitch will pay for killing Frank and sending me away. Then I'll go after her fucking sister.*

# 56

# THURSDAY MORNING, AUGUST 9, 2018

## SHALLOTTE, NORTH CAROLINA

After two nights parked behind the shopping center dumpster, Billy's back and neck were killing him. He needed to find a bed to sleep in tonight. He needed to get to a television to see if his photo was still being broadcast on the local news. As he drove onto the highway, his mind went into high gear plotting his next move. *There's got to be somewhere I can stay where I won't be recognized*, he reasoned. The driver's license he carried displayed a fake name, Roy Marino, but his actual photo. *It's certainly harder to get away with a fake ID today than it was before I went to the slammer*, he reflected.

Turning onto a side street, he scanned the ramshackle homes on either side. Driving slowly past a particularly rundown double-wide, he watched an old lady pick up a newspaper on the unpaved drive. A tattered pink robe, secured by a man's too-big leather belt, wrapped her stooped body, and once-white laceless sneakers covered her feet. Her gray hair held an assortment of pink foam curlers. As she looked toward the street, she noticed Billy's car stop at the foot of the drive, and she waved.

Taking this as a positive sign, Billy backed up slightly, turned into the drive, and halted just shy of the woman. After putting the car in park, he opened his door. "Good morning, ma'am," he said, raising his hand as he exited the car. "Beautiful day, isn't it?"

"Yes, it is," she replied, and Billy noticed she had yet to put in her dentures, if she even wore them. "Do I know you?"

"No, but I heard you need some help around your trailer. I'm here to offer my assistance."

"How'd you know I need help?" she asked, tilting her head suspiciously. "Did you talk to my boy, Andy?"

"Yes, ma'am, I did," Billy improvised. "I ran into Andy at the gas station out on 17." He approached the woman with his hand extended. "My name's Roy, Roy Marino. I'm a handyman by trade."

"Well, this must be my lucky day," she said, attempting a toothless grin. "Come on in, and I'll show you what needs doin'."

Following her into the drab kitchen with its Harvest Gold appliances, dark pine table, and mismatched chairs, Billy contemplated his next move. He was hardly a handyman. And what about her son? Would he be a problem? "Does Andy come around much?" he asked.

"That lazy sum bitch hardly never comes here. He left when he turned seventeen and never looked back. I call him all the time to come fix stuff, but he can't take precious time from his oh-so-important life."

"And your husband?" Billy prompted.

"Benjamin passed five years ago from the gout," she replied, making the sign of the cross. "Nothin's been done 'round this place since."

"Then I'm your man," Billy said and grinned. "There's just one thing, though."

Looking up skeptically, she asked, "Yeah? What's that?"

"I need a place to stay. Any way you can let me crash in a spare room while I do the work?"

Looking a bit put-out, the woman said, "Long as you clean up after yourself and don't eat all my food, you can stay in Andy's old room. It's not being used for much but storage now. Least til the work's all done, that is."

"It's a deal," Billy said, smiling. "Thanks, Mrs....?"

"Jones," she said, looking at him oddly. "If you talked to my Andy, you shoulda known that."

"Sorry, Mrs. Jones. I forgot. I remembered your address but not your last name. Do you want me to call you Mrs. Jones?"

"Nah, we ain't so formal 'round these parts. Just call me Miss Rhona."

"Okie-doke, Miss Rhona, where do I start?"

An hour later, Billy and Rhona Jones had walked through the trailer. She had dozens of projects for him, from cleaning the windows inside and out to defrosting the freezer. Why she couldn't manage that one on her own, he had no idea. At one point, she'd handed him a pad of paper and a pencil to write it all down.

"I don't see so good no more," she said by way of explanation. "Or I'd make the list myself. Don't know why I even bother gettin' that morning paper anymore, since I can hardly make out the headlines."

"No problem," Billy said, scribbling on the notepad. "How about I start by dusting and vacuuming the living room?"

"Good a place as any," she replied. "Feel free to turn on the telly. My shows don't start til after noon anyway."

"Thanks, ma'am," Billy said, and meant it.

Plugging in the ancient Hoover, Billy glanced at the television, where he'd turned on the local news. "Thank goodness she's a blind biddy," he muttered. "I don't have to worry about her seeing my photo in the paper or on TV."

At the top of the hour, the lead story was again about him. Shutting off the vacuum, he turned up the volume. A blond chick with enormous boobs was warning viewers that he was armed and dangerous. *Like that bit of information is gonna protect anyone*, he thought. *Not from me, the stealth villain.*

At 12:30, Miss Rhona walked into the living room to watch her soap. Billy moved to the kitchen to fix himself a sandwich, thinking his new arrangement wasn't too bad. Scarfing down bologna and Velveeta on white bread, he set the chipped plate in the sink and opened the freezer door. Years' worth of leftovers, encased in rock-hard ice and smelling of puke, stared out at him. "This is gonna get fuckin' old real fast," he cursed.

"What's that, Roy?" came Miss Rhona's voice from the living room.

"Nothin', Miss Rhona, just commenting on your lovely china."

"See that you wash that plate and put it back in the cupboard," she hollered. "I ain't got no fancy dishwasher."

"Yes, ma'am, whatever you say," he muttered, rethinking his plan for laying low with Miss Rhona.

# 57

# THURSDAY EVENING, AUGUST 9, 2018

### SOUTHPORT, NORTH CAROLINA

M aria sat quietly in her living room, the television volume turned low. The top story on the evening news had been about Billy Ramone. "Armed and dangerous" it had said, warning all North Carolinians to be on the lookout for anyone matching his description. Shaking her head, Maria stood and walked to the kitchen to make some tea. What she really wanted was a big glass of merlot, but she'd been strong since Sunday night's bender. *I can do this*, she thought. *I'm safe, and I won't let the threat of Billy Ramone throw me off my game.*

John had come over earlier that morning, coffee and Danish in hand. "Not fair," she'd protested. "If I can't get out to walk that off, I can't eat it."

"A small piece isn't going to hurt," he offered.

"Thanks for nothing," she said, laughing. "I saw you speaking with the deputy who came on duty earlier. What's he saying?"

"Nothing yet, but I also spoke with Rouse and Mitchell, who were here all night. They spotted footprints outside your bathroom window, and there'll be a forensic team here in a short while to take a mold and dust for fingerprints. If it proves that Ramone was here, we'll know to focus our efforts in Southport."

"Like I asked you a couple days ago, shouldn't I just leave?" Maria suggested. "I mean, if I sneak out during the day, he may not know I'm gone. He'll still come back, most likely anyway, and you can catch him then."

"We can't take the chance that he sees you leave. Then we'd lose him for good."

"I hate being a sitting duck," she said and sighed.

"Well, after last night, I understand. Which is why we're reassigning a second officer to stay inside with you."

"God, how awful is that going to be? For both him and me."

"He's a she, just so you know. Wouldn't be appropriate for a male officer to take that assignment. Deputy Katrina Anderson will be here at four p.m. this afternoon."

"Should I make up my spare bedroom?" Maria asked.

"No, she won't be sleeping—you will, and hopefully peacefully."

Katrina Anderson now sat at Maria's kitchen table, laptop open in front of her. She was a beautiful woman with skin the color of molasses, dark, almond-shaped eyes, and a small, upturned nose. Her thick brown hair was pulled into a tight bun at the nape of her lean neck. Although no more than five foot two, she gave off a self-assured persona that made her appear much taller.

"Cup of tea?" Maria asked.

"Yes, that'll be nice, Maria. Thanks."

While she waited for the kettle to whistle, Maria laid a few slices of Danish on a plate, setting it and napkins on the table. "So tell me about yourself, Deputy Anderson."

"Katrina, please," she answered. "What do you want to know?"

"Age, marital status, life story. The works. Might as well get to know each other if we're going to be spending all this time together."

"Hopefully," Katrina said, "we won't be together for too long. As soon as Ramone makes his next move, we'll grab him."

"Your lips to God's ears."

"Okay, I'm thirty-three and have been on the department for ten years. My dad and Uncle Martin were both cops, so I naturally followed in their footsteps."

"Naturally," Maria agreed, walking back to the stove to pour the boiling water into two mugs. After placing the mugs, an assortment of tea bags, and a bowl of sugar on a tray, she set it on the table beside the Danish. "The Danish, by the way, is courtesy of Sheriff Franklin."

"Really?" Katrina asked with exaggerated surprise. "I didn't think he had it in him to be nice."

"I disagree," Maria objected. "John, Sheriff Franklin, has been very nice to me. Which, given this awful situation, is much appreciated."

"I've always thought of him as standoffish and abrupt."

"Maybe with colleagues, but not crime victims?" Maria suggested.

"You're probably right, but he doesn't hang with other officers after shift, which is how most of us burn off stress and get to know each other."

"He's a single dad," Maria stated. "It can't be easy to get away when he needs to fix dinner, help with homework, etcetera."

"You're right. I'll try cutting him some slack. He is my boss, after all."

"So, back to you," Maria prompted.

"I have a beau, as my mom likes to say. His name is Jake."

"Is he a cop, too?" asked Maria.

"God, no." Katrina laughed. "He's an insurance broker. Works in Wilmington. We live together just outside the city."

"How long have you been together?"

"Five years, although we've known each other since college."

"Marriage in the works?"

"Yeah, we talk about it all the time, but neither of us is going anywhere, so there's no rush until we're ready for kids. Which we aren't yet."

Maria swallowed back her first response of *don't wait too long*, and asked, "Do you like being a police officer?"

"Very much. The power of the badge and gun is high on my list of likes. Very little hard crime occurs in Brunswick County, but it feels good when I'm able to help someone in trouble. Plus, I'm paid to be a badass." She smiled. "What's not to like?"

"Hmm. You certainly don't look like a badass."

"Don't let my size deceive you. I can be when it's called for—just ask Jake." She laughed again.

"I hope to have that opportunity one day," Maria said with a smile.

Katrina stood and said, "I'm going outside to talk to Rouse. Be right back, but lock the door and set the alarm behind me. When I get back, we'll do our walk-through, and then I suggest you call it a night."

"Will do. See you in a few."

BILLY WATCHED the female officer walk down the drive to the patrol car. "Car Cop" got out of his cruiser, said something into his shoulder mic, and nodded in the woman's direction. *A chick cop*, Billy thought, smiling. *This is going to be more fun than I'd hoped. The two little piggies have left Blondie alone, and she's just waiting for me to come and get her. Hmm, how am I going to do that?*

Billy weaved his way through the overgrown shrubbery of the house across the street and two doors down. He silently cursed as a spider web wrapped around his head. It was too dark to see the spider itself, but Billy knew it had to be near, and he swiped at his face. *What a pussy*, he thought. *It hurt like hell to get my spider web tattoo, and now I'm afraid of a real one.* Still, he vowed to spray himself with bug repellent before coming back.

Peering through the cover of a wax myrtle, Billy could just make out the sidearms strapped to the officers' belts. He felt for the .32 tucked into the small of his back. *It might be tiny*, he thought, *but it'll be deadly when I need it to be*. The ex-con he'd bought it from had given him quick lessons in loading and shooting, but Billy had told him there was no need to show him how to clean the thing. At that, the con had shaken his head, but Billy hadn't cared. He only planned to use the gun twice, and for one purpose.

Catching a slight movement in the bushes across the street, Chick Cop pulled her service weapon and motioned to the other officer. "Not today," Billy whispered, reversing through the neighbor's backyard, careful not to make a sound. Turning when he reached the side of the house, he ran as fast as he could for another block, back to where he'd parked his car. *Soon*, he thought. *One night soon, after Miss Rhona goes to sleep, I'll check off the second-to-last thing on my own to-do list, then I'll find the Bitch and cross off the last.*

# 58

# FRIDAY MORNING, AUGUST 10, 2018

### SOUTHPORT, NORTH CAROLINA

The morning's weather report had Hurricane Jasmine forecast to hit somewhere along the Carolina coast as a Cat 3, maybe as early as Saturday night. Maria frowned as she sipped her coffee in front of the TV. "Unless Billy Ramone is arrested before Jasmine hits, we could be in for a bit of trouble," she said, glancing toward the kitchen.

Deputy Joan Hart, who'd arrived thirty minutes earlier to relieve Katrina Anderson, barely acknowledged the remark with a slight nod from her stool at the island. The older officer, who was overweight—bordering on obese—with an angry, in-your-face disposition, couldn't have been more different from Katrina. She'd made it plain from the moment she walked through the door that she was there to do her job, not to make a friend. She'd all but told Maria to not bother her unless it was an emergency.

"Oh, well," continued Maria, ignoring the slight, "I'm sure Deputy Hart will take good care of us, won't she, Smarty?" The cat stretched her back, then each hind leg, before settling into the corner of the sofa. "Might as well get some exercise this morning while you nap," she said, ruffling the cat's fur.

"Deputy Hart?" she said, a little more loudly. The uniform looked up from her tablet but said nothing. "I'm heading upstairs to use the elliptical for a while."

"Roger that," Hart replied, and resumed whatever she'd been doing on the tablet.

Forty-five sweaty minutes later, Maria reached for her ringing phone. "Hello?" she asked, a bit breathless.

"Maria, it's me, Izzy."

"Izzy, what's up?" She exhaled, wiping perspiration from her face.

"I have an idea."

"Uh-oh. That doesn't sound good."

"Hear me out," Izzy said. "I've booked a flight from LAX to Wilmington for later this morning."

"Izzy, why would you do that? There's a hurricane coming, and you're safe where you are, in more ways than one!"

"That's exactly why, Maria! I'm in no danger out here, but you're in double danger. If I wait any longer, I won't get a flight out. And yesterday, we both agreed we should be together."

"Not so that we're both in mortal danger," Maria chided. "Your plan is ridiculous. I won't let you do this!"

"Good thing you don't have a say in what I do," Izzy said boldly. "I'm calling your sheriff. Franklin, right?"

"John won't permit it!"

"John? So he's John now? Well, he can't stop me either, Maria. I land at nine fifteen p.m. your time. I'll expect one of his deputies to pick me up and bring me to your house."

"Izzy, this is stupid. Please don't come," Maria begged. "The police think they spotted Billy again last night. Across the street, for God's sake, Izzy. There's no sense for us to make his diabolical plan for retribution any easier!"

Ignoring Maria's pleas, Izzy stated, "I'm coming. Think of it as a hurricane party. We'll have fun."

"But we're under a mandatory evacuation," Maria tried, rejecting Izzy's party plan. "The only reason I'm staying is because there's so much security watching me. What does Jack think of your brilliant plan?"

"Jack hasn't been able to tell me what to do or think since the first time he asked me out." Izzy laughed. "And even then, I planned the entire date. When I told him this morning that I was going to visit you, he shrugged and handed me his credit card."

"If I can't stop you, please let me call John first to fill him in on your plans. Text me with your flight information, and I'll make sure you're met at ILM."

"Don't do anything stupid, Maria. If I even sense I'm being taken anywhere but your house, I'll jump out and call an Uber."

"Okay, okay. I'll call you after I talk with John. Send me those details."

"On their way. Talk soon, Maria."

# 59

# FRIDAY EVENING, AUGUST 10, 2018

### SHALLOTTE, NORTH CAROLINA

B illy found an expired bottle of 40 mg Oxycontin in Miss Rhona's medicine cabinet. It had been prescribed for her dearly departed husband, Benjamin, undoubtedly during the last days of his life. *He must have been in real pain, the poor bastard*, thought Billy. When Miss Rhona had asked him an hour earlier to fix her nightly cup of hot tea, he'd gladly done so, stirring in a spoonful of sugar and two Oxy tablets. She'd managed to watch most of *Jeopardy!* before nodding off in her chair. Billy sat on the sofa beside her as Alex Trebek revealed the Final Jeopardy clue. "What is Montpelier?" Billy answered aloud, only knowing the correct response because he'd watched the episode's original airing while still at Central.

After shaking Miss Rhona a few times to make sure she was down for the count, Billy went into her bedroom to rummage through her drawers. In the bottom of the night-stand, he found a wad of money hidden in a man's white tube sock. He whistled after counting out five thousand four hundred twenty-five dollars. *Fair compensation for the work I done this week*, he thought before heading to the closet.

Climbing on a set of oak bed steps, Billy reached to the back of the top shelf and pulled out an old hatbox, its lid secured with rubber bands. Dumping the contents on Miss Rhona's bed, he grinned when he recognized the stacks of US savings bonds. Rifling through them, he noted the various denominations, most issued over thirty years earlier. "Old bat's pretty flush. Who'da thunk it?" He laughed to himself as he gathered the bonds and cash in his shirt and left the room.

After shoving the stash in his backpack, he grabbed a few bottles of water from the fridge and left through the back door, slamming the screen behind him. The wind had picked up since he'd been out cleaning the gutters, a chore that the biddy had insisted was mandatory storm prep. "What a good boy you are, Roy," she'd fawned. "I've always hated hurricanes, and they've only gotten scarier since my Benny died."

"Now, now, Miss Rhona," Billy had soothed. "I'll take care of you during this one."

"Thank you, Roy," she'd said with a sigh. "It'll be nice ridin' out the storm with you by my side."

*Fat chance of that*, Billy had thought. *If I can get into Blondie's house tonight, I won't be back to this dump.*

# 60

# FRIDAY EVENING, AUGUST 10, 2018

### SOUTHPORT, NORTH CAROLINA

Maria paced from kitchen to living room, den to bedroom. Izzy had arrived at ILM less than an hour ago, but with the wind picking up, Maria's anxiety was growing exponentially. There was absolutely no reason they both needed to be in this much danger. Stopping her in the kitchen, Katrina Anderson admonished, "Maria, you're going to wear out the floorboards. Sit down for a few minutes, please!"

"Oh, Katrina, I'm just so torn about Izzy coming here."

"Are you worried for her safety or about seeing her after all this time?" Katrina asked intuitively.

With glistening eyes, Maria admitted, "I guess it's both, really. If we'd only had a more gradual reconciliation, I'd feel better. But it's been nearly twelve years since we were together at Dad's funeral, and we barely spoke then."

"Just be yourself. You're a remarkable woman, Maria. Izzy will see that and remember the sister she's always loved."

"I hope so," Maria said, but before she could continue, the doorbell chimed.

Walking into the foyer, Maria saw Izzy peering through the door's glass panel, John standing behind her. Hesitating for a second, Izzy waved a hand in tentative hello. Tears spilled from Maria's eyes as she disarmed the security and unlocked the deadbolt. Pulling open the door, she spread her arms. Izzy, dropping her pocketbook, walked into them, a sob escaping from deep within.

"Oh, my God, Maria, it's so good to see you!" she cried. "Thank you for letting me come!"

Maria laughed, despite herself. "Izzy, I've never allowed you to do anything!"

Pulling away, Izzy wiped her eyes, searching her pocket for a tissue. "You're right. I gave you no choice, did I?" Looking over her shoulder at John, she continued, "And thanks to your sheriff here, I've arrived safely. Despite, I might add, a stern scolding about what an idiotic decision this has been."

"Come in, both of you," Maria said, backing into the foyer. "Katrina and I were just about to have some tea and cookies. Chips Ahoy, I believe," she added, a twinkle in her eye as she glanced at John.

"As much as I'd love that, my kids are waiting for me to tuck them in," John replied as he rolled Izzy's suitcase in behind her.

"Kids?" Izzy asked dramatically, looking about her sister's home. She noted the uncluttered and welcoming living room with its elegant ivory sofa accented with down pillows in soft shades of green and blue. Two roll-back swivel chairs sat opposite the sofa with a tufted cocktail ottoman in a rich brown leather in between. A tray holding candles, crystal snifters, and a decanter of sherry sat atop the ottoman while end tables of inlaid mahogany held ceramic lamps with tapered linen shades. Light from the lamps reflected across the warm cherry flooring, and a plush rug warmed the intimate conversation area. Layered throughout were comfy knit throws, vases filled with lush hydrangea, stacks of magazines and books, candles and gorgeous artwork.

"Maria, this is beautiful!" she said as she ran her hand along the back of the sofa.

"Thanks, Izzy."

Jumping in, John replied to Izzy's question. "Yes, kids. Two of them, actually. Sam and Jackie."

"You're a blessed man, Sheriff," Izzy replied.

"I agree," John said. "Now I really must leave. You're in good hands with Deputy Anderson here"—he nodded in Katrina's direction—"but I'll be back first thing in the morning."

"We'll look forward to it," Izzy said, nudging Maria playfully.

"Thanks, John, we're fine here with Katrina. We'll see you in the morning. Unless the weather's too nasty, then you stay home with those babies."

"I'll take them to my parents' before I head over. They'll have fun there and can help Dad get the goats rounded up before the storm hits."

"Only if you're sure."

"I'm sure, Maria." Turning to Izzy, he lectured, "Izzy, please listen to any and all instructions from my deputies. What they say goes, come hell or high water. This weekend, we might get both, so no matter who else you won't take direction from, your life depends on listening to them. Agreed?"

"Agreed," Izzy said, pressing her hands against his back. "Now go away and let me catch up with my sister."

# 61

# FRIDAY EVENING, AUGUST 10, 2018

## SOUTHPORT, NORTH CAROLINA

T he looming storm had turned the skies dark and threatening as Billy drove slowly into Blondie's neighborhood. Noting the houses with their boarded-up windows and tightly latched storm shutters, he remembered that Miss Rhona had insisted he get up early tomorrow, as she had phrased it, "to batten down the hatches." *No way in hell*, he thought, scanning the streets for a secluded spot to park.

He noted happily that the neighborhood itself was especially dark tonight. Sensing an opportunity, he turned into the driveway of a house he knew to be just behind Blondie's and pulled under the open carport. It was a two-story brick structure, older than most in Blondie's cushy community. The first-floor windows were boarded up with an assortment of plywood and two-by-fours. "Dumb fucks," he said, exiting the car. "Couldn't even hire someone to cover the second-floor windows."

After concealing the car under a ratty furniture blanket he pulled from a storage locker at the rear of the carport, Billy crouched low to approach the house. Peering through an opening between board and glass, he concluded the house was empty, the homeowners likely riding out the storm farther inland. Just to be sure, though, he rang the doorbell and waited. When bell went unanswered, he smiled. What had his fucking dad always preached? Something about lost opportunity and wasted opportunity. Billy had never grasped the difference.

A memory flashed of the baseball bat his dad had used on him after he'd been cut from the football team his junior year in high school. Frank, on the other hand, had been a real good offensive tackle back then and had been named to the varsity team as a freshman. When Billy'd been sent packin', though, good ol' Frank had quit in solidarity. Billy's dad hadn't cared about that solidarity shit, and he'd taken the bat to Frank as well. Equal opportunity parenting, he'd told the boys, but Billy knew he just liked beating the crap out of them, especially when he was tanked. It had taken fifteen stitches to close the deep gash in Billy's cheek, and his arm had been in a sling for weeks. Poor Frank, though, had never really recovered, what with his left eye always droopy and out of focus and his memory none too good.

Despite the security signs pounded into the front yard and peeling from the side-door window, Billy yanked his sleeve over his fist and waited. When the next gust of wind rattled through the trees, he pulled his arm back and punched out a pane of glass. He listened intently for an alarm to sound but happily heard nothing. *Hmm*, he pondered, *these kind folks must've forgotten to set the alarm when they evacuated. How very convenient for me.*

# 62

# SATURDAY MORNING, AUGUST 11, 2018

SOUTHPORT, NORTH CAROLINA

A ringing doorbell roused Izzy from sleep. The room was dark except for the eerie yellow light glowing along the edges of the window blinds. *What time is it*, she wondered, grabbing her phone from the nightstand. Eight a.m., she read, dropping back onto the heavenly down pillow. Five a.m. California time.

She and Maria had stayed up talking until nearly two. They would have stayed up later, but Officer Katrina had insisted they get to bed and not open that next bottle of wine. Remembering the three bottles they had opened, and emptied, Izzy massaged her temples and groaned.

There was a soft knock on the door, and Maria popped her head in. "Good morning. I was hoping you'd be awake."

"I am now," she replied as Smarty jumped onto the bed. "Who was at the door?"

"Two recruits John sent over to board up my windows. I have storm shutters on the second floor, but none downstairs. You'll be hearing the banging soon, so I figured I'd get you up before they start."

"Good idea. Is John here?"

"No, he called to say he'll be a little later than planned. He needs to help out at his folks' place for a while."

"Coffee on?" Izzy asked hopefully as she sat up and pushed aside the covers.

"Always."

"I'll jump in the shower and be down in a few. Could you bring me up a cup?" Izzy asked. "And maybe an aspirin?"

"Pecan praline okay with you?" Maria asked, scooping up the cat. "Come on, Miss Smarty Pants. Let Aunt Izzy get ready."

"Sorry, Smarty, but you can come back when Mama brings the coffee. And yes, pecan praline sounds divine!" Izzy cooed.

Forty-five minutes later, the sisters sat at the kitchen island sipping coffee and nursing their hangovers. "What were we thinking, wanting to open that fourth bottle?" Maria asked.

"Not in our right minds, for sure. I haven't been that tipsy in years!"

"Wish I could say the same," admitted Maria, "but I have been doing better. Until last night, that is."

"Blame me. We both deserved to enjoy ourselves."

"Agreed, but I'm back on the wagon as of this morning. Ready for something to eat?"

"Something light. Yogurt or hard-boiled eggs will be fine."

"Lucky for you, I have both. I boiled two dozen eggs yesterday in case we lose power."

"Do you think the electricity will go out?"

"Yep, and we'll probably lose water, too," Maria added.

"Oh no, I can't live without water," Izzy cried dramatically, the back of her hand pressed to her forehead.

"No worries, I have four cases of bottled water in the

garage, and John said he'll get someone to set up the gener-ator to keep the fridge running. Deputy Hart?" Maria called to the officer standing guard at the front door. "Want anything to eat?"

"No, ma'am, I ate before I reported for duty this morning."

"Well, you don't have to stand there. Take a seat in the living room, or pull over a stool."

"I'm fine, ma'am."

"Suit yourself," Izzy chimed in, then whispered to Maria, "Not quite as personable as Officer Katrina, is she?"

"Bingo!" Maria agreed.

As the women sat eating their breakfast, they watched with worry as the Weather Channel amped up its coverage of the approaching storm. "Leave now or hunker down for the long haul," came the advice of the meteorologist who, in Maria's opinion, seemed far too enthusiastic about the storm's anticipated severity.

"Guess we hunker down for the long haul, then," Izzy said, concern seeping through. "Glad we're together."

"You'll have to come back when the weather's nice. Southport is such a beautiful town most of the year."

"You're coming to California next," Izzy insisted. "Maybe Christmas? I want to introduce my daughters and grand-baby to their long-lost Aunt Maria."

"We'll see," Maria said quietly as she watched yet another meteorologist brace himself against Jasmine's fierce winds. Angry waves crashed in the surf behind him, while seemingly oblivious curiosity seekers ambled along the ever-shrinking beach.

"Brave souls out there," Izzy noted.

"Crazy souls, if you ask me."

# 63

## SATURDAY MORNING, AUGUST 11, 2018

### SOUTHPORT, NORTH CAROLINA

B illy was pissed. Last night, after he'd thoroughly searched the house behind Blondie's, he'd made the mistake of lying down in the master bedroom. *Just to rest my eyes*, he'd told himself. If the damn bed hadn't been so comfortable, he wouldn't have slept through til morning. Now he'd have to wait til tonight to make his move.

Downstairs in the kitchen, he glanced through a gap in the boarded-up back window. Two men were hammering plywood to Blondie's first-floor windows. The storm shutters on the second level had already been closed and latched.

"Fuck, fuck, fuck!" Billy cursed. He might have trouble breaking into that cunt's house now. "Think, Billy!" he ordered himself. There had to be a way in without those fuckin' cops catching him. *I may have to shoot my way in*, he thought, spinning his gun on the counter, *but one way or another, she's goin' down tonight*.

Yanking open the refrigerator door, he smiled when he saw the fresh-baked peach pie. "Lookie what the missus left me," he said aloud. "Any ice cream up here? This may be my lucky day after all," he said, pulling the pint of French vanilla from the freezer.

After locating a fork, Billy sat at the glass-top kitchen table, eating the pie right from the pan. *No sense makin' a mess for these nice folks. What with their comfy bed and home-made pie and all. Maybe a good night's sleep and a full belly's all I need to perfect my attack plan.*

"I'm coming for you, Blondie," he said menacingly. "Ain't no stoppin' me now."

# 64

# SATURDAY AFTERNOON, AUGUST 11, 2018

## SOUTHPORT, NORTH CAROLINA

J ohn had arrived at Maria's house just before noon, a bucket of fried chicken under one arm, a bag of fixins in the other.

"Oh, you dear man," Izzy said gratefully. "How'd you know this is just the tonic we need today?"

"Honestly? Maria sounded like she'd swallowed a mouthful of cotton balls when I called earlier. Figured you girls tied one on last night."

"To put it mildly," Maria confirmed, accepting the bucket. "Please tell me you brought mashed potatoes and biscuits?"

"Not a Southern meal without them."

As Izzy found plates and set the table, she whispered to John, "I'll set one out for Officer Hart, but ten to one she'll refuse to eat."

"She's one tough nut, all right."

"I guess that's a good trait in a cop?"

"Can be, yes," John acknowledged. He wasn't sure what to make of Maria's sister. A beautiful woman, for sure, with long chestnut hair and dancing blue eyes, she was several inches taller than Maria and lean in a way that made him think she regularly played golf or tennis. With her self-assuredness and expressive mannerisms, she exuded an air of *I am wealthy and well kept.*

Maria poured tea into three ice-filled glasses. After they'd all taken a seat, she asked, "What are you hearing about Jasmine?"

"It's not good," John reported. "As of an hour ago, she's forecast to come in right over Oak Island at a hundred and twenty miles per hour."

"What time?" Izzy asked, licking her fingers.

"She's slowed since yesterday, but best guess is early tomorrow morning, before dawn."

"Couldn't be high noon, could it?" Maria asked sarcastically.

"I've cancelled all leave for the next forty-eight hours. We'll man the storm from the fire department here in town and my station farther inland."

"And the deputies watching us?" Izzy prompted with eyebrows raised.

"I may have to pull the outside patrol, but you'll have an officer inside for the storm's duration. Frankly, I can't imagine Ramone making his move during a hurricane."

"Why not?" Izzy asked a bit testily. "Billy has never been level-headed or sensible. He might see the hurricane as his golden opportunity."

"And if he does, my officers will be armed, Izzy, as is your sister."

"You're right, John, of course. I don't mean to second-guess you or seem ungrateful for your protection," she said sheepishly.

After grabbing a drumstick, John pushed back his chair

and said, "I've got to get back to brief my men. Most have never served during a hurricane."

"Go, then. We'll be fine here," Maria offered. "We have oodles more to catch up on."

She walked the sheriff to the door, and they stepped outside. "John, I truly know we're in good hands, and I don't want to frighten Izzy more than she already is, but when we lose electricity, we lose the alarm system, too."

"As soon as I can spare someone to hook up your generator, I will. In the meantime, you'll be safe, I assure you." Taking her hand, he squeezed it gently before leaning down to softly kiss her forehead.

Discombobulated, Maria said, "That was nice."

Smiling, John took a deep breath, then said, "I'll call you later."

As Maria watched him depart, she jumped when a gnashing gust of wind ripped a bough from a nearby pine tree. "God help us all," she prayed, hurrying inside.

# 65

# SATURDAY AFTERNOON, AUGUST 11, 2018

### SHALLOTTE, NORTH CAROLINA

Rhona Jones stirred in her easy chair, the TV on and broadcasting satellite shots of the hurricane. Her head was achingly foggy, and her mouth tasted of desert dirt. "What the heck happened to me?" she asked aloud, wiping her eyes with the sleeve of her bathrobe. The room was bathed in a ghostly yellow light, making it difficult to determine the time of day. Sitting up, she glanced at the wall clock and gasped. She'd been asleep for eighteen hours. How had that happened?

Standing unsteadily, she called out, "Roy, you here? Why in tarnation did you let me sleep so late?" When no one answered, Rhona made her way into the kitchen. The overhead fluorescent was flickering, and the refrigerator door hung wide open. "Roy?" she called again. "Why'd you leave the darn 'frigerator door open? I ain't payin' to chill the whole house!"

She filled the kettle, placing it on the burner before walking down the short hallway to the bathroom. After relieving herself, she splashed her face with cold water and ran a brush through her thinning hair. Setting the brush on the counter, she noticed the brown pill bottle lying atop discarded tissues in the waste basket. Picking it out, she squinted to read the label, tilting her head in confusion. Had she dropped these in the trash by accident? Had Roy? "Oh, no!" she gasped, realization working its way through the fog. Roy must have slipped her a Mickey Finn!

She rushed across the hall, then stood stock-still in the doorway of her bedroom, taking in the disturbing scene. The drawers of her dresser and nightstands were wide open, clothing and other items strewn onto the floor. Her closet, too, had been ransacked. Seeing the upended hatbox lying in the middle of her bed, Rhona screamed and ran for the phone.

"911, what's your emergency?"

"I've been robbed. That no-good Roy took off with everything!"

"Ma'am, is the robber still in the house?"

"No, he's gone and run off with all my money. He must've drugged my tea last night, and I just woke up."

"Ma'am, an officer is on the way. Stay on the phone with me until he gets there."

"Where else am I gonna go? Oh, dear sweet Jesus, he took it all! How'm I gonna live?"

"Ma'am, is there anyone you can call? You know there's a hurricane heading our way. You should go stay with someone, maybe a family member?"

"My boy, Andy. He's just gonna have to step up and help me out this time. Never did before, but family's family."

"That's right. Give Andy a call after the officer gets there, okay?"

"Here he is now. The police, not Andy. I'll be hanging up."

"Be safe, ma'am."

# 66

# SATURDAY AFTERNOON, AUGUST 11, 2018

## BOLIVIA, NORTH CAROLINA

Sheriff John Franklin listened to his radio as the 911 operator dispatched a deputy to a house in Shallotte where an elderly woman had been drugged and robbed. *Storms bring out the worst in people*, he thought, shaking his head. *Who would want to harm a helpless old lady? Weren't first responders busy enough during a hurricane without having to deal with senseless acts of greed and violence?*

After briefing his team on storm procedures, he'd sent them out to patrol the county's roads, looking for signs of damage or trouble. So far, with the hurricane eye still hours offshore, everything appeared calm. Although a mandatory evacuation had been issued for low-lying areas, including the entire town of Southport, he knew many residents had decided to stay put. He couldn't blame them. He was just glad Sam and Jackie were with his folks. Their farm, on higher ground inland, was a safe distance from any rising flood waters. So long as they didn't lose power for too long, his children would be safe and comfortable until he could bring them home.

John's thoughts drifted to his home, the home he and

Jenny had lovingly restored with their own hands and reso-lute determination. The home they'd been raising their chil-dren in when, in the blink of an eye, Jenny was gone. His beautiful wife, who'd been diagnosed with breast cancer at the age of thirty-five, had died before her thirty-seventh birthday.

They'd met nine years ago, at an anniversary party thrown for mutual friends. John, who'd been in his late forties then, was recovering from a divorce his first wife had wanted but he hadn't. He'd been perfectly content married to Ashley. Turns out, Ashley hadn't been content at all. When she announced, out of the blue, that she was leaving him for another man, he'd been blindsided. It had taken him two years to shake off the funk from their divorce.

Jenny, much younger at only twenty-nine, had insisted their nearly twenty-year age difference didn't matter if they truly loved each other. And loved they had. Jackie was born ten months after they'd said, 'I do,' and Sam had come along two years later. John had wanted to try for a third, but Jenny had asked him for more time. With little warning, there was no more time.

John missed Jenny every waking minute and dreamed of her most every night. At fifty-seven, he now thought of himself as too old to find another great love. He doubted there was anyone he could love as deeply and passionately as he had Jenny. As consolation, he threw himself into his children's lives and his job, falling exhausted into bed every night, praying to see Jenny in his dreams.

Shaking his thoughts of Jenny, John picked up the phone and dialed Maria's number. "Hey, you," she answered, a sultry lilt in her greeting.

"Hey, you," he mimicked. "Everything okay on your end?"

"With the exception of the wind, all's quiet here. Have everything under control there?"

"As much as possible until the storm actually hits. All my patrol cars are on the road now, just waiting for something to happen."

"I've been monitoring the county's Facebook page, and it looks like most folks have evacuated. Izzy and I've been out on the front porch a couple times for fresh air, and the whole town feels deserted."

"Maria, please stay inside, where you're safe. From the storm and Billy Ramone."

"Deputy Hart accompanied us both times," Maria assured him. "And there's still a cruiser in the driveway, so I assume he's not needed elsewhere yet?"

"No, not yet. I'm surprised Hart agreed to your porch visits."

"You know how convincing Izzy can be," Maria laughed. "But Katrina is coming later, right? She's so much more personable than you-know-who."

Laughing, he scolded, "It's not the responsibility of my police force to entertain you, Maria. But, yes, Deputy Anderson will stay with you through the night. And I'll check in when I can."

"Thanks, John, that's comforting. I'm sure your duties as sheriff don't include holding the hands of nervous women, but Izzy and I appreciate all you're doing."

"That's nice to hear. Which reminds me, I should give Chief Roberts a quick call to update him on the Ramone situation and the hurricane."

"Give him our best, John. I'm sure he'll be happy to hear that Izzy and I are together. Tell him I'll call once this nightmare is over."

"Will do. In the meantime, stay put, and I'll try to swing by sometime after dinner."

"We're having doctored frozen pizza, if you're interested. That is, if the electric's still on."

"I'll keep that in mind. See you then."

"Yep, see you then."

# 67

# SATURDAY EVENING, AUGUST 11, 2018

## SOUTHPORT, NORTH CAROLINA

The wind gusts bowed the towering pine trees like pliant blades of grass. Pinecones and branches echoed off the copper porch roof, causing Billy to flinch with each metallic clang. Goddamn, he hated storms, always had. He remembered the one, years and years earlier, when his mom had still been around.

Irma Ramone had been outside taking laundry off the line when a sudden wind gust had wrested a bedsheet from her hands, sending it billowing into a tree in the neighbor's backyard. Watching from the kitchen window, Billy's dad had ordered four-year-old Billy to climb the fence and retrieve the sheet. Problem was, the neighbor's dog, a mean old basset hound named Boo, lived in that backyard, guarding it with his life. Boo would bark and snarl and gnash his teeth if anyone even got close to the fence, let alone tried to jump over it. Boo was already barking like a rabid dog at the flapping sheet when Buck had all but kicked Billy down the back steps, telling him to return with the sheet or not at all.

"Buck, the boy'll get bit," his mom had hollered over the

roar of the wind. "Let me go ask Mr. Jeffers to get it down for us."

"No!" Buck had bellowed. "You coddle that boy, Irma. Leave him be, and get the rest of those things in here before they blow off, too."

Fortunately, old Mr. Jeffers had seen the sheet land in his tree and was already heading out with a rake to pull it down. Billy had sighed with relief and gratitude when Mr. Jeffers had handed over the balled-up sheet. He remembered the old man winking and whispering, "Tell your daddy to get it hisself next time. I'd like it just fine if my Boo took a chunk outta his mean ass."

Billy had smiled up at the man and then turned toward his house, knowing full well he'd still pay dearly for not climbing the fence even though it hadn't been necessary after all.

A particularly wicked gust brought a tree limb crashing down on the roof above Billy, and he jumped in the chair, banging his knee on the underside of the table. "Fuck me," he cursed, rubbing his knee. "Ain't no way I'm going out in this shit."

Turning on the television, he clicked the remote until the Weather Channel appeared. The hot brunette on screen was pointing to the storm's eye and warning, "With winds already gusting to fifty-five, we anticipate Jasmine getting much stronger as the eye nears landfall. With her present speed, we predict that to be around two o'clock tomorrow morning."

"That's right, Melanie," came the voice of a second reporter, standing on the bulkhead overlooking a churning body of water. "We need to remind our viewers that, even though the rain and wind will ease as the eye passes over our area, we can't let our guard down. The worst of this may come on the storm's back end."

*Okay, Billy Boy, just hold on until that eye gets here. Then it's show time.* Checking the wall clock, he calculated he had eight hours to prepare. So long as a tree didn't fall on the house and kill him before then.

# 68

# SATURDAY EVENING, AUGUST 11, 2018

## SOUTHPORT, NORTH CAROLINA

Sheriff Franklin stepped from his patrol car and motioned for Deputy Rouse to unlock the passenger door.

"Anything happening here?" he asked his deputy, handing him the takeout bag of burgers he'd picked up on his way into town.

"No, sir. Quiet since I came on a bit ago. Think Ramone changed his mind once he saw that we're guarding Miss Smythe?"

"Could be, but my money's on him holing up somewhere nearby until we ease up on her protection. We caught a case earlier today of a robbery and assault in Shallotte. Victim's an elderly woman who hired the suspect to help with chores around the house. Said his name is Roy Marino, but her description bore an uncanny resemblance to Ramone. She picked his photo out of an array."

"So he's still in the county."

"I'd pretty much guarantee it," John stated. "Latest on the storm is the eye should arrive after midnight. Will you be okay here until then?"

"Yes, sir. Just radio me if I'm needed anywhere else."

"Will do," the sheriff replied. "Your family okay tonight?"

"With my wife's folks in Leland. Kids think it's a slumber party."

"Hopefully that's what they'll do through the worst of it —slumber."

"Roger that, sir. Amy's a bit nervous about me being so close to the coast, but I told her not to worry."

"Keep in touch with her through the night, if it helps."

"Thank you, sir. Appreciate the food and your concern."

When the sheriff knocked on Maria's door, Deputy Anderson opened it with a smile. "Sir, good to see you tonight."

"Deputy Anderson, likewise. How are your charges this evening?"

"Playing backgammon in the study while the pizzas bake," she replied with a wave toward the study.

"I thought I smelled garlic. Good thing I brought my appetite."

"Yes, it is a good thing, John!" Maria agreed, smiling as she walked into the foyer. "We have a pepperoni and a veggie. Should be ready in about ten minutes. Care for a glass of iced tea?"

"Sounds good to me. No wine tonight?" he asked with a grin.

"Oh, God, no!" Izzy exclaimed, joining them. "I may never drink again after last night."

As Maria filled four glasses with ice, Izzy pulled open the oven door to check on the pizzas. "Mmm, they smell so good."

"Food that's decadent and delicious should always be eaten during a hurricane," Katrina said. "Think we should ask Rouse to come in for a slice?"

"No need. I brought him burgers from that new joint by the station. That's enough decadence for him."

As Maria and Izzy set the table, John and Katrina slipped into the foyer. "All quiet here?"

"Yes, sir. Seems eerily so. When I showed up earlier, Hart said, and I quote, 'Sitting in this house is a waste of my time and talent.' Personally, I'm enjoying my time here, and the more boring it is, the better for me, my considerable talents notwithstanding."

"I might have a talk with Deputy Hart to set her straight on her job priorities," the sheriff said, frowning.

"The girls have been a little stir crazy, but other than that, we're all just fine."

"Good to know. As I told Rouse, the eye should pass over sometime after midnight. Could get a little dicey before then and again as it moves inland. When I pull Rouse, I'll let you know you're on your own."

"Not a problem, sir."

"Dinner's on!" Maria called, and the two officers headed back into the kitchen.

While the salad was dished out and the pizzas sliced, the Weather Channel advisories hummed steadily in the background.

"Mind if I turn on some music?" Maria asked, getting up to retrieve the remote. "I doubt much will change in the twenty or thirty minutes it takes us to eat."

"If you're taking requests," Izzy suggested, "I'd love to hear some smooth jazz." As the music played quietly, she added, "Can almost imagine we're having a nice, intimate dinner tonight instead of a hurricane party."

"Under different circumstances, this would be nice," John agreed, looking discreetly at Maria. "Unfortunately, the reality of our situation is a bit grim."

"More so than when we spoke earlier?" Maria asked with concern.

"I haven't told Deputy Anderson this yet, but it seems so. An elderly woman in Shallotte was drugged and robbed by a man she hired to help with some household chores. He gave her a different name, but his description fit Billy Ramone to a T, including his tattoos and scarred cheek. She identified his photo, and the ID's strong."

"Where's Shallotte?" Izzy asked, the hand holding her pizza shaking slightly.

"About thirty minutes west of here. The suspect spent Thursday night in her spare bedroom, but last night he drugged her tea with Oxy that had been prescribed for her deceased husband. After she passed out, he cleaned her out."

"Any idea where he went after that?" Maria asked.

"No sightings today, but the good thing is we now have a vague description of his vehicle. According to the vic, who can't see all that well, he's driving a gray four-door sedan with tinted windows."

Racking her brain to recall if she'd seen a car matching that description, Maria asked, "No idea on model or license plate?"

"No. We're lucky we got that much from her."

"Still victimizing women after all these years," Izzy said, sighing heavily as she hung her head. "I've tried so hard to move past the horror of what happened to us, but being here has brought it front and center again. It's as fresh in my mind today as if it took place last week."

Maria reached across the table and grabbed Izzy's hand. "You and me both, Izzy. As soon as this is all over, we'll go on a long tropical vacation somewhere. Forget that Billy Ramone ever existed, then or now."

"Let's make it a spa-cation instead of this god-awful stay-cation," Izzy said, a tear slipping down her cheek.

"Didn't mean for dinner to take such a maudlin turn," John apologized. "Anyone want to change the subject?"

"Yes, let's talk about your children," Maria suggested, getting up from the table when the house phone rang. "As soon as I get this."

"Hello?" she answered, listening as a recorded voice warned of the impending storm surge. When she returned to the table, John was pushing back his chair, plate in hand.

"Going so soon?" she asked dejectedly.

"Duty calls. Thank you for the delicious pizza, ladies. Should be just as good for breakfast tomorrow, so if you don't eat it all tonight, I'll have a slice in the morning."

"You're more than welcome, John," Izzy said, taking the plate from him. "Maria, why don't you walk him out?"

Stepping onto the porch, Maria whispered, "As I feared, Izzy's coming here wasn't such a good idea. It was bad enough when I had to deal with this on my own, but now it's twice as awful with her going through it with me."

"Maybe you need to look at it as being twice as strong together, not twice as weak."

"I don't think we're weak, exactly, just doubly exposed. But you're right. We survived all those years ago because we had each other. We supported each other, fought for each other, and lived to tell the story."

"Remember that," he said, pulling her into a firm, yet tender, embrace. "You're a strong and beautiful woman, and in my humble opinion, you're quite the formidable force all by yourself."

"That's sweet of you to say, John." Resting her head against his chest, she inhaled deeply, taking in his rich, masculine scent. A wave of longing, held in check for years, rippled through her.

Tipping her chin up with his finger, John placed his lips against hers, tasting the lingering flavors of tomato sauce and garlic. "Yum," he murmured. "You taste good."

"So do you," she responded, opening her mouth hungrily to accept his probing tongue.

Seconds later, his radio squawked, and John groaned quietly, reluctantly pulling himself away. "Damn, woman, you make a man forget everything else around him."

"I could say the same about you," she admitted with a smile and a push toward the steps. "You'd better get out of here."

"And you'd better get back inside and bolt the door. I'll be back to finish this as soon as I can."

"I'll hold you to that, John. Stay safe."

# SATURDAY EVENING, AUGUST 11, 2018

### SOUTHPORT, NORTH CAROLINA

With the leftover pizza wrapped and refrigerated, Izzy and Maria returned to the study to resume their game of backgammon while Katrina remained at the dining table, typing away on her laptop. Maria's study was the perfect combination of business and style, femininity and practicality. Her writing desk, with its rich, satin finish and inset leather blotter, was accented with ornately carved cabriole legs. The game table, a spectacular find from last April's High Point Market, had drop-in game boards for backgammon, checkers, chess, and Monopoly. The chairs, where the sisters now sat, were bentwood café chairs with double-caned seats.

As Izzy rolled the dice, Maria glanced at the television, muted now but tuned to the Weather Channel. You could take only so much of the ridiculously gleeful reporters as they warned of the doom and gloom to come.

As Izzy moved her checker, Maria exhaled deeply. "Izzy, you know I love you and appreciate your wanting to be here."

"I feel the same way. Your home is truly lovely, and I can

see why your design blog is so popular. How many readers do you have?"

"I average about fifty thousand page views per month. Brings in just enough mad money to keep me happy. Have you read my blog?"

"I have," Izzy answered thoughtfully. "It's how I've been able to keep tabs on you."

"I didn't realize you wanted to keep tabs on me."

"Until you called this week, it was the only way I knew how to without actually picking up the phone."

"You could have asked Mom how I was doing," Maria protested.

"I did," Izzy confessed, "but she'd never tell me anything. She'd just say I had to call you myself, and then she'd change the subject."

"I guess it was time," Maria said. "As I was saying, I've loved having you here and hearing all about your life in California."

"But," Izzy prompted. "I sense a *but* coming. Spit it out, Maria."

"There's no *but*, really. I just feel we need to talk about the past, get it off our chests, so to speak. What you said at dinner, about not being able to move beyond what happened to us."

"Oh. I don't know where that came from," Izzy said with a wave of her hand. "It does incense me, though, that after all these years, Billy Ramone's been released to threaten us again. It just boggles my mind."

"I agree completely. But let's go back to then, Izzy. Why'd you leave and not come back home? Why'd you cut me out of your life like I'd never been your sister? Like you'd never loved me?"

Izzy hesitated, taking a deep breath before explaining, "I

didn't plan it that way. Not right away, anyway. But after months of Mom and Dad treating me like an invalid, or worse yet, an infant, I had to leave. I needed to get back to being a twenty-one-year-old independent woman. Didn't you feel completely smothered by them?"

"A little, yeah. Which is why I went back to Shippensburg that fall. It was far enough away, but I could still go home when I wanted. You didn't just leave Mom and Dad, you know. You left me too, Izzy."

"You were a reminder of them."

"Them? Mom and Dad or Billy and Frank?"

"Billy and Frank," Izzy answered, tears welling in her eyes. "Every time I looked at you, I flashed back to the cabin. I wasn't able to focus on getting myself healthy or how you'd started moving on. Instead I was consumed by memories of being tied to that bed, of you, bloody, beaten and crying. You were my little sister, and I'd allowed that to happen. I just couldn't live with the guilt anymore, so I left."

"I'm still your little sister, Izzy," Maria said as tears of her own fell. "You had nothing to feel guilty about. We weren't responsible for what they did to us. We were victims."

"And by the time I left," Izzy said forcefully, "I was sick and damn tired of being a victim. Everyone in town knew what had happened to us. I had to leave, or I'd never have gotten myself back."

"But once you 'got yourself back,'" Maria said, using her fingers as quotation marks, "you should have come home. Called or written me, at the very least."

"I know, and I told myself that same thing over and over, but the longer I stayed away, the harder it became. Until I finally convinced myself that staying away was best for both of us."

"You didn't have the right to decide that on your own!"

Maria insisted. "Do you know how much it hurt when you'd get in touch with Mom and Dad but not me? They went to your wedding, but you didn't even invite me, for God's sake!"

"You didn't miss much," Izzy said, attempting to lessen the sting. "After I learned I was pregnant with Marybeth, we married at the courthouse in front of the justice of the peace."

Maria stood, knocking her chair against the bookshelf. "Dammit, Izzy! I still should have been there! Then, and when Marybeth was born!"

"Get mad if you need to, Maria. I know I hurt you, but that was never my intention."

Maria sighed, then after grabbing a tissue from her desk and blowing her nose, she sat back down. "I'm over being mad at you, Izzy. It took a long time, but when Mike and I fell in love, my sorrow and disappointment at losing you faded away."

"Was Mike your first true love?"

"Oh, I dated a lot before him. Thought about marrying a couple of them, actually. Glad I didn't, though if I had, I would've learned about my infertility much sooner."

"I hate them for taking that away from you." Izzy bristled.

"Me, too. Sadly, after tests proved that scar tissue from my injuries had caused all my miscarriages, I died inside. I couldn't stop crying, couldn't eat, couldn't forgive. Mike wasn't to blame for any of it, but the sadness that had dissipated when we married came back with a vengeance. It's why he finally left."

"I'm so sorry," Izzy said, shaking her head. "What finally allowed you to move on again?"

"At some point, I realized I either had to kill myself or get over myself. I found a really great therapist and just kept moving forward, a little bit each day. Still am, though as you know," Maria continued awkwardly, "I have a bit of trouble with the bottle."

"You come by it honestly. And who can blame you if you lose yourself from time to time."

Grimacing, Maria admitted, "It's way beyond 'time to time.' But I think reconnecting with you might be the catalyst that enables me to take control of my drinking —finally."

"If we're confessing here," Izzy admitted, "I've spent a fair amount of time in treatment myself over the past decade."

"Really? For what?"

"Percocet and Oxycontin are, um, were my drugs of choice."

"Izzy, I had no idea. I wish Mom had told me at least that much. Maybe I could have helped?"

"She didn't know either. By the time I finally confided in her, after my last stint in rehab, I was done with the pills. I'd had enough."

"When was that?" Maria asked.

"Christmas two years ago," Izzy said, shifting uncomfortably in her chair. "I became hooked after my hysterectomy, which was about ten years ago, give or take. I liked the way the drugs made me feel. Oblivious to the pain, to the past, to the present. An escape from reality. Jack's been a saint, standing by me each time I screwed up."

"He's a good man. Seems we've both been dealing with our demons in not-so-healthy ways," Maria offered, swiping at fresh tears.

"Maybe, but I like your suggestion that finding each other again will help us stay sober."

The lights flashed, and the printer on the desk reset

itself. Maria said, "I'd better get the flashlights and candles. Stay here."

As she walked into the kitchen, Katrina looked up from the table. "You two okay in there?"

"Finally having the talk we should've had forty years ago. I'm getting flashlights and candles for when the electricity goes out for good. Need anything?"

"No, I'm fine here. Been charging this all along," she said, nodding to her laptop, "so I can stay connected to the department."

Returning to her study, Maria watched Smarty Pants pounce into Izzy's lap and knead her belly. "Ya know, she only does that to people she likes."

"She's a beautiful cat, aren't you, Smarty?" Izzy scratched the cat's chin and throat. "We had a cat named Gabby until Amy was born. When she broke out in hives, Amy, not Gabby, her pediatrician suggested the possibility of a cat allergy, so we gave Gabby to Jack's sister."

"You could get another now that the girls have moved out."

"I don't think so. We travel so much, it really wouldn't be fair."

"Well, you're welcome to visit Smarty Pants any time you want."

"Am I really welcome, Maria?"

"Of course you are, Izzy. We've lost so much time already. And I don't know about you, but I'm not getting any younger."

"I agree. But let's not talk any more tonight. Between last night's bender and tonight's waterworks, I'm exhausted. If you don't mind, I'll take one of these flashlights and head upstairs."

"I'm a little tired myself. Here, take a candle and

matches, too. The battery's fully charged, but you never know. Need anything else?"

As Smarty jumped from her lap, Izzy stood and held out her arms. "A hug?"

"Gladly," Maria said, returning her sister's embrace.

# 70

# SATURDAY NIGHT, AUGUST 11, 2018

## SOUTHPORT, NORTH CAROLINA

B illy sat in the darkness of the master bedroom watching the flickering of lights from behind the window blind. Blondie's house was shuttered and boarded up, but he could still see glimpses of light and shadow in the few remaining gaps.

He'd been downstairs watching the news until ninety minutes ago, when he'd headed upstairs for a quick nap. Not wanting a repeat of the night before, he'd figured out how to set the alarm clock on the nightstand. It had gone off only moments before. *Not much longer*, he thought as he headed into the bathroom. Flushing the toilet, he glanced in the shower and shrugged. *Why not,* he thought, pulling the shirt over his head. *Maybe even find me some clean clothes.*

After lathering his head, he grabbed a razor from the soap dish and carefully shaved his scalp before moving on to his chin. He'd grown the goat patch in the joint to hide a botched attempt at a skull tattoo that had turned out looking more like a clown. *Fuck it*, he thought now, *clowns are every bit as scary as skulls.*

As he stepped from the shower, the lights flickered once,

then blackened altogether. Reaching for a towel, he jammed his toe on the corner of the vanity, shooting a lightning bolt of pain through his cursed bad knee. Swearing, he felt his way to the toilet and sat until the throbbing subsided. Retrieving his pants from the floor, he pulled a disposable lighter from the pocket and flicked on the flame. After allowing his eyes to adjust, he inspected his bleeding toe.

He wiped away the blood with a bath towel and then searched the medicine cabinet for a bandage before limping into the bedroom. With the bleeding at bay, he pulled on his pants, held the lighter out in front, and shuffled to the closet. Finding a Duke University jersey tossed over a hook, he smelled the pits before pulling it over his head. After unearthing a clean pair of white socks in the bottom drawer of a tall chest, he laced up his shoes, relit the lighter, and worked his way through the hall to the stairs.

Once in the kitchen, he proceeded to open every drawer and cupboard until he found a battery-powered flashlight. He flicked its switch, and the kitchen was bathed in a dull yellow light. *Let's hope this battery is fully charged*, he thought. Pulling what was left of the peach pie from the fridge, he sat at the table to recharge his own battery.

With a smack of his lips, Billy dumped the empty pie pan into the sink. *I should probably eat some protein if I want to make it through tonight*, he thought. Finding an unopened container of chicken salad, he checked the expiration date before snapping off the lid and digging in. *Damn*, he smiled, *this is good shit. Thanks again, folks!*

With his belly full, Billy returned to the master bedroom and peered out the window at Blondie's house, as dark now as the one he was in. Going over the plan in his head, he focused his attention on the crawl space running the length of the house. He recalled that, although obscured by shrubs and darkness, it was enclosed by a lattice of white wood. His plan was to race to the side of the house, crawl through the lattice, and find an access point inside. All he had to do was wait for the eye of the hurricane to pass overhead.

As he sat looking at the house, his dick stirred at the thought of sucking the plump breasts and dark snatch he'd seen beneath Blondie's nightie. Dropping his pants, he grabbed his cock as his thoughts drifted to that first night in the cabin when he'd fucked both Blondie and the Bitch. Shuddering a few moments later, he flopped backward onto the bed. Staring into nothingness, he spoke aloud, "That was some great pussy, wasn't it, Frank? Damn, I wish you was with me tonight, buddy, but I'll fuck her good for you, too. Okay?"

# 71

# SATURDAY NIGHT, AUGUST 11, 2018

## BOLIVIA, NORTH CAROLINA

The sheriff's radio signaled, and a distraught voice came over the line: "Sheriff, this is Mitchell. I'm on Highway 87 in Boiling Spring Lakes. The lake's washed out the bridge, and surrounding structures are flooded. We need to evacuate the town, especially downstream. I'm afraid the dam's gonna fail."

"Roger that, Mitchell. I'll have the county issue an immediate order to evacuate."

"BSL fire department is on scene and knocking on doors. Could use some PD backup."

"I'll call in all available and head there, too. Are you north or south of the washout?"

"North, sir, in the parking lot of Dollar General."

"Got it. Be there soon."

Without hesitation, John radioed for all available cars to report to BSL for evacuation and, God forbid, rescue. "Rouse, that includes you. I'll notify Anderson."

"Roger that, Sheriff," Rouse responded. "On my way."

Once all available officers had confirmed, John called

Katrina on her cell. "You're on your own, Anderson. Boiling Spring Lakes has flooded, and the town's being evacuated."

"Got it, Sheriff. All's calm here. Both women are sleeping. No sign of the suspect."

"Good. Stay safe."

"You too, sir."

# 72

# EARLY SUNDAY MORNING, AUGUST 12, 2018

## SOUTHPORT, NORTH CAROLINA

After drifting off, Billy jolted up from the mattress and scrambled to the window. Trees no longer bowed in the wind, and he could just make out a few stars flickering in the black sky. Looking toward the clock, he chuckled when he remembered the power was out. Regardless, it was time to move. Turning on the flashlight, he jumped to his feet, cursing as the pain in his toe forced him to hop on one leg.

Shoving the .32 in his front pocket, he followed the flashlight's yellow beam down the steps and into the garage. Spotting a box cutter on a workbench against the wall, Billy dropped it into a back pocket. He extinguished the flashlight, secured it through his belt, and stepped outside.

The calm was creepy. After his vision adjusted to the darkness, Billy took off through the backyard. As he weaved through the tangle of trees and shrubs, he stopped suddenly when a branch cracked loudly underfoot. Holding his breath for a count of five, he moved forward until catching sight of the white lattice beneath Blondie's house.

Smiling wickedly, Billy crouched and surveilled the

yard. A flagstone patio abutted French doors centered on the back of the house. The doors were boarded, as were the windows to the right and left. He identified a single window on the far right as the one into Blondie's bathroom. Recalling her fearful expression when she'd caught him peeping in at her, he rubbed his palms together in anticipation of things to come.

Exhaling deeply, Billy dropped to his hands and knees and crawled in the direction of the air-handling unit sitting atop a raised platform. Pausing a moment to listen for movement inside the house, he grabbed a sheet of lattice, pulling it away from the foundation until the fretwork snapped. Scooting to an adjacent area, he yanked until it, too, broke. With one final tug, a jagged hole large enough to crawl through was formed.

Aiming the flashlight through the hole, Billy fanned the beam through the dark space, noting first the muddy floor and then the multitude of spider webs hanging from the floorboards overhead. Damn, he hated spiders! *Suck it up, Billy Boy*, he chided himself. Reaching his arms through the opening, he tossed the flashlight to his right before sinking his hands through the muck. Supporting himself on hands and toes, he inchwormed his way forward. As his shoulders and chest crossed the threshold, a sudden gust of wind swept through the space. Billy shuddered as the dreaded spider webs danced across his face. Reaching out his right hand to bat them away, his left arm slipped out from under him. His torso dropped onto the jagged pieces of wood, dangerously close to his crotch, and his chin slammed into the mud. Pain spasmed through his entire body as he chomped down on his tongue. Spitting out a stream of blood, he pushed onto his elbows and dragged his body through the opening.

With a silent groan, Billy rolled onto his back, lying still while his thundering heart calmed. When his breathing quieted, he picked up the murmur of voices above. Sweeping the flashlight back and forth, he searched overhead for a possible access point into the house. When the beam of light settled on the HVAC ductwork in the far corner, Billy slithered toward it through the slime.

# 73

# EARLY SUNDAY MORNING, AUGUST 12, 2018

## SOUTHPORT, NORTH CAROLINA

Maria dreamed of skeletal hands grabbing at her in the darkness. As she spun in circles, trying to see where the hands were coming from, she dizzied and fell to the ground. Craggy fingers pulled at her hair and clothes while sharp, black-painted nails raked her face and throat. She screamed and attempted to stand, but as a hideous laugh cackled from the murky depths, her trembling legs buckled beneath her. She labored strenuously to escape, but with every twist and turn, more and more fingers plucked at her. Covering her eyes, she cried out in pain and anger, "Stop it!" The hands receded into the shadows until only one remained. This one gently brushed the hair from her face.

"Maria, wake up. You're having a nightmare."

"Izzy?" Maria asked, opening her eyes. A faint beam of light reflected off the ceiling fan above.

"No, Maria. It's Deputy Anderson. Izzy's asleep upstairs. Here, take a sip of water." She helped Maria to a sitting position and pressed the glass to her lips.

Maria swallowed and pushed the glass away, laughing self-consciously. "Oh my, that was a doozy."

"I could tell from your scream. Want to tell me about it?"

"Not really. Did you think I was in danger?"

"I have to admit, I did, but once I cleared the room, I realized the only threat was your bedsheet."

Falling back onto her damp pillow, Maria asked, "What's it doing outside?"

"The eye's overhead now, which is why it's so quiet, but power's been out for over an hour."

Kicking off the tangle of sheets, Maria swung her legs to the floor. "Might as well get up and wait it out with you. There's no way I want to chance having those hands come back."

"Hands?" Katrina asked. "Never mind, I won't ask."

"Suffice it to say, I'm getting a good manicure when life gets back to normal around here."

"Alrighty then," Katrina said. "How about I put some water on for tea. Sound good?"

"But you said the electricity's out."

"We can light your gas stove with a match."

"I didn't know that. By all means, I'd love a cup. I'll be right out."

Maria walked into the bathroom using her phone to guide her. Placing it on the vanity, she splashed her face with water. She pulled off her sweat-dampened nightie and slipped on a cool satin bathrobe, tying the sash tightly. As she brushed her hair, she shuddered at the unnatural way her face reflected in the dimly lit mirror. With a quick glance at the window, she hurried from the bathroom.

# 74

# EARLY SUNDAY MORNING, AUGUST 12, 2018

## BOILING SPRING LAKES, NORTH CAROLINA

Police and fire department personnel had walked door to door, urging residents to evacuate, while Sheriff Franklin had cruised through neighborhood streets, repeatedly calling over his loudspeaker, "Evacuate your home now. The dam is failing. Move to higher ground." He'd watched as panicked parents carried their children, many wrapped in blankets, from their homes.

Now, as patrol and fire vehicles congregated in the Dollar General parking lot, first responders watched in awestruck fascination as the water level in the upper lake sank dramatically, exposing a muddy, tree-stump-littered lake bed. For those residents who had waited to evacuate, which the sheriff knew to be the case with many of the town's more storm-hardened old-timers, it was now too late to leave. The dam had crumbled, sending millions of gallons of water rushing through the streets, flooding homes, businesses, and everything else in its wake.

Stepping from his vehicle, John signaled for Deputy Rouse to join him under the building's awning. "Need you to stay here to coordinate rescues with the fire chief."

"No problem, Sheriff, but shouldn't someone be backing up Anderson?"

"I'll head that way after I assess the damage here," John replied, glancing skyward. "This calm is deceiving, and the wind and rain will kick back in soon enough."

"Be nice if it were over all together, but there's more coming for sure," Rouse agreed.

John walked over to a group of firemen gathered by a ladder truck. After pulling aside the BSL fire chief to discuss their coordinated efforts for the remainder of the storm, the two men shook hands, and John returned to his cruiser. As he backed out of the parking space, a fierce gust of wind propelled a limb from a nearby oak through his vehicle's windshield. Glass shattered with such force that a large shard pierced John's windbreaker, slicing into his chest.

"Goddamn it!" he cried, opening the door and falling to the pavement.

"Sheriff! You all right?" a voice called over to him. Several arms reached down to lift him to his feet.

"Got me in the chest," he muttered, angrily pulling off his jacket.

"Got your face and hands, too, sir," a female officer added.

When an EMT team wheeled over a stretcher, John waved them away, but after wincing at the blood oozing through his shirt, he allowed them a closer look. "I'm not going to the hospital, so whatever you're thinking of doing, get to it here," he demanded.

"Yes, sir," the younger of the two medics agreed before helping the sheriff onto the gurney. As the EMTs carefully plucked the jagged glass from his chest, pulling out more than a few hairs along with it, John swore under his breath.

"Sorry to be hurting you worse, sir, but this really needs suturing."

"Screw that. Just tape it good for now. I'll get it stitched after the damn storm is over."

After cleansing and bandaging the chest wound, the EMTs tended to the cuts on his face and hands. Peering around a medic, Rouse laughed and said, "Boss, you look like you were shaved by a two-year-old."

"Don't you have somewhere to be, Deputy?"

"Yes, sir. Heading back out now."

Grimacing, John called to the retreating officer. "Rouse, leave me your vehicle. Can't drive mine in that condition."

"How am I supposed to get around, if you don't mind my asking, sir?"

"Ride with someone else. Now give me your keys."

"Want my shirt and jacket too?" Rouse teased.

"Won't be necessary," the sheriff replied. "Got spares in my trunk."

Rouse tossed his keys, and John grabbed them from the air.

# 75

# EARLY SUNDAY MORNING, AUGUST 12, 2018

## SOUTHPORT, NORTH CAROLINA

T he voices overhead were indecipherable, and as the
wind and rain picked up again, Billy lost them all
together. *Just as well*, he thought. *If I can't hear them, they
can't hear me.*

Tugging gently on the flexible ductwork snaking above
him, Billy determined it must lead inside the house, somewhere. Planting the flashlight in the muck, he aimed the
beam at the shiny silver tubing. Using the box cutter, he
began striking the thin material where it connected to the
rigid framing.

It was slowgoing as he stabbed the blade through
multiple layers of aluminum and insulation. Despite a
steady flow of wind, sweat rolled into his eyes and down his
back. Pausing to wipe his face, a messy feat given his mud-
covered hands, Billy peered out through the lattice. Rain
was falling in near horizontal sheets, and a steady wind
stooped even the tallest trees. Branches crashed onto the
driveway, sending pinecones and acorns skittering across
the pavement. *So glad I took that shower earlier*, he thought to
himself with a smirk. After breaking off the blunted knife

blade, he ratcheted in a fresh one and returned to his cutting.

Twenty more minutes of slicing severed the round length of coiled duct, and Billy dropped it to the ground. After a quick breather, he went to work on the round-to-square adapter attached with a thick coating of mastic to the upper housing. Once it, too, separated, Billy pocketed the box cutter, grabbed the flashlight, and grinned up into the opening that would lead him straight to Blondie.

After hooking the flashlight through his belt, he wiped his hands as best he could on the underside of his muddy shirt, raised his arms, and ducked into the hole. With head, arms, and shoulders inside the dark cavern, an unanticipated wave of claustrophobia washed over him. He hadn't experienced these suffocating symptoms in years, not since he'd done his first, and only, stint in solitary.

He'd been at Central only a few weeks when another prisoner, a badass Hispanic looking to make a name for himself, had cornered Billy in the shower, grabbing his dick. He'd slipped out of the spic's grasp and jumped on his back, riding him to the wet tile. With his rage unleashed, Billy had smashed the man's head over and over as a stream of blood mixed with the water before spiraling down the drain.

Billy'd been dragged off the man by two very pissed-off guards who'd thrown him in an isolation cell for three torturous weeks. The Hispanic had lived but had been transferred to another cell block. Last Billy'd heard, the fucker had died a year later after being shanked during a melee in the yard. While the Hispanic had failed to make a name for himself, by defending himself in the shower, Billy had succeeded. No one messed with him again.

Shaking off the feeling, Billy felt around for a spot in the smooth metal he could grab onto to pull his body up and inside. Nothing. Retrieving the flashlight, he directed the beam overhead. Two feet above his outstretched arm was a right-angle bend in the ductwork. Careful not to clang the flashlight against the hollow metal, he again lowered himself and looked around for something to stand on. Outside the lattice, on the back patio, was a low wooden table turned upside-down so the wind couldn't grab it. The only problem was, he'd need to leave the crawl space to get it.

Cursing, Billy crabbed back to the hole he'd made in the lattice and reached his arms and head through. There, just to his right, sat a concrete block. *What luck*, he thought, congratulating himself on his fortuitous site selection. With the utmost care, he balanced as before on hands and toes. Extending his arm, he muttered a "Fuck me!" when he realized how heavy and unyielding the damn thing was, especially in his precarious position. Straining the muscles in his arm and shoulder, he inched the block toward him. Once it was positioned below the opening, Billy hoisted it up and through the hole, shuddering as a black snake slithered from the spot where the block had just lain. *Spiders and snakes! What else is creeping around here?*

# 76

# EARLY SUNDAY MORNING, AUGUST 12, 2018

## SOUTHPORT, NORTH CAROLINA

K atrina Anderson's cell phone vibrated as she and Maria sat talking in the kitchen. Swiping her finger, she opened the text and frowned.

"What's wrong?" Maria asked, seeing her furrowed brow.

"It's Sheriff Franklin. He's been injured by a falling limb but will be heading our way within the hour."

"Is he hurt badly?"

"Doesn't say, but if he's okay to drive, I guess it can't be too bad."

"The folks in BSL must be so frightened," Maria sympathized. "It's scary enough just listening to the storm outside, but having to evacuate in the middle of it must be a nightmare."

"From what I've been reading on the county's website, it's pretty bad out there. It'll be months, if not years, before the bridges and dam are repaired."

As Maria took a sip of tea, she tensed when a loud bang sounded outside. "What was that?"

"Probably a branch hitting the house. Anything loose out there is a projectile in these winds."

"Just jittery, I guess, but I think I'll get my gun."

"No need," Katrina said, patting Maria's hand. "I have mine, and no one's getting through that front door unless I let them."

Looking at the ceiling, Maria wondered aloud, "I don't know how Izzy's sleeping through this racket! I should look in on her."

"All right. While you do that, I'll check the weather service to see how much longer Jasmine will be hanging around."

As Maria ascended to the second floor, the flashlight guiding her way, ghostly shadows danced around her. *What a strange and creepy night*, she thought before chastising herself for letting the storm unnerve her so. *Or is the threat from Billy Ramone causing this nagging sense of dread?* Regardless, she needed to get her emotions under control. If only John were here. She felt so calm and comfortable in his presence, almost as if they'd been close friends for years. She'd be terribly hurt if he disappeared from her life once Billy was captured. *Oh well*, she thought, *whatever's meant to be will be.*

Pausing outside the guest room, Maria tapped lightly before twisting the knob. As she aimed the light on the bed, she saw Izzy, eye mask in place and chest expanding with slow and rhythmic breaths. Smiling, Maria decided against waking her. After covering her sleeping sister with the blanket that had slipped off the bed, she returned to the first floor.

"Sleeping?" Katrina asked.

"Like a baby," Maria said. "She must have been exhausted to not hear the commotion outside."

As she pulled a throw around her shoulders, another thud, this one louder than before, startled the women.

Katrina, pulling her gun from its holster, whispered, "That sounded like it came from inside. You stay put while I check it out."

"Could be a branch hitting the roof like before," Maria suggested nervously.

"Could be, but I need to make sure."

As Katrina walked through the house, searching each room and closet, Maria tiptoed into the living room. After lighting the trio of candles on the cocktail tray, she snuggled into the corner of the sofa, pulling her legs beneath her.

When Katrina signaled that she was heading to the second floor, Maria nervously glanced around her before hurrying to the staircase. Perching on the bottom step, she hugged her knees. When another clang sounded below her feet, she hopped up a few steps. Leaning over the banister, Katrina gave her a questioning look. Pointing to the floor, Maria mouthed, "It came from down there."

With a finger at her lips, Katrina silently descended the stairs, motioning for Maria to follow her into the kitchen.

"Could an animal be in your crawl space?" she whispered.

"I suppose a possum or raccoon could have gotten under there," Maria said. "It's too low for a person and not at all clean. I've been thinking about getting it conditioned, but right now it's just a muddy dirt floor."

"Okay, let's go on the assumption that an animal has taken shelter there. It can't get into the house, so we'll just wait it out."

Breathing a sigh of relief, Maria asked, "What time is it?"

Checking her phone, Katrina replied, "Two. The

weather report says the storm should be gone by daybreak, so we have about four hours to go."

With a shiver, Maria walked to her bedroom, retrieved her pistol from the nightstand, and returned to the living room.

"Feel better?" Katrina asked with a shake of her head.

"Yes, I do, thank you," she replied, smiling. "Now, what were we talking about?"

# 77

# EARLY SUNDAY MORNING, AUGUST
## 12, 2018

SOUTHPORT, NORTH CAROLINA

Navigating the metal ductwork was trickier than Billy had anticipated. Once he'd dragged the concrete block across the muddy floor, he'd stood on his toes to reach the bend in the pipe. Although he'd spent hundreds of hours in the prison gym over the years, upper-body workouts had never been his strong suit. He was old now and paying for it. To pull himself up and in, he'd need to jump as high as he could, praying he didn't slide right back out. There was no way he could do so quietly, so fuck it.

His first attempt failed miserably, his awkward landing twisting his bum knee painfully. Sitting on the block while he massaged away the pain, he realized that turning the thing on its end would garner him several more inches.

Stepping onto the upturned block, Billy tested his balance before grasping the ledge of metal. He was sweating, and the cold surface was slick beneath his fingers. Bringing his hands down, he blew on his fingers, then wiped them again on his filthy shirt. With a single motion, he launched himself upward, grabbing the ledge and pulling his legs up and into the ductwork. He was, essentially, wedged in place.

The feeling of suffocation returned briefly, but Billy wasted no time dwelling on it. Using his hands, knees, and feet, he inched his body upward until, at last, he lay horizontally in the metal tunnel. The clamor he'd made had been deafening to his ears, and he listened intently while his breathing steadied. Footsteps sounded overhead, but when they retreated toward the rear of the house, relief washed over him.

There was no room in the tunnel to do anything but shimmy forward, and Billy did just that until the duct opened into a slightly larger area. Separating that space from the adjoining room, a room *inside* the house, was a louvered grate. Feeling the edges, Billy estimated the grate to be about two feet wide by two feet high.

*Easy-peasy*, he thought. He could taste her now, smell her pussy and see the terror in her eyes as he plundered her over and over and over. With more freedom to maneuver, Billy adjusted his pants, giving his erection room to expand. *Hang on, Big Guy*, he thought, grinning. *I'll let you out soon enough.* Pulling the box cutter from his pocket, he ran the blade along the edge of the grate, searching for a means to open it.

# 78

# EARLY SUNDAY MORNING, AUGUST 12, 2018

### BRUNSWICK COUNTY, NORTH CAROLINA

Sheriff John Franklin had left the parking lot of the BSL Dollar General, heading north out of town. With bridges and dams out, he had to navigate his way to NC 211, taking his chances that it would provide a clear shot into Southport. Within minutes, a downed tree forced him to pull over and fire up the chainsaw he'd remembered to grab from the trunk of his cruiser. After sawing the tree into easier-to-move logs, he'd dragged them to the side of the road, rolling them into the fast-moving waters in the ditch below.

Between the Lockwood Folly bridge, where the waters swept over the roadway, and the Midway Lowes, it had been necessary to repeat his Paul Bunyan act two times. Slowing him down, too, were other vehicles attempting to negotiate the dangerous conditions. He'd stopped each one with a flash of his roof light, delivering a stern warning to get off the roads as quickly and safely as possible. He hoped they'd all heed his advice.

Crossing into Southport over the Duke Energy bridge, he noticed with grave concern the raging waters below.

Stopping in the center of the bridge, he hit his emergency flashers and exited the cruiser. Peering over the railing, he watched tall pine trees, roots to branches, churn in the rising waters like socks in a washing machine. He wondered briefly how many unsuspecting critters, deer, squirrels, and even gators had been lost in the maelstrom. With a shake of his head, he returned to the vehicle.

The Southport Fire Station was crowded with vehicles as he drove past. Making the right at Tenth Street, he parked behind a red Ford F250 he recognized as belonging to the fire chief. A strong gust of wind grabbed the door as he exited the vehicle, nearly snapping the hinges. Yanking the door closed, he grimaced at the thought of reporting two damaged cruisers to the county board of commissioners.

Inside the FD building, he followed the smell of chili into the mess, where he found the chief stirring a large pot on the commercial-size gas stove. "Obviously not much going on in town tonight," John noted sarcastically. He'd known Chief AJ Wright for over twenty years, and Jenny and AJ's wife, Angie, had been close friends.

Looking over his shoulder, the chief replied, "I could say the same thing about Brunswick County in general, Sheriff. Ain't there better places for you to be right now?"

"Nah, I heard you were making chili and wanted to get me some," John deadpanned.

As Wright turned from the stove, John saw that his left arm was in a temporary cast and his forehead sported a large square of gauze. "Stirring chili's all I'm good for tonight. But then it appears you're no better off than me."

"What the heck happened to you?" John asked.

"We were cutting down a tree out on Bethel Road that'd fallen on some electric wires. Darn limb snapped back and hit me in the head. I fell outta the bucket, hit the road, and snapped my arm near in two. Thank the Lord the hospital stayed open through this. What about you?"

"You got me beat. A limb came through my windshield's all."

"Thanks for not calling us out to rescue you. All my men and trucks have been busier than an October bee on sweet tea."

"Didn't have to. An EMT crew from BSL was on scene. We were evacuating the town before the dam broke when this happened," John said, pointing to his face.

"Can't say you're any better looking than you were before." Wright laughed. Placing a bowl in front of his friend, he asked, "Jackie and Sam up to your folks?"

"Took them early this morning. Haven't spoken to them since, but knowing my dad, he had them so tuckered out from rounding up the goats, they're sleeping right through this ruckus. Yours?"

"Drove up to Angie's dad's place in Raleigh yesterday. Took 'em forever with the traffic," Wright said. "Heard you have a tough case with a woman here in town. That why you're here?"

"Heading there as soon as I finish this," John said, blowing on a heaping spoonful. "How'd you hear about it?"

"You know how everyone in this town knows everybody else's business. Maria Smythe is a good lady. Hope you catch the shite bag before he causes her any more pain."

"That's my goal," John said, smiling. After finishing the chili, he rinsed out the bowl and placed it in the dishwasher. "Thanks for the hot chow, AJ. Take care of your arm and head."

"You do the same with your ugly mug," Wright said. "Come to dinner once this all calms down, will you?"

"Yeah, I'll do that. Give Angie a kiss for me."

# EARLY SUNDAY MORNING, AUGUST 12, 2018

## SOUTHPORT, NORTH CAROLINA

M aria, as wired as she'd been moments earlier, yawned and scooched deeper into the sofa cushions. "Katrina, I won't tell the sheriff if you want to nod off awhile."

"Thanks, but no can do. On-duty naps are severely frowned upon. I could use the powder room to splash cold water on my face, though."

"Absolutely," Maria replied. "I left a gallon of spring water under the sink. If you want, use that until we get an all-clear on the tap water."

Watching the beam from Katrina's flashlight disappear down the hallway, Maria closed her eyes and sighed deeply. She was so damn weary and wanted nothing more than a few moments of peace and quiet. From the storm, from Billy Ramone, from the intrusion of the police, as sweet as Katrina Anderson was. And, she had to admit, from Izzy. She was thankful she'd reconnected with her sister, but their emotional conversation from earlier had been draining. Fortunately, Izzy was fast asleep upstairs.

A featherlight breeze stirred Maria's hair, and she sat up

quickly, watching as the candle flames danced in the darkness. "Smarty Pants?" she called quietly, thinking the cat might have brushed by. "Hey, sweetie, come here." When the cat failed to appear, Maria picked up the flashlight and her P238. Following the flashlight beam down the hall, she knocked on the powder room door.

"Katrina, you okay in there?"

A moment passed before Katrina spoke, her voice a bit shaky. "Uh, yes, Maria. My stomach's just a bit upset. From the pizza, I guess."

"You sure? I have Imodium or Alka-Seltzer if you need them."

"No, I'm good," Katrina said quickly.

Hesitating, Maria was tempted to wait outside the bathroom door, but when the toilet flushed, she said, "Okay, take your time. Let me know if you need anything."

Returning to living room, she directed the flashlight around the room. Smarty Pants lay where she'd been for the past hour, atop her perch by the French doors to the patio. *Where had that breeze come from*, Maria wondered with a shiver. The house was locked up tight and the power was out, but she'd definitely felt the movement of cool air and seen the candle flames sway. Reaching for the throw that had dropped to the floor, she sensed movement to her left.

"Katrina, is that you?" she called out. Aiming the light in the direction of the movement, she squinted at a shadow hovering just inside the hallway to the powder room. "Katrina, come on. You're scaring me."

Stepping from the shadows, Billy Ramone grinned wickedly into the bright beam. "Don't be scared, Blondie, it's only me."

Screaming, Maria pulled her gun from the pocket of her robe and fired. Billy ducked around the corner as the round ricocheted into the darkness. Turning to run, Maria yelled out, "Help! Katrina, Izzy!" Her slippers tangled in the throw, sending her flailing into the cocktail ottoman. The tray flew through the air, the sherry service and candles crashing to the floor a second before she did. Her gun and flashlight scattered across the floor in opposite directions.

Racing into the room, Billy jumped on Maria's back and clamped his hand over her mouth. The rank smell of mud filled her nostrils as she struggled to breathe beneath his suffocating weight.

"Shhh, Blondie, it's just you and me now," he taunted, tightening his grip. "Sorry, but Chick Cop ain't comin' to the rescue. Luckily, I heard her go in the can, but too bad for her, she didn't lock the door. She's left a nasty mess for someone to clean up."

*What did he do to Katrina*, Maria wondered, her panic escalating. Frantically looking around, she spotted the flashlight shining from beneath the bombé chest by the fireplace. Her gun was nowhere in sight. As she bucked upward in an effort to knock Billy off her back, she felt the muzzle of a gun against her cheek, and she stilled.

"I see you're as feisty as ever, cunt, but if you don't want your pretty head blown off, keep your fuckin' mouth shut." Removing his hand from her mouth, he forced her onto her back, securing her arms under his knees. Pulling the flashlight from his belt, he shined it on her face, grinning. "Mmm-mm, Blondie, I like what I see. You may be old, but you ain't half-bad." Squeezing her right breast, he asked, "Are you still a decent fuck?"

Maria lay silent, eyes closed against the assault and blinding light.

"I asked you a question, Blondie. Open your fuckin' eyes when I talk to you!" When she did, he leaned in to cover her mouth with his. His kiss was brutal, his breath rancid from teeth untouched by a dentist in forever. Gagging, she struggled to turn her head, but Billy gripped her hair to hold it steady. When he kissed her again, she bit down hard on his already-damaged tongue.

Billy's head and body jerked back, and he screamed in pain, releasing her hair to probe his mouth. As he stared at his bloodied fingers, Maria pulled an arm free and smashed her fist into his ear, stunning him. Before he could recover, she drove her hand straight up and into his nose.

"Fuck you, cunt!" Billy bellowed as he reared back, blood spurting everywhere. Re-pinning her arm, he smashed his flashlight into her skull. Maria went limp.

"I oughta shoot you now," he lisped angrily. Lifting Maria in his arms, the satin fabric of her robe slipped away, exposing her right breast. Despite his pain, his erection was instantaneous, and he lowered his mouth to her nipple, biting down hard and leaving it smeared with his blood.

Maria whimpered as Billy carried her to the bedroom and tossed her atop the tangled sheets. Yanking off her robe, he used the sash to bind her hands to the headboard. "Takes me back, Blondie," he muttered, unzipping his fly.

# EARLY SUNDAY MORNING, AUGUST 12, 2018

### SOUTHPORT, NORTH CAROLINA

I zzy's eyes flew open, and she whipped off the mask. *What was that*, she wondered. *Did someone just scream?* Even with the eye mask removed, the room was pitch black. Remembering the flashlight on the nightstand, she reached over and switched it on. There, there was that noise again. It was hard to make out over the wind wailing outside. Not so much a scream now as a deep cry of pain. *Oh, my God*, she thought. *Is Maria in trouble?*

Her body shaking, she slid from the covers and stood beside the bed. *Where is Deputy Katrina? Wasn't she supposed to stay through the storm?* Quietly cracking the door, Izzy took a moment to orient herself. Yes, she could definitely hear a voice, but it was a man's voice now. Had John come back? No, it wasn't John, but it sounded vaguely familiar.

Revulsion turned her stomach as she recognized the taunting voice of Billy Ramone. Flashlight in hand, she crept down the stairs, stopping on the landing to listen.

With dread, she heard Maria's pleading. "Stop, Billy. You don't have to do this." Revulsion overcame her fear, and she moved further down the stairs. Fanning the light into the living room, she caught a glint beneath the sofa.

Tiptoeing into the room, she reached under the sofa, pulling out a gun. *Is this Katrina's? Maria's?* She couldn't be sure, but holding it gingerly, she edged down the hallway. The voices became clearer as she approached the master bedroom, and seeing a dim light shining from the room, she extinguished her own.

Peering around the doorframe, Izzy watched in horror as Billy, straddling Maria, forced apart her legs. When he hammered a filthy fist into her belly, Maria cried out in agony, which only excited him more. Grabbing her exposed breasts, he pinched her nipples while she twisted beneath him.

"See, you do like it, don't you?" he boasted. "And I haven't even gotten started."

With a rage she hadn't felt since the cabin, Izzy approached the bed, aiming the gun ahead of her. "Get off my sister, you fucking monster."

Billy stiffened before responding with a sharp back-thrust of his elbow that connected with Izzy's extended hand. Shrieking as the gun flew from her grasp, she lunged at Billy, pummeling him off Maria and driving him from the bed.

Jumping to his feet, Billy hissed, "If it isn't the Bitch herself." With one hand holding his withering erection, he extended the other in invitation. "Come on, play nice. I've got enough here for both of you. Like before, remember?"

Izzy shuddered as Billy tugged at his penis. With the bed between them, she chanced a look at the floor, hoping to spot the dropped gun. At her feet, barely visible under Billy's discarded pants, was a small black revolver. Using her toe to push aside the fabric, she bent quickly, straightening with the gun aimed at Billy's crotch.

Glancing up from his burgeoning cock, Billy's lusty grin disappeared. "Hey, now. Don't do anything rash."

Izzy's hands shook slightly, but drawing in a deep breath, she pulled back on the trigger. Blood erupted from Billy's hand. "You bitch!" he roared, dropping to his knees.

Izzy moved quickly around the bed. Placing the muzzle to his temple, she hissed, "Tell Frank we say hi," before calmly pressing the trigger a second time. Billy's brain exploded against the wall of Maria's beautifully decorated bedroom.

Izzy mused at how natural the gun felt in her hand before carefully setting it on the nightstand. She crawled over the mattress to where Maria lay, eyes staring at the ceiling, and gently untied her sister's wrists. Lying beside her, she held on tightly as desperate sobs of sadness and relief racked them both.

# EARLY SUNDAY MORNING, AUGUST 12, 2018

## SOUTHPORT, NORTH CAROLINA

John pulled into Maria's driveway and approached the front door, gun drawn. He'd tried calling Katrina Anderson when he'd left the fire station, but she hadn't picked up. Although he hadn't wanted to wake Maria, he'd tried her cell, but it, too, went unanswered. With a sinking feeling, he'd rung AJ Wright and requested an ambulance be dispatched to Maria's address. AJ had agreed and said he'd be there himself as soon as he could.

John peered through the glass and tapped lightly. When no one appeared at the door, he used his tactical flashlight to shatter the glass and reached in to unlock the deadbolt. Barging through the door, he called out, "Maria? Izzy? Where are you?"

"In here," came a quavering voice. "We're in the bedroom."

John cleared the living room before heading down the hall to Maria's bedroom. Stepping through the doorway, he stopped short when the beam of light took in the two women on the bed. Izzy, wearing a long white nightgown splattered with what appeared to be blood, lay beside Maria, who was naked, her blond hair matted with blood.

He rushed over and knelt beside the bed, his voice trembling as he asked, "You two okay? What happened here?"

Pointing to the far side of the bed, Izzy stated, "Billy's over there. Dead."

"Glad to hear it." John gulped. "Is the blood on your nightgown his?"

"Most of it," she replied. "But Maria's hurt and needs a doctor."

"I'll be okay," Maria insisted as tears streamed down her face. "But I think Katrina might be dead. She went to the powder room and never came out."

Squeezing Maria's hand, John said, "I've got an ambulance on the way. You two stay here." Gently pulling the comforter over the women, he strode to where Billy Ramone lay motionless and bloodied, a look of sheer terror in his still-open eyes. Two bullet holes were immediately evident. The one to his groin appeared to have blown off his penis and testicles. The other, through his left temple, was the apparent source of the blood and brain matter splattered on the walls.

Kicking the body lightly, John muttered, "He's dead all right," before heading out of the room.

Passing through the kitchen and into the short hallway leading to the powder room, he smelled the putrid odors of feces and blood. Beaming the light through the open door, he blanched at the sight of Katrina Anderson slumped on the tile floor, her head angling oddly to the side. Her uniformed trousers were bunched at her ankles, a pool of blood spreading from the toilet seat to her polished black shoes.

John backed from the room, turning to draw in a breath

of fresher air. He'd seen dead bodies before, but never one with its carotid artery slashed wide open. *She must have been terrified*, he thought, making the sign of the cross.

Seeing lights flashing outside, he walked to the door as two medics rushed up the front steps. "In here," he said, directing them into the master bedroom. While the medical team ministered to Maria, asking questions as they worked, Izzy stood at the foot of the bed, and John paced the hallway.

When one of the medics left to retrieve the stretcher, the other walked into the hall and whispered to John, "She'll be okay, even though I can't rule out a concussion. She took a pretty brutal hit to the head."

"Was she...?" John stammered.

"If you're asking if she was raped, there's no evidence to suggest he got that far."

"Thank God," John prayed.

When the EMT returned with the stretcher, John retreated to the living room. As he continued to pace, AJ Wright and Deputy Rouse walked through the open front door. "Heard the call over the radio, Sheriff," the young deputy explained. "Headed right back." Looking around at the disarray, he asked, "Where's Anderson?"

"She's gone, Rouse. Billy Ramone slit her throat," John replied, choking up.

"Oh, God, no!" Rouse cried in anguish. "I shouldn't have left her."

"You followed my direct order, Deputy. If anyone's to blame, it's me."

"It's nobody's fault," AJ said, grabbing John's shoulders. "Except this Billy Ramone. Where is the bastard, anyway?"

"He's dead, too. Maria's sister shot him. Once through the cock and once through the temple."

"Karmic justice," AJ observed with a shake of his head.

As the medics departed with Maria, John and AJ held a blanket over the gurney to protect her battered body from the wind and rain, diminished as the storm now was. When Izzy said she was riding with Maria to the hospital, John offered to bring fresh clothes for them both. Watching the ambulance back from the driveway, he clenched his fists in anger before returning to the house to secure the scene.

## SUNDAY EVENING, AUGUST 12, 2018

### SOUTHPORT, NORTH CAROLINA

I zzy sat by Maria's bedside, composing a text to her husband in California. She'd tried to reach him earlier, but her calls had gone straight to voicemail. He was likely lost in one of his many projects, she reasoned, tapping *send* and returning her phone to the pocket of her jeans.

Maria rested comfortably under a mound of blankets, staring blankly at the television. A harried woman, wearing the requisite yellow rain slicker and dancing under an inverted umbrella, warned viewers of Hurricane Jasmine's imminent destruction of Cape Cod and surrounding islands. With annoyance, Maria jabbed at the remote until settling on a repeat episode of *Fixer Upper*.

"Had enough of Jasmine?" John asked, walking into the room.

"Hey there." Maria smiled up at him.

"How're you doing tonight?" he asked, gently smoothing the hair from her forehead.

"She's doing great," Izzy said, rising from her chair. "So great, I think I'll head to the cafeteria for a snack. Can I bring anything back for you two?"

"Ice cream?" Maria asked with a grin.

"You got it. John?"

"Nothing for me, Izzy," he replied, turning his attention back to Maria. "You look one hundred percent better, but I'm glad they're keeping you overnight."

"I'll be just fine. I'm only staying so they can monitor my concussion. I'll be going home in the morning."

"Maria," John said, frowning, "you can't go home tomorrow, and probably not til next week, at the earliest. Your house is a crime scene, and we can't let you back in until the forensics team finishes up."

"When will that be?" she asked with alarm.

"They should be done by Tuesday, but remember, there's quite a bit of cleanup needed. Not to mention the repairs."

"Repairs? I figured there'd be a mess to clean up, but I didn't consider any real damage. Just how did Billy get into the house?"

"I'll be happy to tell you everything tomorrow once you and Izzy are settled into the hotel suite I've booked. It accepts pets, by the way, so Smarty can go, too. We found her under the guest bed upstairs. She's at my house temporarily."

"She must have been so frightened."

"She was, but Jackie and Sam are in heaven having her around. You might not get her back."

"Not a chance. Now what is this about a hotel suite? How lovely of you to have taken the liberty of booking one for us."

"You're being sarcastic, aren't you?" John asked sheepishly.

"Yes, I am. But I do appreciate your thinking ahead. God knows, my head's so muddled, I actually thought I'd be going home from here."

Taking her hand, John whispered, "I'm sorry, Maria."

"For what? Doing your job?"

"No, for not being there when you needed me. Ramone would never have broken in, let alone killed Anderson, if I'd stayed with you."

"Maybe not last night, but he'd have eventually found a way to get to me. Not even you could have protected me around the clock forever."

"If you'll let me take you to dinner one night soon, I'd be happy to discuss that," John said, his eyebrows lifting impishly.

"That might be interesting," Maria mused. "Let's talk about it once I'm out of here."

"Look what the storm washed up," Izzy announced as she walked into the room with a man on her arm.

"Jack, when did you get here?" Maria asked as he bent to kiss her cheek.

"Maria, so great to see you again. Sorry it's under these circumstances. You doing okay?"

"I am, but how'd you find out what happened? Izzy said you weren't answering her calls."

"I was in the air," he said, pulling his wife into his arms. "A Sheriff Franklin called in the middle of the night and told me what happened. I hopped on the first flight out, and here I am."

"Well, wasn't that nice of Sheriff Franklin?" Izzy noted, reaching out to hug John. "Jack, meet Sheriff John Franklin."

As the two men shook hands, Jack patted John on the back. "Thanks for watching out for these two, John. They seem to find themselves in the most unpleasant predicaments."

"I suppose so, but it seems they managed fine on their own before I even arrived on scene."

Crawling onto the bed beside Maria, Izzy beamed up at the two men. "That's what sisters do."

# AFTERMATH

AUGUST 13 THROUGH NOVEMBER 30, 2018

M aria was released from the hospital the following afternoon. On John's insistence, he picked her up, delivering her to the hotel where Isabella and Jack had stayed the previous night. Her suite was just down the hall from theirs, and after John had made sure she and Smarty, who he'd brought with him, were comfortable, he said good-bye.

After unpacking the suitcase Izzy had packed for her, the sisters went down to the swimming pool. The weather was beautiful with clear skies and low humidity.

"Maria, if this is Southport's typical weather, I may have to talk Jack into moving here once he retires!" Izzy said, reclining into a chaise longue.

"It is, I swear," Maria said and laughed, reaching for her sister's hand as she settled into her own chaise. "And today's about as pretty as it gets."

"As are we!" Izzy laughed. "You okay there? Can I get you anything?"

"A masseuse?" Maria grimaced. "No, seriously, I'm just a little wobbly still."

"So what would you think about my staying until your house is livable again?"

"You can stay as long as you like, Izzy, but won't Jack need to get back to LA?"

"He will, but there's no reason I can't stay on. Only obstacle would be my limited wardrobe," she said, smiling. "But I'm sure I can convince Jack that *you'll* heal better with some serious shopping and spa therapy."

"Sounds heavenly to me. And I know a few shops that'll be more than happy to oblige."

---

THE FUNERAL SERVICE for Katrina Anderson was held Thursday morning, a bright and optimistic sun shining upon the small, beautiful church. Jack, Izzy, and Maria sat several pews behind the grief-stricken family. As the strains of "Ave Maria" sounded from the balcony, a tall, handsome man of about thirty wiped tears from his eyes before blowing his nose.

Leaning into Izzy, Maria whispered, "That must be Jake, Katrina's boyfriend."

Following her sister's gaze, Izzy noticed the young man struggling to maintain his composure, and she squeezed Maria's hand.

Katrina's fellow police officers, including John, were serving as pallbearers and sat directly behind the family. In dress blues, John and his deputies made Maria's heart swell with a mix of pride and sorrow. Their job was a selfless one, and watching as they memorialized one of their own reinforced just how dangerous a job it was as well.

Although the entire congregation had been invited to the gravesite, Maria and Izzy had decided earlier they wouldn't attend. The events leading to Katrina's death had been well publicized, and they felt their presence at the cemetery would be an unwelcome distraction. As soon as the casket was placed in the sleek black hearse, they drove back to Southport.

JACK FLEW home Saturday morning after negotiating with the various contractors who'd be conducting the repairs and improvements to Maria's house, both inside and out. At Izzy's prompting, he'd generously offered to cover the cost of conditioning and enclosing the crawl space. Once completed, nothing, animal or otherwise, could gain access to it or the house. Maria had been touched by the gesture but had later confided to Izzy that she wasn't sure if she wanted to stay in the house after Billy had desecrated it.

"Well, there's no need to make a rash decision on that. Let's just see how it feels once it's been cleaned up and painted. It's such a pretty house, and you've made it such a beautiful home."

"I know it is, or was, anyway. At the very least, I'll need new bedroom furniture."

"Let's start shopping, then, shall we?"

AND SHOP THEY DID, in Southport, in Wilmington, in Myrtle Beach. Most shops had reopened quickly after Jasmine, and many were offering post-hurricane specials. Bags and boxes filled their hotel suites, and Maria was having more fun than she'd had in years. It was nice having someone special to do things with. She'd convinced herself that she already had everything she needed to be happy. That was until Billy Ramone had nearly taken that everything away.

John called early each morning to see how she was feeling and again in the evening to see how her day had been. Although she wouldn't admit it, she felt better, happier even, after talking with him. With so much after-the-storm cleanup, plus the massive red tape surrounding Billy and Katrina's deaths, he hadn't been by the hotel since he'd dropped her off.

Over the course of their conversations, Maria had learned how one of John's deputies had spotted Billy's car under her neighbor's carport. After the police had contacted the homeowners and received permission to enter, they'd discovered a great deal of unpleasant DNA evidence in the kitchen, master bedroom, and master bath. Learning that, her neighbors had arranged for a thorough professional cleaning of the entire house before they'd returned from their son's home in Atlanta.

---

WHEN JOHN CALLED Saturday morning three weeks after the storm, Maria asked if he'd like to join Izzy and her for dinner at Mr. P's Bistro. "Izzy leaves tomorrow morning, and I know she'd love to see you before she goes."

"That'd be nice, but can I make an alternative suggestion? How about you come to my house this afternoon for a little barbecue? It'll give you a break from restaurant food and an opportunity to meet my children."

"Sounds wonderful to me, but let me check with Izzy, and I'll call you back."

At four o'clock that afternoon, after following John's detailed directions, Maria drove up a treelined drive that led to a charming two-story cottage centered on a rise overlooking the Intracoastal Waterway. With its white clapboard siding, black shutters, authentic with their clasps and brackets, and a wraparound porch, it offered spectacular views in every direction. A slat-back swing hung by a chain from the ceiling to the right of the door, and two rockers sat invitingly to the left.

Standing on the porch, waving as the car pulled to a stop, were John and his two beautiful children. Maria's stomach fluttered, and she placed a hand over her heart.

"You okay?" Izzy asked.

"My heart just jumped a little."

"I know," Izzy whispered. "It's the portrait of a perfect family with their perfect home."

"Pretty much what I see, too." Maria smiled.

Izzy reached across the seat to caress Maria's shoulder. "One step at a time, sis. You okay to get out?"

Patting Izzy's hand, Maria unfastened her seat belt and took a deep breath. "I'll be fine. For a second there, I had a vision of...I'm not sure how to describe it exactly, but I saw myself on that porch swing."

"Oh, Maria, I can see you there, too. But if we don't get out now, John and his children will think we're nuts."

With a laugh, Maria opened her door and stepped from the car.

***

MARIA RETURNED to her house in mid-September, spending the first few nights roaming from room to room, attempting to recapture the sense of tranquility she'd always felt there.

Smarty Pants seemed to perceive the change as well, and she wandered behind Maria until they'd both fall into a restless sleep just before dawn.

In mid-October, a jaunty red convertible pulled into her driveway, a casually dressed woman with spiky blond hair and big round sunglasses waving to Maria from the vehicle.

"Hey, there, Maria! Shall I join you?"

"By all means, come on up, Janet! I have tea for us."

"Oh, good," Janet replied, stepping up the freshly painted stairs.

After exchanging pleasantries and sipping on sweet tea, Janet said, "So you really want to put this on the market?"

"Yes, I do. I've been thinking about it for weeks, and now that I've been back awhile, I know it's the right decision."

"Have you considered where you'll go? Despite what happened here, it's a beautiful home and most likely will sell quickly. Especially if we price it right."

"I'd like to rent temporarily, if you can help me with that. Nothing too big or too much trouble. Where I ultimately end up depends on several things presently in motion."

"Is John Franklin one of those *things* in motion?" Janet asked with a grin.

"Might be...but no matter where our relationship goes, it's time for me to move. I loved this house with my whole heart, but what happened here has made me realize that people, not places, are what's important."

After discussing and agreeing on a fair asking price, Maria signed the paperwork. As she hugged Janet good-bye, an errant tear escaped, but she quickly wiped it away.

---

Maria's house sold in ten days for above-asking price after

two interested buyers got into a bidding war. They'd both been made aware of the crimes that had taken place there, but when Maria had agreed to include the bulk of her beautiful furniture in the deal, neither of them had hesitated to make an offer. The final bid came from a husband and wife retiring from Maryland, and she couldn't have been happier to learn their large extended family would be visiting often.

Settlement was to be on December 15th, and after looking at several rentals, Maria signed a six-month lease for a small, but comfortable, fully furnished townhome off Fish Factory Road. With barely any packing needed, she and Smarty planned to move in right after Thanksgiving.

When John readily offered to help lug the boxes from her house to the townhome, his parents suggested that they take Jackie and Sam for the long weekend, which was forecast to be sunny and in the midsixties. Perfect North Carolina fall weather.

On Black Friday morning, John pulled up in a fifteen-foot U-Haul. Watching him reverse the truck up her driveway, Maria stood on the porch, laughing.

Stepping down from the truck, he called up to her, "What do you find so amusing, might I ask?"

"Not a thing," she replied. "Just questioning my sanity in deciding not to hire professionals."

"Oh, ye of little faith," he said, heading up the steps. Taking her in his arms, he kissed her long and hard.

Maria's head swooned, and when she pulled away, she looked up into his eyes. "Tonight?"

"I do believe we've waited long enough," he replied with a devilish grin. "I suggest we get this moving over by midafternoon, because what I've planned starts promptly at four thirty."

Although they'd been seeing each other quite steadily

since the barbecue at his house, they hadn't yet been intimate. They'd come close on several occasions, but with Jackie and Sam sleeping in rooms next to his, and Maria's disquiet in her own home, the optimal opportunity had yet to present itself. And Maria wanted their first time to be optimal.

When the last box had been hauled inside, Maria and John sat on the top porch step, sipping from bottles of cold beer.

"So tell me about our plans tonight," Maria asked a little nervously.

Looking at his phone, John replied, "You'll have two hours to pack an overnight bag, shower, and dress. Slacks and a sweater will be fine," he finished, anticipating her next question.

"And then?"

"I'll pick you up here, and you'll learn more after that."

"Alrighty, Sheriff Franklin. Leave me be so I can get ready."

Turning and kissing her deeply, he then sighed and said, "Just a taste of what's to come."

Promptly at four thirty, John knocked on Maria's door, a bouquet of chrysanthemums in hand. When Maria opened the door, he took a deep breath and grinned.

"You are beautiful, Maria."

"Well, thank you for the compliment and the flowers. We should take them with us, though. Smarty's good for a night on her own, but since this is her first night here, I'm afraid the flowers won't survive her nocturnal explorations."

"By all means," he replied. "You carry the flowers, and I'll take your bag."

As they headed into town, Maria looked over and asked, "Will you tell me more now?"

"Impatient, aren't you?"

"Yep, now 'fess up. What's your dark plan for me?"

"First, we're having an early dinner at Mr. P's. Front window table, I might add."

"Sounds great."

"Then we're catching the last ferry for a holiday concert at the Fort Fisher Aquarium."

"I read about that," Maria said. "It sounded wonderful, but I didn't think we'd be able to go."

"I purchased tickets a few weeks before you planned your move, but the timing's going to work out perfectly."

"And then?"

Pulling in front of the restaurant, John said, "We have reservations at the Greystone Inn in Wilmington. Two nights, actually."

"I'm not sure I packed enough for two nights, John," Maria said, frowning.

"No worries. Whatever you need, we'll buy."

"But Smarty will be alone all weekend."

"I thought you said she'd be fine for a night on her own."

"I did, but—"

"But nothing," John interrupted, grinning. "I gave my folks the spare key to your townhouse—remember you had me run to the hardware store for one? They'll bring the kids by your place over the weekend to play with and feed her."

"And clean her litter box?"

With a laugh, he opened her door and held out his hand. "Yes, and to clean her litter box."

An overwhelming sense of warmth and love blossomed in her chest, and she leaned into him. "Thank you for thinking of everything."

"You're welcome, Maria. I've been waiting a long time to do just that."

# EPILOGUE

———

The late afternoon sun glimmered through the branches of the ancient live oak on the lawn of Fort Johnston. A container ship, huge and imposing, maneuvered through the cut and plowed north up the Cape Fear River. A small gathering of people sat in folding lawn chairs under a white canopy strung with twinkling lights while a trio of violinists played softly off to the side. When the music paused, the voices under the tent quieted and heads turned to the building behind them. As the strings resumed, a door opened, and John Franklin, wearing tan slacks paired with a soft blue shirt, stepped onto the lawn.

John turned to hold out his hand, and when Maria appeared, Izzy hugged her mother and squeezed Jack's hand so tightly he cringed. Maria wore a full-length gown in a slightly lighter shade of blue than John's shirt. Fitted at the waist and bodice, it flowed delicately from her hips in filmy layers of fabric that swirled in the spring breeze. Her hair was pulled into a loose chignon, and she held a delicate spray of wisteria and baby's breath. Beaming down at her, John took her arm, and they walked toward the canopy. As they passed through the assembly of family and friends, tears glistened in the eyes of many.

John's children, sitting in the front row, joined the couple on a small raised platform, with Jackie standing beside Maria and Sam next to John. AJ Wright, fire chief *and* ordained minister, stood before them all. Smiling broadly, he cleared his throat and announced, "We have gathered here today to witness the union of Maria and John in holy matrimony. As their family and friends, we are asked to bless them as they begin this journey together and to support them along their way."

Sam did a little jig beside his dad, and once the laughter subsided, AJ continued. "John and Maria do not enter lightly into this marriage, and their vows will be offered with a determined commitment to love each other for the remainder of their days. At this time, I ask if anyone here knows why these two cannot marry today?"

As the guests looked about uncertainly, two brilliant ibises landed on the lawn, pecking at the grass as they meandered under the tent.

"It's a sign of true love," Jackie whispered, giggling. "My teacher said that ibises marry for life, too."

"I guess that means there are no objections?" John laughed nervously, bending to kiss Maria.

With the sun dropping low in the sky, AJ continued, "Then let us proceed."

## ALSO BY CAROLYN COURTNEY LAUMAN

DECEPTIVE WATERS, coming Winter 2020

Read the prologue for *Deceptive Waters*, the first book in Carolyn's new series, on the next page.

# DECEPTIVE WATERS

PROLOGUE

**September 2019**

The woman's long silken locks swirled about her head and shoulders. A shimmery shade of platinum, surely store-bought, the tresses glittered like diamonds in the beams cast by the night's full Harvest Moon. Gentle waves caressed her body as she undulated upon the cool water. Face down.

Thirty feet below, a sleek white Genesis G90 lay wheels-up, its roof buried in the soft sand, its windshield shattered.

At two forty-three a.m., the exact moment the luxury sedan crashed through the guardrail, few other vehicles had been making the twenty-mile trek across the lower Chesapeake Bay. While headlights pointing north toward the eastern shore of Virginia were now visible, the jagged gap in the southbound span had yet to be discovered.

As the body bobbed in the rippling waters, a man in black jeans and hooded sweatshirt stood on the beach two miles to the northeast, his feet so close to the water's edge that the incoming tide sucked at his gator skin Lucchese boots. Adjusting the sights on his tactical binoculars, he watched as a CBBT transit vehicle, its yellow rooftop lights flashing, approached the crash site. Smiling to himself, the man turned and retreated toward the dunes.

# ABOUT THE AUTHOR

Carolyn Courtney Lauman is an emerging author of crime and suspense thrillers. *Against Their Will* is her first novel. She lives in Southport, NC with her husband and three spoiled cats.

**f** **◎**

Printed in Great Britain
by Amazon